STORMING OLYMPUS

THE UNDERWORLD SAGA, BOOK NINE

Eva Pohler

Eva Pohler Books
20011 Park Ranch
San Antonio, Texas 78259
www.evapohler.com

Publisher's Note: This is a work of fiction. Names, characters, places, and incidents are a product of the author's imagination. Locales and public names are sometimes used for atmospheric purposes. Any resemblance to actual people, living or dead, or to businesses, companies, events, institutions, or locales is completely coincidental.

Book Layout ©2017 BookDesignTemplates.com

Book Cover Design by B Rose Designz

Storming Olympus/ Eva Pohler. -- 1st ed.
Paperback ISBN 978-1-958390-43-6

For my readers.

Contents

"This is what parents are supposed to do for their children. Not threaten them. Not swallow them. They're supposed to be willing to die for them—or in our case, since we can't die, to suffer for them."

--POROS

CHAPTER ONE

Morpheus's Return

Still bleeding from where his silver wings had been ripped from his back, Morpheus stumbled across Iris's rainbow from Mount Olympus toward the depths of the Underworld. He could hardly see through his tears. He couldn't think. He wasn't even sure if he was breathing. The horrible vision kept playing over and over in his mind: Zeus opening his great mouth and swallowing Persephone before throwing Demeter into the bird cage that had been Morpheus's prison.

He could still hear Zeus's threat: "I will spare Iris and give you back your wings if, and only if, you do something for me."

Then the king had said: "I want you to report back to me on everything you see and hear. You will use the helm of invisibility and Iris's rainbow to travel back and forth."

But, worst of all, Zeus had said: "If you fail me, I promise I will take pleasure in ripping those pretty little wings from your pretty little girlfriend. Then I will defile her in ways you can't imagine before I paralyze her and hide her at the bottom of a river, where she will spend eternity, just like Phaeton. Do you understand?"

Then Zeus had forced Morpheus to swear on the River Styx that he would obey, and Morpheus, full of fear and dread, had sworn.

Had it really happened? Or had it been a horrible nightmare in the Dreamworld that had passed through the Gates of Ivory, and not through the Gates of Horn?

Morpheus's knees quivered as he walked beneath the helm of invisibility. He'd never flown without his wings. His beautiful wings. Were they really gone?

He strained to see his back. No wings. Only fresh blood. So much blood.

He wondered if he would ever see his wings again, or if he was doomed to suffer the same fate as Iris's sister, Arke.

Poor, sweet Iris. The memory of her lovely face twisted with fear and agony brought a new wave of tears to Morpheus's eyes. She'd been a faithful servant to Zeus, and the king couldn't care less. Morpheus had once believed that if you were a good and loyal subject, the king would always protect and reward you. But now he knew that wasn't true. Unlike her sister, Iris had done nothing to deserve the threats against her. Persephone may have taken her chances against her father, but what had Demeter done to deserve imprisonment?

Zeus used people. He didn't care about fairness and justice. He only cared about power. That's why he had swallowed Athena's mother in the first place. He was no better than *his* father, Cronos.

Morpheus felt like an idiot for ever trusting his king. Why, oh, why hadn't Morpheus trusted his father? If he had, maybe he and Iris would be safe, and none of this would be happening.

When Morpheus reached the throne room in the palace of Hades and Persephone, he found it empty. He followed the sounds of voices to one of the meeting rooms, where there were many gathered, including his parents. Hades and the Furies and Pete were there. Apollo and Artemis were there. Poseidon, Than, and Therese were there. Huddled in a corner, near the flickering fires of the Phlegethon, were two Asian kids fast asleep. Hermie and Hestie were each lying on a bed in the middle of the room, where the table usually was, and they were *glowing*.

Morpheus forgot that he was beneath the helm. He stared with wonder at the glowing bodies of his cousins and of the blond boy hovering in the air above them, who Morpheus now realized must be the son of Zeus, Poros.

Artemis said, "That can only mean one thing."

Poseidon glanced around the room. "Poros is stronger than Zeus."

Morpheus wasn't sure what he had heard. He felt as if he was in the Dreamworld witnessing a bizarre nightmare. Dazed, trembling, perplexed, he fell to his knees. He wanted to tell his family the truth, even if it meant that the Maenads would rip him to shreds every year; but he couldn't bear the thought of his sweet Iris paralyzed at the bottom of a river for all eternity.

And yet, if he *didn't* tell his family what Zeus had made him swear to do, what worse thing would Zeus do to *them*? Was it right for Morpheus to put his and Iris's happiness above all of theirs? And could he really trust Zeus *not* to harm Iris, even if Morpheus kept his word?

"The mortals are in danger because of my presence," Than said. "I better go."

"No," Pete said. "I'll go. I'll take them to Tartarus and keep them safe. You need to stay here, with your family."

Pete took the hands of the Asian kids, and the three of them disappeared.

Family. That's what this was about. Pete was right. They all needed to be with their family, and Zeus was definitely *not* family. Family members didn't threaten, torture, and imprison one other.

No, Zeus was not to be trusted. Morpheus had to tell his family the truth. But what would it matter, in the end?

He covered his face with his hands and wept. He was convinced that they were all doomed, whatever path he chose.

***

Hypnos was thrilled by the transformations taking place before his eyes. Therese and Than's twins had fulfilled their destinies. A power shift from Zeus to Poros had been the result, and now, the rebellion had a fighting chance.

Hip smiled across the room at his brother, once again in his rightful role as the god of death. He was altered since the last time he had served, having aged to an appearance more like their father. But his dark wavy hair and solemn blue eyes reminded Hip of the boy he'd once been, of the boy Hip still appeared to be. It was strange and jarring to think about it.

Beside him, Therese, also older in appearance than she'd been the last time she was the goddess of animal companions, looked just as radiant and fierce, her red curls falling about her shoulders and quiver full of arrows, her green eyes determined and expectant. She hadn't hesitated in the fight against the loyalists, as if she'd never stopped fighting. Hip was happy for his brother and relieved that Than and Therese would return to the pantheon and live eternally with their Underworld family, who'd missed them. Even their children, Hermie and Hestie, could now join them, thanks to the power of Poros.

Smiling, Hip said to Than, "It will be quite a treat to finally visit with my niece and nephew outside of the Dreamworld."

"It's a miracle," Therese murmured, still in shock over the unexpected transformation of her children into gods.

As pleased as Hip was, he was worried for Morpheus and Persephone. He wouldn't rest until his son and mother were safely returned. He could tell by Jen's expression that she was feeling the same. He was about to suggest a rescue plan, when he noticed drops of blood falling from thin air, creating a trail across the room.

The other gods noticed it, too. In a flash, Hades held the helm of invisibility, and beneath it, on his knees and covered in blood, was Morpheus.

Jen screamed into her hands as Hip rushed to Morpheus's side. Jen followed, the three of them on their knees in a huddle of misery.

Hestie sat up in her bed. "Morpheus!"

"Oh, my gods!" Therese flew to the other side of Jen.

Hip couldn't believe how much blood covered his son's beautiful bronze skin and the black curls on his head. It was now on Hip's hands. He stared at it, half-dazed.

"What happened?" The stern voice of Hades brought Hip back to his senses.

With his head bowed, Morpheus cleared his voice and said, "Zeus…he…"

"He took your wings!" Jen cried.

"How barbaric!" Apollo scoffed.

"But why?" Tizzie asked.

"Leverage," Alecto said with disgust.

"He made me swear…" Morpheus began, his silver eyes troubled.

Apollo raised his hand. "Don't break your oath."

Morpheus looked at Apollo and the others with disbelief. "But if I don't tell you…"

"We already know what he wants from you," Poseidon said, with a toss of his long, sun-bleached hair. "He wants you to spy."

Morpheus turned to Poseidon, searching his turquoise eyes. "How did you…"

"Don't say another word about it," Apollo said again.

"I can't believe Zeus would do this to you," Jen said to Morpheus. "After you obeyed him and everything."

"I can," Artemis said with a scowl, her forest green eyes narrowed.

"I'm so sorry." Therese stroked Jen's long, blonde hair, trying to comfort her.

Hip could only gape, still unable to process what had happened.

"What about Persephone?" Hades asked. "If she doesn't have the helm, she must be exposed."

Hip was afraid of the answer.

New tears rushed from Morpheus's eyes, and his chin quivered. "Zeus…he swallowed her."

Hades stumbled back and fell into a chair, his face pale.

The room filled with gasps. Hip could barely process the looks of shock on the faces of the others in the room. Speechless, he stared in horror at his father, who seemed suddenly crushed. The giant, confident leader Hip had always looked up to was now hunched over in his chair on the verge of weeping.

Hip couldn't bear to see his father like this. It was almost as disturbing as the image of his bleeding son. How had things come to this?

"This is an outrage!" Poseidon shouted. "We won't tolerate it, Hades. We'll get her back. I promise you."

"Don't make promises you can't keep, brother," Hades managed to say.

"Poor Mother!" Meg wailed. "I can't bear it."

Tizzie flew to Meg and threw her arms around her. "We'll get her back. I know we will."

Thanatos crossed the room to his father's side. "Poseidon and Tizzie are right, Father. We *will* get her back." He turned to Hip. "And we'll get his wings back, too," he said of Morpheus. "I didn't return just to be defeated. We have power on our side." Than turned to Poros. "We have destiny on our side." He glanced across the room at Apollo. "We have foresight." He turned to Poseidon. "And we have the most powerful brothers." Then he met the faces of every single person in the room. "The time for change has come, and we are that change."

***

Hermie was moved by his father's speech, but he was still trying to understand what had happened to him. Hermie's body was *glowing*. He was sitting up in the bed, gazing at his hands, wiggling his fingers. He was feeling a little creeped out.

We're gods, Hestie's voice said directly into his brain.

She hadn't spoken out loud, but he'd heard it as clearly as if she had. He stared at her transformed body, glowing like his. Her red hair seemed thicker and shinier, and her muscles more defined. Was he more muscular, too? He checked his abs and gaped. Yes. He was a lot more buff than he'd ever been.

Can you hear me? he said to his sister telepathically.

Looking at him, she nodded.

I feel funny, he said.

Hermie noticed tears in his sister's eyes as she said, *We'll get to be with Mom and Dad forever.*

He hadn't thought of that. Everything was happening so fast. But it was true. He smiled as he realized it. They would be a family forever.

But he frowned as quickly as he had smiled. What would it mean to be a god? The others were talking about a revolution. Would this mean that he and Hestie would be expected to go into battle? Their parents had trained them to fight ever since they were babies, but he'd always thought of it as a sport, like live action role play. He wasn't sure if he had the guts to wield a sword against a real person, much less a god. He wondered if it was possible to be turned back into a mortal.

Thinking of being mortal reminded Hermie of Mina and Jinsoo. Pete had taken them to Tartarus, where all the evildoers go. He hoped they weren't freaking out. He wished he could go with them and tell them everything was going to be okay, though he wasn't convinced that it was true.

He wondered where Prometheus was and then remembered someone had said he was with Hecate, who was recovering from being tortured by the Titans. He'd heard that even her father, Perses, had participated in her suffering. Hermie shuddered. Torture seemed to be a common theme among the immortals. Hermie hoped Prometheus would return soon and take Mina and Jinsoo someplace away from here—someplace safe, if such a place existed.

Artemis crossed the room and stood before Hades. Like Therese and Apollo, she wore a quiver full of arrows. "I imagine your first thought is of rescue."

"Yes," Hades said.

"But we can't rush in," Artemis insisted. "We need a plan to overtake Mount Olympus."

Poros moved to Artemis's side. "I agree. You might not want to hear this, Lord Hades, but Persephone is safe where she is."

"She's been *swallowed!*" Hestie cried, as if that fact hadn't already been known.

"My mother survived in my father's belly for centuries," Poros continued. "She could hear everything Zeus said. She could even hear his thoughts."

"Persephone could be of use to us where she is," Apollo said.

"Telepathy is impossible with someone who's been…" Meg's voice trailed off.

"And think how miserable she must be!" Tizzie cried, just before her white wolf howled.

Poseidon crossed his arms. "We know firsthand. Don't we, brother?"

"It's *pure* misery," Hades said, looking as if he were in a daze.

Hermie had to agree. His Grandma Persephone must be terrified, lonely, and uncomfortable, if not in outright pain. Could she breathe? Could she see? Could she move? She must feel like she was buried alive. He shuddered again.

"We have to get her out of that tyrant as soon as possible!" Alecto's red hair became flames, and her snake, coiled around her neck, hissed.

"We have to get her out," Artemis said, "but not yet."

Hermie frowned. "But when?"

"Let's give her time to know Zeus's mind," Apollo suggested. "Then, once we do free her, she can help us with our next move."

Poseidon turned to Apollo. "Being swallowed has a way of…changing a person."

"We can't leave her there, Father," Meg pleaded.

As if in agreement, her falcon squawked.

"We need to think of a way to free her as soon as possible," Hades said.

"Uranus," Hip said. "That's how I recovered Ares's leg from the dragon. Uranus gave me an herb from Circe's stash."

"Maybe he can tell us where to find more," Hermie's mom suggested.

"With the helm, Morpheus can sneak it into Zeus's cup before Hebe serves him," Poseidon said.

"Why must it always be Morpheus?" Jen complained.

Hermie glanced at his cousin, feeling sorrier for him that he'd ever felt for anyone or anything. He'd been mutilated, his girlfriend was imprisoned, and now he was expected to play the dangerous role of double agent in a war between gods.

"Poseidon is right, I'm afraid," Hades said. "We'll have to use Morpheus in the same way Zeus meant to."

"Are we sure we can trust him not to play both sides?" Artemis asked.

"What?" Morpheus gave Artemis a surprised look and then glanced at the faces of the other gods in the room for the first time. "I wouldn't do that. I swear."

"But you've sworn your allegiance to Zeus," Poseidon pointed out. "Even if it was under duress."

A chill crept up Hermie's spine as he recalled the way Morpheus had turned him over to Zeus. If Morpheus hadn't done that, things might have turned out differently.

Apollo turned to Hades. "I sense the boy is telling us the truth, but we need to keep him ignorant of our strategies, so that Zeus can't force the information out of him. We've said too much in front of him already."

"We'll have to tell him something, though," Hip said, "or Zeus will know that we're keeping him in the dark."

"And if Morpheus is no longer useful to Zeus…" Artemis's voice trailed off.

Nausea formed in the pit of Hermie's stomach. He loved his cousin, even after all he'd done. Hermie knew Morpheus had only been doing what he thought was right.

"Wouldn't Zeus leave him alone?" Jen asked, hopefully. "Morpheus wouldn't be able to spy for us, but he'd be safe."

"Not if he'd already heard too much of Zeus's plans, I'm afraid," Hades said.

"Then let's keep him here," Jen said. "He's just a boy."

"I'm almost twenty," Morpheus argued.

"You're still so young," Tizzie agreed with Jen.

"I *want* to go, Mom," Morpheus said. "Iris is still there, and Persephone. Zeus put Demeter into my cage, and she didn't even do anything wrong. If I don't go back…"

Hermie covered his mouth. He wasn't sure what shocked him more—that Morpheus wanted to go into danger, or that Demeter had been imprisoned.

"He's imprisoned Demeter?" Meg asked.

"Oh, no!" Hermie's mother cried.

"He's lost it." Poseidon turned to Hades. "Our brother has lost it. Who knows what's next?"

"We need a plan," Hermie's father said.

"Send Morpheus to the Dreamworld, so we can get on with it," Poseidon said.

Morpheus looked to his father and mother.

"Just for now," Hip said.

"I'll go with him," Jen offered, before taking Morpheus's hand.

Prometheus and Hecate entered the room just as Morpheus left with his mother. Hermie gasped at the sight of Hecate. She was covered in cuts and bruises, and dried blood surrounded her eyes.

The Furies and Therese rushed to her side, asking if she was okay.

"I'll be fine," Hecate said with a half-smile.

She didn't look fine to Hermie. Tears filled his eyes, and he swiped them away. He was an effin' god, but he'd never felt more afraid.

CHAPTER TWO

Lynn's Dream

Hestie sat on the sofa beside Poros in the rooms that had once belonged to her parents but that were now inhabited by Tizzie and Pete. Her father had assumed the chambers that had been his for centuries would be returned to him, but nothing had been settled yet. Her parents and Hermie had just left, leaving her and Poros alone to digest everything that had been said.

Hestie and Hermie must find a way to serve the world or humanity in some way, or they would turn back into mortals. And they only had three months to figure it out.

"Is there a god of fashion?" Poros asked.

Hestie rolled her eyes. "That's not what I want to be."

"I thought you *loved* fashion."

"I do, but I don't want to be the goddess of it. Besides, don't you think that's part of Aphrodite's realm?"

"You could be right."

Hestie sighed. This was going to be a lot harder than she thought. Everything was already taken.

Poros squeezed her hand. "Don't worry. You'll figure it out."

"I want to do something with my gift with languages, but Hermes is already the god of communication."

"He's the god of a lot of things," Poros said. "Maybe he'd give you that."

Hestie shook her head. "Since when has any god given up power?"

"Is it power, though? Or is it responsibility?"

Hestie cocked her head to the side. "Hmm. Good point."

"Hermes was the god of death before your dad was born," Poros pointed out.

"But no one wants *that* job."

"True."

Hestie wondered what her uncle Pete was going to do. If he didn't find a new purpose within three months, would something happen to him, too?

"What about you?" Hestie asked Poros. "What are you going to be?"

Poros shrugged. "That's easy. I'm destined to replace my father."

"You want to be the king of the gods?"

Laughing, Poros said, "No, no, no. No way. I want to keep doing what I've *been* doing. Life on the open sea, diving for treasure, helping people."

Hestie furrowed her brows. "How can you take over from your dad *and* go to sea?"

"You don't have to be on Mount Olympus to rule the sky," Poros said. "I think the sea affords the best view of it, anyway."

Hestie grinned. "Sounds like you got it all figured out, Poros, god of the sky."

He took her shoulders and squared himself to her. "You will, too. Don't worry."

She met his eyes. They were the same stunning gray as Athena's. *Dang, you're hot*, she thought as she felt herself blushing. She shouldn't be thinking of him like that. There was too much going on to be distracted by thoughts of love.

"You forget that I can hear you," he said, moving his lips toward hers.

She pulled away.

He frowned. "What's wrong?"

She jumped up from the couch and paced the room. "What's *wrong?* Are you seriously asking me that? One set of my grandparents is dead. Grandma Persephone has been swallowed by Zeus. My parents and brother and I were just turned into gods. *Gods!* My cousin got his wings ripped off. And now, we're expected to find a purpose for the rest of our lives while overthrowing the king of the Olympians. What's *wrong?* What's *wrong?*"

Poros stood up and took her hands. "Calm down. I'm sorry. Please. Take a deep breath."

Hestie stopped pacing and took a deep breath. Then she slowly blew it out.

"Good. Better?"

She shrugged. "It doesn't change anything."

He squeezed her hands. "I know things seem bleak right now, but this is the beginning of the change. It's only going to get better."

"What if it gets worse before it gets better?"

"It might. But it *will* get better."

"How can you be so sure?"

He cupped her cheeks in his hands. "Because I believe in the rebellion."

She could tell he wanted to kiss her. *Don't,* she said to him telepathically.

His eyes widened with surprise, and he let her go, taking a step back. "I'm sorry," he murmured, looking hurt.

Hestie folded her arms across her chest. As much as she liked him and was interested in him, it just wasn't the time. There was too much going on for her to think about love.

***

Morpheus followed his mother to the Fields of Asphodel.

"I'm so sorry, my sweet, sweet son," she said to him as she washed the blood from his back. She rinsed the cloth in a bowl of water and then rinsed his hair. "I can't believe this has happened to you. You've always been so good and obedient."

Morpheus gave her a half-smile. "I should have listened to Pops."

"You didn't have the big picture," she said as she dried him with a clean towel. "Or you would have. I know it."

Morpheus hoped she was right.

Then she said, "I can't believe Zeus is such a dick."

"Me either."

"But don't you worry," she added as she brought forth a soft white blanket made of wool and carefully wrapped it around him. "We've got all the good people on our side. We'll win this, and we'll get back your wings, and we'll get Iris and Persephone and Demeter, too."

Morpheus wished he could believe her. "You really think so?"

"Yes, I do."

"How can you be so sure?"

"Because dicks like Zeus eventually piss off everyone around them," she said. "Nobody wants a leader like that. You just wait and see. Once we get Athena and some of the others to our side, the rest will be history."

He really hoped she was right, but he still couldn't believe that anything good would come of this. There were always casualties in war, even on the winning side, and Iris seemed doomed to be one.

"Let's try to get some rest," his mother said before she kissed his cheek. "We both need to recharge our batteries, okay?"

"Okay."

"I love you, son."

"Love you, too, Mom."

Morpheus lay in the wool blanket beside his mother in the asphodel and closed his eyes. He was glad for the chance to return his focus to the Dreamworld. Although the power to be in two places at once had been gifted to him, so that he could be in the Dreamworld and still have a life outside of it, the pain and trauma he'd been experiencing had made it difficult for him to carry out his duties. Reintegrating with himself in the asphodel brought him a certain degree of peace.

He loved how he could become anyone or anything as he visited the dreams of mortals. In one moment, he was a dragon and, in another, a butterfly. He could swim among fish, fly among birds, and dance among clouds. Being the god of dreams gave him a freedom like no other. And, more importantly, he was good at his job. His Pops had told him again and again: "Morpheus, you were born to be the god of dreams." Those words had filled him with a sense of purpose.

But that sense of purpose had been shaken by Zeus. Morpheus wondered what would become of the Dreamworld—or any world— after the rebellion was squashed or was triumphant. If squashed, would Zeus throw the rebellious gods into the Titan Pit and give their duties to others?

Although he wanted nothing more than to dream about Iris, Morpheus's thoughts dwelled on what life would be like in the Titan Pit. The Titans hated him and his family. Would their eternal existence be nothing but torment and conflict?

Too distracted to conjure up peaceful dreams of Iris, Morpheus searched the Dreamworld for Zeus. It was the one time when Morpheus had the upper hand. And boy, oh, boy, did Morpheus have plans for the tyrannical king of Mount Olympus. He searched and searched and, not finding Zeus, looked for his loyalists, wanting some sweet revenge; but he was sorely disappointed. The only deities asleep, besides his mother, were a few of the Muses. Tormenting them wouldn't bring Morpheus any kind of release.

He wished his sweet Iris would close her eyes and find sleep—not only because she needed it, but because he needed her. The Dreamworld was the one place where they could be together.

Iris, he prayed to her telepathically, knowing she wouldn't hear him in the bird cage, but hoping she would, anyway.

When he received no reply, Morpheus, tired of lies and deceit, flew through the Gates of Horn, where dreams of truth were formed. The dreams that came through the Gates of Horn were usually past events. Sometimes they were pleasant memories that gave solace to the dreamer. Sometimes they were traumatic events—like experiences in war, natural disasters, child abuse. Both the good and the bad were helpful to the dreamer, pushing the mortals to work through their emotions.

Morpheus was caught off guard to find himself in a dream belonging to Lynn—Hermie and Hestie's cousin in Colorado. He was surprised because she wasn't dreaming of a past event. Her dream was of the second type to pass through the Gates of Horn: a dream of prophecy. This kind of dream came only from the Fates.

He could tell it was a dream of prophecy because the event had never happened. Moreover, Lynn wasn't an agent in the dream. Like Morpheus, she was watching from the sidelines.

In the dream, figments appeared in the forms of Hermie, Ares, and Hermes. The gods were on a dry riverbank beneath a cluster of poplar trees near a rock wall. One event played out over and over in gruesome detail: Hermes swung his sword across Hermie's neck. Morpheus watched in horror as the body and head of his cousin dropped to the grass beside a tortoise, and blood sprayed across the tortoise and the trees.

Then the dream reset, and Morpheus saw it happen again.

Why were the Fates showing Lynn this dream?

Morpheus left the awful vision and searched for his mother. He found her on the Horn side reliving a memory from his early childhood, not long after he'd been made into a god.

In his mother's dream, they were playing Night Frisbee above the island of Crete with Asterion and Ariadne. Pops was there, too. Asterion had captured the frisbee and had thrown it miles away, up into the night sky, so that it had been difficult to predict where it would return. They played on teams, and the goal was to either steal the disc from the throwing team, or to keep it from being stolen. New to the game, Morpheus had been placed on his parents' team, playing against Asterion and Ariadne. The Minotaur's strength seemed to make up for the difference in the number of players.

As they waited for the red disc to return, the gods scattered. Morpheus spotted it first and swept up into the sky, intercepting it from Ariadne.

His mother shouted, "You're a natural, son!"

His father gave him a fist bump. "You're almost as fast as Hermes."

"It's those beautiful silver wings," Ariadne said. "He's really grown into them, hasn't he?"

"It was just beginner's luck," Asterion teased. "Now throw the disc, Morpheus. Let's see if you're any good."

Morpheus watched as a figment in his form hurled the red frisbee into the night sky.

"Nice!" his mother shouted before kissing his cheek.

The real Morpheus watched his mother enjoying her dream with the figments for a moment longer before he interrupted her.

"Mom, come on," he said, taking her hand. "This is important."

"Figment," she said, "I command you to show yourself."

"It's me. Come on."

He led her to Lynn's dream, where the scene with Ares, Hermes, and Hermie was still replaying, in an ongoing loop.

"Oh, my gods," his mother whispered. "I'd forgotten."

Morpheus turned to his mother. "Forgotten what?"

"Back when I was still a mortal human, something happened," she explained. "All the souls were unloosed from the Underworld…"

"Wait. What? How could that be?" This was the first Morpheus had ever heard of such a thing.

"Zeus had attacked…"

"Zeus attacked?" Morpheus threw his hands up in the air. "And you never thought to tell me this before?"

"I didn't want to scare you."

"Mom, I might've known better than to trust that lunatic if you'd told me this! Oh, gods!"

"I'm sorry. Geez. Parents try their best to protect their children, and they make mistakes, okay? I'm sorry. Now get over it."

"Tell me what happened."

"Pete had the ability to see the ghosts. None of the rest of us could—except Lynn."

"What?"

"Therese told me. Lynn could see the ghosts, too. Which means…"

"What, Mom?"

"Lynn's a seer."

***

Therese fell back on her old bed in the Underworld and gaped up at Jen. She had just returned from visiting the souls of her parents in the Fields of Elysium. She'd realized that the first time they'd died, back when she was fifteen, she hadn't truly grieved for them. She'd distracted herself with Than and had focused on becoming a god, so she could see them in the Underworld. Now that they'd gone from her a second time, she wanted to grieve them properly. But it seemed her grief would have to wait.

Speechless, she looked from Jen to Morpheus and back to Jen again.

"And you think this is a prophecy because…why?" Than, standing beside the bed, asked.

Morpheus, whose back had become one long scab where his wings used to be, heaved a heavy sigh, as though all of this was his fault.

It wasn't his fault. Therese decided to say it out loud, in case he hadn't heard her telepathically. "This isn't your fault."

"I've said that to him 'til I was blue in the face," Jen said.

"Lynn's dream came through the Gates of Horn," Morpheus explained. "It wasn't a memory, so it had to be…"

"A prediction," Than finished Morpheus's sentence.

"Yeah," Morpheus said.

"But only the Fates know with certainty," Therese said.

"It comes from the Fates," Morpheus said.

Therese stopped breathing as tears flooded her eyes. What did this mean for poor Hermie?

Than sat on the bed beside her. "Sometimes the Fates use symbols. The dream may not mean what it seems to mean."

"He's right," Jen said.

Morpheus's silence said more. Therese looked up at him, but he avoided her eyes. She was pretty sure that symbolic dreams passed through the Gates of Ivory, not of Horn. Dreams from the Horn were literal and true.

"Besides, he's a god now," Than added. "Even if the dream comes to pass, his death will be temporary."

Therese didn't say what she was thinking: A god could be forced to remain in Tartarus without his body if the head was hidden someplace where the body couldn't reunite with it. What if that was what Hermes and Ares had in store for her son? What if one of them swallowed her son's head?

"I want to talk to Lynn," Therese said. "Maybe she's had other visions that we don't know about."

"I'll go with you," Than said.

"You can't," Jen pointed out. "Remember?"

Therese frowned, wondering if Carol, Richard, and Lynn would have to wait to die before they would ever see Thanatos again.

"I'll go with you," Jen said.

Suddenly Hestie, followed by Poros, entered the room. "Whatever you do, don't tell Hermie. It will totally freak him out and probably paralyze him with fear."

"What will?" Hermie asked, as he pushed his way past Poros through the door.

Therese jumped up from the bed. "Nothing, honey. Hestie's exaggerating."

"Then tell me," Hermie said.

Therese turned to Than, hoping for help.

"Your mom has to go to Colorado," Than said.

Hermie crossed his arms and narrowed his eyes suspiciously. "And that's terrifying because?"

"Because she's going there to tell Grammie and Grampie about Nana Lin and Papa Ger," Than said of Therese's parents.

Hermie wiped his eyes. "That makes me sad, but it doesn't paralyze me with fear."

"Yeah, Hestie," Morpheus said. "Leave my boy alone."

Hestie glanced at Poros and put her hands on her hips. "I thought the trip down there would…you know, after what happened the last time you were in a chariot, and since it's too dangerous for god travel…"

"He was brave," Poros said. "Jumping out after the laptop. Dude!"

Hermie grinned. "You heard about that?"

"Tell me," Morpheus said. "I haven't heard the story yet."

"It was epic," Poros said.

"We wouldn't have been able to fulfill our destiny if it hadn't been for Hermie," Hestie said.

Therese sat down on the bed and watched her children interacting. She and Thanatos exchanged smiles. It was a dream come true for them to be together in the Underworld. But Lynn's prophetic dream had her worried. What would drive Hermes to do such a thing to her son?

"Oh, and I'm pretty sure I've thought of my purpose," Hermie said, after he'd finished telling Morpheus the story.

Therese jumped to her feet. "Really?"

"What?" Morpheus asked.

"I want to spread technology to third-world countries," Hermie said. "All kinds."

"What a great idea," Jen said.

"Do you think it will offend Hermes or Hephaestus?" Hermie asked.

"Hermes is more about messages and letters," Than said. "He used to oversee telegrams, and he still helps out the postal services. But I think he's given up on social media."

Everyone laughed.

"And what about Hephaestus?" Hermie asked. "The god of the forge is sometimes thought of as the god of technology."

"His focus is more on the craftsmanship," Therese said. "And on weapons and simple machines—not so much on the applications of complex machines, like computers, right Than?"

"Right. And that's right up your alley," Than said. "I'm proud of you, son."

Therese nodded as tears filled her eyes. "Me, too."

"Gosh, Mom," Hermie said. "Don't cry."

"The god of technology," Hestie said. "That has a nice ring to it."

"What about you, Hestie?" Therese asked, wiping her eyes with the backs of her hands. "Any ideas yet?"

Hestie shook her head.

"You've got plenty of time," Than reassured her.

"It'll come to you," Therese said, recalling her own struggle to find her purpose. She'd had no ideas whatsoever, until it suddenly dawned on her in the middle of a chariot ride to Mount Olympus.

"I came here to ask what the plan is for Mina and Jinsoo," Hermie asked.

"Prometheus wants them to stay in Tartarus until he's ready to set sail again," Poros said.

"He wants to go back to *The Marcella*?" Hermie asked, surprised.

"I think so," Poros said. "That's the plan, at least."

"Why don't you go back and keep them company?" Than suggested to Hermie. "Your mom and I need to talk before she leaves for Colorado."

"We really are proud of you," Therese said as Hermie turned to leave. She glanced at Hestie. "Of both of you."

Once Hermie had gone, Hestie said, "I want to go with you to talk to Lynn."

"Not this time, sweetheart," Therese said.

"I have to know what she knows," Hestie insisted. "This is Hermie we're talking about. Please, Mom. Take me with you, or I'll just go on my own, anyway."

"Hestie," Than said in a warning tone. "Don't talk to your mom like that."

"It's all right," Therese said.

"Can I come, too?" Poros asked.

Therese glanced at Jen. Who could say no to the most powerful god in existence?

CHAPTER THREE

The New Seer

Hermie returned to Tartarus and found Mina and Jinsoo in a conversation with Pete and Tizzie. Tizzie was demonstrating how a Fury fulfilled her duties as an avenger of the Underworld.

When Tizzie's black ringlets transformed into hissing snakes, Hermie said, "Um, maybe that's too much."

"No, it cool!" Mina said. "I want snake hair, too! And a wolf!"

Tizzie and Pete laughed.

"What about you?" Jinsoo asked Pete. "Your hair do anything cool like that?"

"Nope," Pete said. "I'm boring compared to Tizzie."

"Oh, hush," Tizzie said as she kissed Pete's cheek. "You're far from boring, my love."

"He was the god of death," Hermie explained to the mortals. "My father was for centuries, until they switched fates."

"You really the god of *death*?" Mina asked Pete.

"Not anymore," Pete said.

"My dad is now," Hermie said. Then he turned to Pete. "Do you know what your new purpose is going to be?"

Tizzie frowned.

"Not yet," Pete said. "I'm still trying to figure that out."

"Maybe he could become a fourth Fury," Tizzie said.

Pete rolled his eyes. "I doubt Hades will go for that."

"You never know." Tizzie nudged her elbow against Pete's side. "With all the bad people in the world, my sisters and I really could use another set of hands."

"Is that something you're interested in?" Hermie asked Pete.

"I used to be a seer, but I haven't been able to *see* since I got my eyes back."

Hermie furrowed his brows.

Pete laughed. "I guess I wish I could use my natural talents in some way, you know?"

"What are your talents?" Hermie asked him.

"I sing and play the guitar," Pete said. "And I'm good with horses."

"I like horse, too!" Mina said.

"And I like guitar!" Jinsoo said.

Tizzie brushed Pete's dirty-blond hair from his eyes. "Apollo and Poseidon wouldn't go for either of those, my love."

"It's not going to be easy," Pete said. "But the best things in life usually aren't." He winked at Tizzie.

"I've got mine figured out," Hermie said, turning to Mina and Jinsoo. "You're now looking at the god of technology."

"That make sense!" Mina cried. "You so good with computer and internet!"

"I know Hermes is the god of communication and Hephaestus is the god of the forge, but technology encompasses much more than that. I'm talking about advances in biomedical, ecological, computer, and transportation technologies. I want to bring it all to third world countries," Hermie told them.

"How?" Jinsoo asked.

"Maybe Captain can help!" Mina said. "You come back with us on the ship!"

Hermie grinned. He'd like nothing more than to go back to sea with Mina. Just a few months ago, if someone would have told him he'd want to be a sailor, he would have died laughing; but now it would be a dream come true.

"I hope so," he said.

"We dive for treasure together," Mina said. "And watch *Naruto* and help people."

"Sounds like a plan," Hermie said with a grin.

Tizzie mussed Hermie's hair, like she did when he was a baby. "Congratulations, Hermie! I'm so happy for you!"

Alecto and Meg suddenly appeared.

"What's going on?" Meg asked.

Tizzie told them Hermie's news, and the other two Furies added their congratulations to the mix, giving Hermie kisses and high fives.

"Can I be god, too?" Mina asked.

Hermie turned to the Furies. "Can she?"

"I suppose Poros is the one to ask," Alecto said.

"Don't make such a decision lightly," Meg warned Mina. "Being a god has its perks, but it isn't easy."

"And eternity is a long time," Alecto added.

Hermie swallowed hard. He hadn't been given the choice. Poros had made him a god to save him from death. Hermie was grateful, but he was also afraid. He now wondered if he'd been too hasty in claiming his purpose. If he'd waited, he would have reverted to a mortal—at least, that's what his parents had told him. A mortal life would have meant being away from his family, but he wasn't so sure that he was cut out to be a god, especially when they always seemed to be at war with one another. What kind of immortal life would Persephone have if the other gods weren't able to rescue her from the belly of Zeus?

Mina took Hermie's hand. "What you think, Hermie? Should I ask Poros?"

What if Mina became a god, but they didn't get along as well as he'd hoped? What if this crush he had on her didn't last? Or, worse, what if another deity swallowed her or paralyzed her for all eternity?

"I don't know," Hermie finally said. "Let's think about it."

Mina frowned. He could tell he had hurt her feelings, but he didn't know what else to say.

***

Hestie rode in the chariot between her mother and Poros as her mother directed Swift and Sure from the Underworld to their home in Colorado. Her Aunt Jen hadn't come along after all. Uncle Hip had needed her for something important.

The sun was dawning over Lemon Reservoir, and even though it was late May or early June—Hestie had lost track of time—it was still cold in the mornings. Hestie was surprised that even though she was aware of the chill, it didn't bother her. She wasn't actually *cold*. She wondered what other perks she had to look forward to as a goddess.

As Hestie saw their home in the distance, she searched for the red birds in the treetops. Then she remembered. The death of her grandparents hit her again, and she felt nauseous. Their sacrifice had saved her parents' lives, but it hadn't made it easier to accept the loss. She would miss their daily chats on the back deck of their log cabin in the San Juan Mountains. She'd miss their sweet songs and their beautiful red feathers. She'd miss Papa Ger's jokes and Nana Lin's quirky remarks. It was hard to believe they were gone.

Her eyes filled with tears as her mother parked the chariot near their house.

"You okay?" Poros whispered.

"I will be." She wiped her tears and cleared her throat.

Her mother climbed from the chariot. "Let's check on our animals before we go see Lynn and Grammie and Grampie."

"They know we're here," Hestie said of the animals, her grief replaced by joy at being with them again. She'd just seen them the previous day, but it had been a quick and dangerous trip, and they were probably worried sick about her. "I can hear them talking about us."

"I can, too," her mother said, crossing the deck to the back door.

"You can?" Hestie was shocked.

"Me, too," Poros said. "All gods can understand all creatures, remember?"

"Oh, yeah."

Hestie followed her mother through the back door, where they were greeted by Clifford, Noodle, and Kitty. Chidori's tweets filled the air, and Jewels waved from her sandbox. Hestie kissed each one of them, assuring them that she was fine, and then ran upstairs to let Katniss and Prim from their cage. They ran up her arms and perched on her shoulders, full of excitement to see her.

Poros, who'd followed her up, grinned. "You're adorable."

"Can you make them immortal? So, they can come with us?"

"I don't know," Poros said. "I'm still not sure how I did it to you and your brother."

"I can," her mother said as she entered the room, followed by Clifford and Noodle.

"What?" Hestie blinked. "I thought only Zeus, and then Poros…I don't get it."

"I'm the goddess of animal companions," her mother explained. "I have the power to make pets immortal."

Hestie beamed at her mother. "Do it! Noodle and Kitty and Chidori, too!"

"The Underworld is going to be a little more crowded after this," her mother said with a smile. Then she took an arrow from her quiver, loaded it onto her bow, and struck Prim in the heart.

Hestie gasped. "Did that hurt?"

"Did what hurt?" Prim asked.

"She can't see or feel my arrows," Hestie's mother explained as she pulled the arrow from Prim's heart.

Hestie was impressed. "Wow, Mom."

Her mother did the same to Katniss before heading downstairs and repeating the process with Noodle, Kitty, and Chidori. Like Clifford, Jewels was already immortal.

Clifford couldn't believe his ears when they told him the news: they were all immortal and were returning to their home with Cubie and Galin. He ran up and down the stairs with Noodle on his tail, barking like a crazy dog. Kitty fainted and fell from her perch on the TV. She would have landed with a hard plop on the hardwood floor had Poros not flown across the room to break the fall.

"Good save!" Hestie shouted, moved by his kindness to her pets. She wasn't going to let herself fall in love with him, but it was still nice that he cared about her friends.

Hestie's mother said to the animals, "You wait here while we go talk to Lynn."

"What?" Noodle looked at them as though his bubble had burst. "How long?"

"Maybe an hour or two," Hestie's mother replied.

"We've waited this long," Jewels said. "What's one more hour?"

"I'm convinced time is meaningless for a tortoise," Clifford barked.

Hestie and Poros laughed as they followed her mother from the house.

***

Therese led Hestie and Poros on foot down the dirt road to Carol and Richard's house. She needed the stroll. Seeing her childhood home flooded her with memories and with grief. The trees seemed empty without her two favorite red birds hopping from branch to branch, singing their favorite songs. When she reached the gravel drive, she was a sopping mess.

"Mom?" Hestie asked, noticing her state.

"I'm okay," Therese said. "Let me do the talking, though. Okay?"

Hestie nodded before following Therese up to the screened porch.

When Carol came to the door, the floodgates opened, and Therese broke down in tears.

"Therese? What's happened?" Carol asked, opening the door for them. "Where's Hermie and Than?"

"They're okay," Hestie said. "By the way, this is Poros."

"Nice to meet you," Carol said. "Come in."

Therese entered the living room and found Richard sitting at the bar in the kitchen, drinking a cup of coffee.

"Therese!" he said gleefully. "You're back!"

Then, noticing her expression, he set his mug on the bar and stood up. "What's wrong?"

After giving her aunt and uncle a hug, Therese plopped onto one end of the sofa, leaving room for Hestie and Poros. "We better sit down. Where's Lynn?"

"Still asleep." Carol took the chair near the fireplace. "It's the first day of summer break, and she wanted to sleep in. Should I wake her?"

"I'm afraid so," Therese said. "What I have to say concerns her, most of all."

"Why most of all?" Richard asked from where he stood near the bar.

"She's a seer," Therese said. "She can see the future, and Morpheus told me about a dream she had—a terrible dream about Hermie."

"I'll go wake her up." Carol took the stairs to Lynn's bedroom—the same room where Therese had spent her childhood.

"Promise me you won't put your sister in harm's way," Richard said.

Therese bit her lip. "I only want to ask her a few questions."

But in the pit of her stomach, Therese knew that if word got out to Zeus and the loyalists that Lynn was a seer, Lynn's life *would* be in danger. Than had said as much to Therese telepathically before she'd left. Zeus and the loyalists had lost Apollo, and they had no access to Tiresias or to Pete. Thanatos wanted Therese to bring Lynn to the Underworld for safekeeping, but Therese didn't want to disrupt the lives of her aunt and uncle and sister needlessly. If they kept Lynn's gift a secret from Zeus and the others, Lynn would be fine. Besides, even the Underworld offered no guarantees. There were plenty of dangers there for a mortal girl. Plus, transporting Lynn to the Underworld would attract attention, unlike visiting her family to tell them about her parents' deaths.

Therese hoped she was making the right decision.

Carol returned with a yawning, sleepy-eyed Lynn on her heels.

"Good morning," Lynn said. "Welcome back. Hi, Poros. Where's Hermie?"

"You've met?" Richard arched a brow.

"Yesterday," Lynn said. "When I was feeding the animals."

"We were wondering why you didn't come to see us," Carol said to Hestie.

"It's a long story," Hestie said. "We had to rush back to the Underworld, didn't we, Poros?"

"Yes. Sorry," Poros said. "We were under attack and…"

"What?" Richard spilled his coffee on the bar and quickly dried it with a towel.

"In a game," Therese lied, not wanting to worry them. "They were playing a game with some of the other gods."

"Oh, what a relief," Carol said.

"Sorry to make you get up on your first day of summer break," Therese said to Lynn as she crossed the room for a hug.

"That's okay," Lynn said. "I've been worried. I'm glad you're here."

"Let's all have a seat," Carol said as she returned to her chair.

Lynn took the other remaining chair, and Richard sat on the arm of it as Therese returned to Hestie's side on the sofa.

"First, I have some really sad news." Therese spoke through a new wave of tears as she explained the sacrifice her parents had made for her and Than to live.

"I guess it's a little easier this time," Carol said when Therese had finished. "I felt like I lost them years ago, you know? Since I couldn't really talk to them without Hermie and Hestie."

"I know," Therese said.

"Wait, I'm confused," Richard said. "Are you saying that you and Than are gods again?"

Therese nodded.

"But if Than is the god of death," Lynn said, "does that mean he can't be around us anymore? Not even his own kids? I thought you said that's why y'all became mortal…"

"He can be around me and Hermie," Hestie said. "We're gods now, too."

Carol flinched. "What?"

"How is this possible?" Richard asked.

Therese explained as best as she could, trying to get to the real reason why she'd come.

Carol took Hestie by the hand and pulled her up to stand in front of her. Carol studied her face and hair, inspected the more prominent muscles in her arms.

"How do you feel?" she asked Hestie.

"Grammie, it's amazing. I can fly now, though I haven't had much time to practice. And I can talk to other gods telepathically."

"I have more news to tell you," Therese interrupted. "Please sit down. It concerns Lynn."

"Me? Why me?" Lynn's eyes looked about to pop from their sockets.

"You're a seer," Hestie said as she returned to the sofa beside her mother.

Telepathically, Therese said to Hestie, *I said to let me do the talking.*

Okay, Mom. Sorry.

"What's a seer?" Carol asked.

"It's a person with a special gift," Therese explained. "The gift of prophecy."

"What?" Lynn fell back in her chair. "Quit joking around."

"She's not joking," Hestie said.

"Pete is a seer," Therese said. "And you're like him. It's nothing to be afraid of, but it's probably best not to tell anyone."

Therese decided to ask Pete to visit Lynn, to offer some guidance on how to handle her gift.

"Why not?" Lynn wanted to know.

Therese hesitated, choosing her answer carefully. "Because you don't want people to use you."

"Therese said you had a bad dream about Hermie," Carol said to Lynn.

Lynn gawked. "Wait. How did you know that?"

"Morpheus told us," Hestie replied.

"I've been having it a lot lately." Lynn's face paled. "My dream didn't come true, did it? Oh my God, where's Hermie?"

"He's fine," Therese said. "But we don't want him to know anything about this. That's why we didn't bring him along."

Tears had built up in Lynn's eyes. "Do you really think I saw the future?"

"That's what Morpheus thinks," Hestie said, much to Therese's chagrin.

"What happened in the dream?" Richard asked.

Therese didn't want to upset her aunt and uncle, but she didn't want to keep lying to them, either. She'd already lied about why the kids had to rush off the previous day. As it turned out, Lynn answered before Therese could decide what to do.

"I saw Hermie get beheaded by another god," Lynn said.

Carol gasped. "Oh, my word!"

"Therese, tell me that won't happen," Richard said, looking as though he was about to be sick.

"He's a god now," Poros said. "He can't die."

"Is that right?" Carol asked.

"Yes," Therese said. "He's immortal."

"Then why would another god behead him?" Richard asked.

"To make him weak, maybe," Hestie said.

Let me do the talking, Therese reminded Hestie telepathically.

Sorry, Hestie replied.

Therese took a deep breath. "When a god is beheaded, he or she does die temporarily. The soul goes to Tartarus until the body heals."

"But what if the body is prevented from healing?" Richard asked.

"Can that happen?" Lynn asked.

Therese hesitated before saying, "Yes, it can, but it's very rare. Chances are that Hermie will be fine. I just wanted to hear the details of the dream from Lynn, so we can be prepared."

"Can you remember anything about the setting?" Poros asked Lynn.

"It was dusk," Lynn said. "And it was hot."

"Good," Therese said. "What else?"

"The riverbed was dry and long, except for a small spring," Lynn said. "And it was near an old wall of rock. There might have been buildings in the distance, on the other side. I'll try to pay attention the next time."

"The next time?" Carol asked.

"I've been having the dream every night for a week," Lynn said.

"Can you recall any other details?" Poros asked. "Maybe about the gods?"

"There were two of them," Lynn said. "I recognized Ares, since he used to work for the Holts."

"The other was Hermes," Hestie said. "According to Morpheus."

"Hermie was holding something in his hands," Lynn said. "It looked kind of like a light saber."

"Seriously?" Hestie asked.

"How strange," Therese muttered.

"Ares was laughing at him," Lynn said. "I couldn't hear everything he was saying, though. It was kind of muffled, as if I was listening to him through a wall."

"Where were you in the dream?" Therese asked.

"I was right in front of them, but I don't think they could see me." Then she lifted a finger in the air and added, "I think I saw a tortoise."

"Anything else?" Hestie asked.

Lynn shook her head. "I just have this awful feeling about it, like it's going to happen very soon."

"Don't talk about this to anyone," Therese said. "I don't want you to draw attention to yourself."

"Who would she tell?" Carol asked.

Richard stood up, his hands on his slim hips. "Is there anything you're not telling us, Therese?"

Therese sucked in her lips as Hestie and Poros both glanced her way.

"There is, isn't there?" Richard said without inflection.

"We just have to be careful," Therese said. "We don't want the other gods finding out."

"Is Lynn in danger?" Carol asked.

Lynn's eyes were wide.

"No," Therese said dismissively. "I just want to be extra careful, that's all. I don't want other gods to find out about her, because they may want to use her for her gifts, that's all. Just don't talk about it, and everything will be fine."

Lynn nodded, and Richard returned to his seat, but Therese could sense that they weren't satisfied with her answer. They were worried, as they should be.

CHAPTER FOUR

Prisoners and Allies

Morpheus was sweating beneath the helm of invisibility as he climbed Iris's rainbow from the Underworld toward Mount Olympus. Because he had sworn to report back to Zeus all that he'd learned from the rebels, he hoped what he knew wasn't crucial to their plans to unseat the king. He was still debating whether he should break his oath and face the Maenads.

When he reached the main palace and entered the throne room, he found Zeus, Hera, Hermes, and Ares at home. He wondered where the other loyalists, such as Athena, Aphrodite, Hestia, and Hephaestus, were. Demeter and Iris were still locked in the golden bird cages in the center of the room. Demeter sat with her back against the bars, with her face in her hands. She wasn't sleeping. Iris, on the other hand, lay on her side with her golden wings spread like a blanket around her. He could feel her in the Dreamworld, searching for him. Finally! He tried his best to find her, but he was focused on what he was doing here, on Mount Olympus, which made it difficult for him to concentrate in the Dreamworld.

But he wouldn't stop searching. He hoped she'd remain asleep long enough for him to find her.

He crept up to her cage and gazed down at her. If only he could god travel into her prison and hold her beneath the protection of the helm. But he knew that, even if he could god travel in, he wouldn't be able to god travel out.

He remained beneath the helm, hoping to learn something that could help the rebellion. Carefully, he moved closer to Zeus, who was speaking with his wife and sons.

"But you've had a connection with Apollo since you were an infant," Zeus was saying to Hermes. "Ever since he caught you stealing his cattle. Surely if anyone can bring him home, you can."

"I've tried everything," Hermes said. "He's convinced that the prophecy he and Prometheus have seen will come to pass, and he sees no point in fighting it."

Ares lifted a finger in the air. "Only the Fates know with certainty…"

"That's what I said," Hermes pointed out.

"Keep trying," Hera said. "Use your charming sense of humor and remind him that we're his family."

Morpheus frowned. So that was their big plan? To win back Apollo?

"So, you think I'm charming?" Hermes teased Hera.

The queen scoffed.

"Has anyone heard back from Athena?" Ares asked.

Zeus sighed. "No, and I'm worried. I fear she loves her mother more than her father."

"Her wisdom will guide her to do the right thing," Hera said. "Metis must be found and captured if we're to make any headway with her bastard son."

Ares smirked, but Hermes didn't look pleased, probably because he was a bastard son, too.

Morpheus waited to hear more about their plans to capture Metis, when, unexpectedly, Hermes went down on his knees before Zeus.

"Father, please hear me out."

Zeus narrowed his eyes. "What have you done?"

"Nothing. I've done nothing. It's what *you've* done."

Hera blanched. "How dare you!"

"You may be the only one who loves my father better than me," Hermes said to Hera.

"Don't be too sure about that, brother," Ares said haughtily.

Hermes, still on his knees, looked up at Zeus. "We've been on many great adventures together throughout the centuries, haven't we? How many times have we disguised ourselves as men to play tricks on the mortals, to test their character and their loyalty? How many laughs have we shared?"

"Too many to count," Zeus said, visibly moved by Hermes's words.

"Then please believe me when I say I love you," Hermes said. "And I want you to be my king."

Ares rolled his eyes. "What are you getting at, Hermes?"

"I believe you," Zeus said to Hermes with tears in his eyes.

Morpheus realized for the first time that Hermes loved Zeus just as Morpheus loved his Pops.

"And do you love me back?" Hermes asked Zeus.

"How can you ask such a thing?" Zeus said, but not in anger.

"Does that mean yes?" Hermes asked.

"Yes," Zeus said. "Of course."

Hermes stood and put a hand on his father's shoulder. "Then please don't be the kind of father to your children that your father was to you."

Zeus took a step back from Hermes and broke free. "How can you accuse me of such a thing? I love my children!"

Hermes looked at Zeus with eyes full of tears. "If that were so, you wouldn't have swallowed your daughter."

With a red face and wide, defiant eyes, Zeus shrieked, "She betrayed me! She deserved it! Unlike my brothers and sisters, who were innocent!"

"Like Morpheus was innocent?" Hermes asked.

Morpheus gasped beneath the helm and quickly covered his mouth, not wanting to be discovered.

Then Hermes said, "And what about your loving sister, Demeter? Or Iris? What did they do?"

"Collateral damage," Ares insisted. "It happens in every war. But our father did not start this war."

"He's only trying to defend what is rightfully his," Hera agreed.

"By punishing his loyal servants?" Hermes asked.

Zeus looked at his prisoners, who had climbed to their feet to watch the exchange. Morpheus, partly annoyed that Iris had awakened, noticed their hopeful expressions.

"Father," Hermes said, taking another step closer to Zeus. "Let Iris and Demeter go. Give Morpheus back his wings. I fear you'll lose the loyalty of your remaining supporters if you don't change your ways."

Rage flashed across Zeus's face. "Is that a threat?"

Hermes shook his head. "Of course not. Please listen to me, my lord. Like you, I worry Athena loves her mother more than you. I wonder where Hephaestus has gone. And you know how much Aphrodite loves Hypnos and Thanatos."

"Aphrodite would never go against us," Ares said.

"Because of her love for *you*, maybe," Hermes said. "But not because she agrees with what our father has done. Your supporters, whether they admit it or not," Hermes glanced at Ares before turning back to his father, "must be wondering who's next. Who else among us will you imprison? How many of us will be collateral damage?"

"If I free the prisoners, I'll lose my leverage," Zeus said.

"Maybe," Hermes said. "But you'll gain the love of your followers, and, right now, you need to inspire loyalty more than fear. Please, Father, do the right thing."

Zeus turned to Ares. "What do you think? Should I free the prisoners?"

"We should question Morpheus first," Ares said. "Let's see what he knows and go from there."

Morpheus didn't want them to know that he'd been there, listening. He rushed across the room to the door of the palace and jumped inside the rainbow, catching his breath. He was excited and scared. There was a chance Zeus could be convinced to free the prisoners—to free Iris!

***

Thanatos was surprised when Hecate opened her door before he had knocked.

"You look improved," he said, noticing the dried blood was gone, leaving behind small blue bruises that were quickly healing.

"I am, though my bones still hurt. Come in."

Than entered her sitting area. He'd expected to see Cubie and Galin on the big bed at the back of the room, but he'd forgotten that they were still on Mount Olympus, probably scared sick. "Where's Prometheus?"

"Meeting Athena. He hopes to win her over. Have a seat."

While Athena's support wouldn't guarantee a victory, it would make Thanatos feel a thousand times more confident.

He took a chair. "Do you think he has a chance?"

She sat opposite him "I do. Athena loves him."

"What?" Than had never heard of this.

"You do know that he was the one who rescued her from Zeus's head?"

"I didn't think anyone knew she was the cause of his headache until after Hephaestus used the axe," Than said.

"Prometheus knew. He has visions. Foresight. He convinced Hermes to help him talk Zeus into freeing Athena."

"I didn't know."

"Back then, Prometheus was loved by Zeus for siding with him during the war with the Titans."

"That much I knew."

"He held Zeus's head in his hands as Hephaestus struck Zeus with his axe."

"Did Hermes tell you this?"

She nodded. "When Athena sprung out, fully formed, Prometheus was the first person she laid eyes on. She knew he was responsible for saving her, because she had heard all that Zeus had said and all that had been said to him. She had even heard Zeus's thoughts."

Than scratched his jaw. "Did he love her, too?"

"Very much," Hecate said. "It was obvious to everyone."

Than wondered why Prometheus had never come back for Athena.

Hecate crossed her legs and sat back in her chair. "Once she stops being angry at him for not telling her where he's been all these years, she might listen to what he has to say. We'll see."

"If she could forgive her father for all he did to her—swallowing her and her mother, using Medusa to turn her to stone, and ordering Poseidon to hold her prisoner—well, I have a feeling she'll forgive Prometheus, too, especially after all he's done for her brother, Poros."

"Her love for Prometheus is different than the love she feels for her father. It's easier for us to forgive our parents than it is our lovers. I should know."

Than wondered if she was referring to Hermes, which was the reason why Than was here.

"Speaking of Hermes," he said with a smile.

Hecate laughed. "You see right through me, don't you?"

"Only when it comes to your heart," Than said. "You wear it on your sleeve."

Hecate laughed again. "True enough. What about him?"

"You remember Therese's sister, Lynn?"

"Of course, I do."

"She's a seer."

"I think I knew that. So?"

"She had a prophetic dream from the Gates of Horn. Morpheus saw it."

"What did she see?"

"Hermes beheading my son."

Hecate gaped. "He would never harm your children, or you, for that matter. He loves you."

"I know he does, but Morpheus says her dream comes from the Fates. Have you had any visions that could shed some light on this?"

Hecate shook her head.

"War changes people," Than said.

"Not Hermes. Not like that. Whatever he does, he must have a good reason."

"Maybe," Than said. "But I can't let him harm my son. You understand, don't you?"

"Why are you telling me this?"

"I need your help."

She studied his face. "What do you want me to do?"

"Question Hermes," Than said. "See if he and the others have something planned. Get him to open up to you."

"He knows we stand on opposite sides. I doubt he'll tell me anything."

"Will you try?"

She sighed. "Yes. I'll do my best, but don't get your hopes up."

***

After fifteen or more minutes had passed since he'd curled up inside Iris's rainbow, Morpheus removed the helm of invisibility and returned to Zeus's palace.

"Speak of the devil," Hera said.

Morpheus did not like being called a devil. He wanted to be good. He wanted to do the right thing by his family, by Iris. He glanced at Hermes, whose eyes were still full of tears. Ares looked annoyed. Hestia had returned to her brother's side in Morpheus's absence. Demeter and Iris continued to cling to the bars of their cage, watching the events unfold with hope in their eyes.

Morpheus met Iris's gaze and said telepathically, *Everything's going to be okay.*

"Tell us what you know," Zeus demanded. "Though, I'm sure they suspect you. Did they say anything of their plans in your presence?"

Reluctantly, Morpheus nodded.

Ares crossed his arms at his chest. "Spit it out!"

"I don't know where to start." Morpheus was stalling, hoping for a way around revealing all he knew. He had to tell them *something*, or they would become suspicious.

"Do they have a plan to rescue Persephone?" Hera asked.

Morpheus averted his eyes and cursed to himself, wishing he had never sworn that stupid oath.

"Speak!" Ares demanded.

"There's talk of making Lord Zeus vomit."

Zeus laughed. "They really expect to use a trick from my own playbook? Don't they know I'll recognize the herb I got from Gaia?"

Morpheus closed his eyes and opened them again, not sure how much he should say.

"What?" Ares demanded. "You know more."

"They plan to use the herb Uranus gave to my Pops to get your leg from the dragon."

Zeus smiled. "Good work, Morpheus."

"Even so," Ares said. "How do they expect to get my father to ingest it?"

Morpheus glanced back at Iris. This wasn't going as he had hoped. What had happened to the idea of freeing the prisoners?

"Spit it out!" Ares demanded.

"They want *me* to do it," Morpheus said, unable to think of a lie. He decided he would have to break his oath. It was the only way. He would refuse to tell them anything else.

"Do they suspect you're working for Zeus?" Hermes asked.

"Yes. They don't know if they can trust me."

"You need to *make* them trust you," Hera said. "Or you'll be of no use to us."

"I told them I would never betray them," Morpheus said.

"Good," Ares said. "Keep telling them that."

"Apollo will see right through it," Hermes insisted.

"Wait," Hera looked from her son, Ares, to Morpheus. "How do we know he isn't lying to *us*?"

"He swore an oath," Zeus said.

Hera arched a brow. "And no one has ever broken one?"

"We don't have Apollo to confirm that the boy speaks the truth," Ares said.

Zeus studied Morpheus's face. "What else have you heard? Has Apollo shared any visions?"

"No," Morpheus said truthfully. He wasn't about to tell them what Lynn had seen in her dream.

"We need Metis, and we need Apollo," Hermes said. "Why don't we offer a prisoner exchange? Demeter and Iris for Metis and Apollo."

"Brother!" Demeter cried from her prison. "If you have any love in your heart for me, then give me back my daughter!"

"I can't do that," Zeus said. "She committed treason against me. How would it look to the other rebels if I forgave her for that?"

"You might be surprised," Hermes said. "You might win some of them back with your kindness and mercy."

Zeus looked at Hera and Ares. Then he turned to Hestia. "What do you think, sister? Should I release Persephone?"

Morpheus's heart picked up speed as a glimmer of hope moved through him. Surely Hestia would agree.

"No," Hestia said. "It will make you look weak."

Hermes glanced back at Morpheus with his mouth hanging open, making Morpheus feel as though he were looking into a mirror. How could Hestia be so cold?

"Curse you, Hestia!" Demeter screamed from her cage. "Curse you!"

"You can free her when your kingdom is secure," Hestia said. "She's probably safer in there than anywhere, and she can't make any more mischief for us."

"Please, brother!" Demeter cried.

"I'm afraid I agree with her," Zeus said to Demeter. "But I will free you, in exchange for Apollo."

"Let me be with my daughter!" Demeter cried. "Swallow me, too, so I can comfort her. You never knew what it was like. Your sisters and brothers know, don't we, Hera? Don't we, Hestia? Convince our brother to swallow me, too!"

"I think that's a fair request," Hestia said.

"I don't," Hera said. "What do the rebels care about Iris? We can't use her in a prisoner exchange."

"They care about her because I care about her," Morpheus said. "They know I love her."

"But would they turn over Apollo?" Zeus asked.

Morpheus shrugged, doubting it.

"No," Ares said. "The answer is plain on his face."

"I doubt they would turn over Apollo for any reason," Morpheus said. "But what if I told you there's another seer? A mortal girl in Colorado? Would you give me Iris in exchange for her?"

CHAPTER FIVE

Gifts

Hip and Jen flew to the Island of Crete, near Asterion's labyrinth, to meet Hephaestus at dawn. Several miles away, Artemis and Apollo watched from Apollo's chariot in the sky. Helios was also on guard, should there be a trap or an ambush of any kind awaiting them.

Ariadne emerged from the caves, her black hair flowing about her shoulders in the early morning breeze. Next, her brother, his bull face grim, appeared. Otherwise the ancient ruins were devoid of people. The crowds of tourists had yet to arrive. As a precaution, the deities were in invisibility mode.

"Is he here?" Hip asked.

"Not yet," Asterion replied.

"I'm here!" Hephaestus called from his chariot, as he passed the mountaintop overlooking Heraklion.

Hip gripped the hilt of his sword, just in case.

After Hephaestus had brought his red stallions to a halt on the rocky terrain a few yards away, he lifted his arms in the air and said, "I come in peace, bearing gifts."

Let's not be too eager to believe him, Asterion warned telepathically.

The ugliest of the Olympians—though quite beautiful when compared to mortals, even with his slight hunch and limp—crossed the rocky path to stand before them, his arms still raised in the air.

"I've made a sword, shield, and armor for Poros," Hephaestus said.

"Why would you do such a thing?" Hip asked.

Hephaestus pulled off his riding gloves and stuffed them into his trouser pockets. "Because, believe it or not, I want the rebellion to succeed."

"Then why don't you join us?" Jen asked.

"For the wellbeing of my wife and children," the god of the forge replied. "Algaia and our daughter Cinny remain Aphrodite's constant companions and are too devoted to her to leave her side. We have other daughters on Mount Olympus as well."

"Have you tried to persuade them?" Ariadne asked.

"I'm afraid to speak freely. I don't want them to be used against me in the same way Persephone…" He stopped short. "I took a great risk coming here as it is. Now, let me leave my gifts and go."

"How do we know we can trust you?" Asterion asked with a snort. "What if your gifts are tricks, like the chair you made for your mother centuries ago?"

Hephaestus's brows pushed together, and blood rushed to his cheeks. "If Poros doesn't want my gifts…" The god turned to go.

"Wait," Hip said. "You must understand how difficult it is to know who our friends are."

Hephaestus turned to face him. "How many times have I sided with you against my own father?"

Hip hung his head.

"I'm sorry," Asterion said. "I shouldn't have questioned you, Lord Hephaestus."

"Please don't punish Poros for my brother's mistake," Ariadne pleaded. "I'm sure the boy will be pleased to receive gifts from you, especially since he's been so sorely treated by your father."

"Fine," Hephaestus said. "I'll retrieve them from my chariot."

Seconds later, Hephaestus reappeared with a sword, shield, helmet, and breastplate glinting in the rising sunlight. The hilt of the sword was made of rings of gold, ending with the shape of a lion's head as the pommel. In the lion's mouth was a purple stone.

The scabbard was made of bronze and silver, with scenes engraved on both sides: A lion leaping from a field of grass to clasp an eagle by the talons. Or was the eagle carrying the lion off? It was difficult to tell.

The shield was also engraved with images. Four concentric rings each held a different scene. The center circle held the sun, moon, and stars. This was surrounded by a ring of water, in which fish were depicted. Beyond the water were mountaintops and birds. And along the outer rim were fields full of cattle and men. The shield reminded Hip of the one once belonging to Hercules.

The helmet and breastplate, though less ornate, were beautiful, too. Made of bronze, silver, and gold, the same gold rings on the hilt of the sword were carried over on the chafe of the scabbard, the handle of the shield, and the rim of the breastplate and helmet, so that they were clearly a set.

"You truly are a master," Hip said to Hephaestus.

"They're beautiful," Jen agreed.

"The Alexandrite stone in the pommel of the sword is for empowerment and hope," Hephaestus explained. "The images on the shield represent the entire world, which I believe young Poros holds the fate of in his hands."

He didn't say whether the lion was vanquishing the eagle, or whether it was the other way around, and Hip didn't want to offend the god by asking.

"I wish you could have given these to him yourself," Hip said.

They hadn't wanted to risk exposing Poros to a potential trap.

"We'll be sure to tell him all you said," Jen said. "Thank you."

"Please know that my prayers are for your success with minimal casualties," Hephaestus said. "I hope you understand why I put the safety of my wife and daughters first."

"Of course, we understand." Ariadne glanced at her brother. "Family first."

***

Hermie left his friends behind in Tartarus and headed back to his parents' abode—or was it Pete and Tizzie's? He wasn't sure.

He began to imagine how he might carry out his duties as the god of technology, brainstorming for ways he could inspire third-world countries to develop it, given their limited resources.

He loved the idea of contributing to the good of the world, but he was still fearful of the other ramifications of being immortal. Although he loved to play video games depicting battles—both modern and medieval warfare—he didn't consider himself an aggressive person. He didn't look forward to fighting real battles.

A memory of his mother teaching him to use a bow and arrow came to mind. He liked shooting paper targets but could never imagine aiming at a living one. It was the same when his father had taken him to the shooting range. His father had been proud of Hermie's natural gift with a gun. He was a good shot. But Hermie had attributed that to his use of a scope in the video game *Battlefield*.

A chill went down Hermie's spine at the thought of using a weapon to hurt or injure someone in real life.

As he passed the palace, near Hecate's rooms, he overheard someone say his name. Curious, he stopped to listen.

"You know I would never hurt Hermie—or any of you, for that matter."

Hermie recognized the voice of Hermes.

"You hurt all of us by standing against us," Hermie heard Hecate say.

"This conflict did not start on Mount Olympus. I'm only defending my home."

"How can you say that, after all the treachery your father has done? After what happened to me in the Pit?"

Hermie shuddered, recalling the rings of dried blood around Hecate's eyes.

"Defense mechanisms," Hermes said. "He's defending his throne, as anyone would."

"Not anyone," Hecate argued. "Only tyrants swallow their children. My poor Persephone."

"I'm working on that," Hermes reassured her. "I promise you she won't remain in his belly for long. He was backed into a corner. And even though he's made mistakes…"

"Huge mistakes."

"Yes. I agree. Huge mistakes. But he's my father. I love him. And he has good in him. He's only a monster when he feels threatened."

"We both know that's not true," Hecate said. "Remember what he did to Melinoe? To my entire Underworld family?"

"Must you remind me of that every minute of every day?"

"You never think of it unless I do."

"I suppose you're right. I suppose I don't want to. We've all made mistakes. He's my *father*. Didn't he make up for it by taking the punishment from Thanatos, the oath breaker? Doesn't that show his remorse?"

"Why did you come here, Hermes?" Hecate asked.

"To bring you this gift, and to ask for a favor."

"What a beautiful necklace. Thank you. Now I'm afraid to hear what favor you ask of me."

"A simple locator spell, that's all."

"Who are you looking for?" Hecate asked.

"Metis. Zeus said that necklace once belonged to her."

"Hermes, no. How can you ask that of me?"

"I fear for your safety, if you don't cooperate."

"Are you threatening me?" Hecate's voice had become shrill.

"Of course not, my love. I'd never do such a thing, I'm warning you. I can't control what the others do."

"But you can control your own actions. Don't ask me again, if you want me to speak to you. And don't say a word to anyone about Therese's sister's prophetic dream about you and Hermie, or I'll never forgive you. If word gets out…"

Hermie covered his mouth. Lynn had had a prophetic dream about him? Is that why Hermes had said he'd never hurt him, because Lynn's dream had foretold that he would?

Why would they care about his cousin's dream?

Hermie pulled his cell phone from his trouser pocket. It was dead. Of course, it was dead. He wondered who else knew about the prophetic dream. Surely, if anyone did, it was Morpheus.

"Someone's listening," Hecate said suddenly.

Full of panic, Hermie unwittingly focused on his bedroom in Colorado. In the next instant, he was there.

Once he recovered from the shock of accidental god travel, he called out for his pets. When no one answered, he went looking for them. They were nowhere to be found.

What the heck? He guessed his mom had taken them back with her to the Underworld after her visit to Grammie and Grampie.

He thought of the redbirds and frowned, putting their deaths out of his mind.

He went to his room to check his email and social media accounts. He might as well, while he had the time. He replied to a few tweets and Instagram posts. He read through some other posts on his subreddit, making sure his app had translated them properly. He also checked out the video he'd made of Hestie and Poros on Youtube. Over three million views!

He knew he should god travel back to the Underworld, but he was terrified of screwing it up. To deter him and Hestie from taking Aphrodite's robe and attempting god travel without them, his parents had spoken of the perils of god travel with poor concentration. They could land inside rock, fire, an ocean, and other places of danger. They'd warned him and Hestie often, and now he was afraid to attempt it alone. He'd just landed in his house successfully, without even trying. Surely, he could go back without incident, couldn't he?

Or he could stay and try to get to the next save point in the game he'd been playing before all hell had broken loose. Just as soon as the idea had occurred to him, he was flooded with guilt. The other gods were fighting for their freedom from Zeus's tyranny. How could he sit here and play video games?

He closed his eyes and tried to think of Mina and Jinsoo in Tartarus. He took a deep breath, wishing he could roll a natural twenty and ensure his chances of success, like in *Dungeons and Dragons*.

He felt the extreme pressure of god travel crush against him and release. When he opened his eyes, he was surrounded by stone, but it wasn't any kind of stone he'd seen in the Underworld. No, he recognized this place. It was the dungeon in his favorite medieval video game.

His heart hammered in his chest. How was this possible?

***

As soon as Hestie had returned to the Underworld from Colorado, she and Poros took her animal friends to Tartarus to meet Mina and Jinsoo.

"Where's Hermie?" Hestie asked Mina.

Mina was already on her knees, loving on Clifford and Noodle. Kitty was too interested in the souls strapped to the tables, where the Furies did their work—though none of the Furies were present at the moment.

"He come back soon," Jinsoo said before he, too, joined in the fun with the dogs.

Chidori, who'd been perched on Hestie's shoulder, flew and landed on Jinsoo's hair.

Jinsoo flinched. "What the…"

"Sorry," Hestie said. "She's very friendly. Jewels is too, but she's shy. Aren't you, Jewels?"

"Don't be sorry," Jinsoo said, laughing. "This good. So boring before."

"Now if only we had food," Mina said. "I'm starving."

Hestie hadn't thought about food since becoming a god. She supposed gods didn't need as much.

"We'll find you something to eat," Poros said.

"I'm already on it."

The kids turned to see Prometheus with paper sacks from Mr. Burger.

"Captain!" Jinsoo cried gleefully. "Oh, man. Thank God!"

"You're welcome," Prometheus said as he handed over the bags. "Be careful not to spill the drinks. We don't want to get on the bad side of the Furies."

"So that's where you've been?" Poros asked. "Picking up food from Mr. Burger?"

"That and repairing the ship," Prometheus replied. "In fact, I'm here to take Mina and Jinsoo back to *The Marcella*. Tartarus is no place for mortals."

"Thank God!" Jinsoo said again.

"What about the rebellion?" Hestie asked.

"I'll be ready when I'm needed," Prometheus said. "But I can't ignore my other responsibilities. You saw how important my work is. Humankind has always been my priority."

"I want to come, too," Poros said.

"Can he?" Jinsoo asked with a mouthful of food.

Hestie's chest tightened. She wanted to stay and help with the rebellion, and she wanted Poros to stay, too—not because she was falling in love, she told herself.

"You're needed more here," Prometheus said, and Hestie's chest became less tight. "Your destiny is here."

Poros crossed his arms. "But…"

"I need you to come with me today, however," Prometheus added. "Just for today. Then you need to rejoin the rebellion. Okay?"

"Why?" Poros asked. "What's special about today?"

Hestie was wondering the same thing, but before Prometheus could reply, Hip and Jen appeared with armor in their hands.

"We bring gifts for Poros," Jen said.

"From Hephaestus," Hip added.

"What?" Poros's eyes were wide with surprise.

"What stunning craftsmanship," Prometheus said as he fingered the scabbard.

"Will Poros go to battle?" Mina asked before taking a sip of soda through her straw.

"Eventually," Hip said.

"Can Hephaestus be trusted?" Poros asked Hip and Jen.

Hip nodded. "He's always been there for us."

"Try it on," Hestie said.

Poros took the helmet and put in on his head. It was an open-faced, bowl-shaped helmet with a peak—like the comb of a rooster in shiny gold. It also had a neck collar in bronze and silver, trimmed in rings of gold. He looked incredibly handsome to Hestie, his gray eyes gazing at her from beneath the bronze visor.

He put on the breastplate. It was trimmed with the same rings of gold and bore the head of a lion at its center.

"You look like a proper warrior," Prometheus said.

"You look amazing," Hestie added, without thinking. Then she turned away, to hide her blush, pretending to look for Kitty. "Here, Kitty."

"Did Athena agree to meet you?" Hip asked Prometheus.

Hestie scooped up Kitty and returned to the group, wanting to hear more.

"She wants to meet her brother," Prometheus said. "Today, on my ship."

"It could be a trap," Jen said. "Couldn't it?"

"Maybe," Prometheus said, "but I don't think so."

Hestie exchanged looks with Poros.

"Jen and I should follow," Hip suggested. "Just to be safe. Apollo and Artemis could come, too."

"Athena might question our intentions if she senses you," Prometheus said. "Besides, Metis is meeting us, too."

"Really?" Poros's face lit up. "I haven't seen my mother in…forever."

"She's eager to see you, too," Prometheus said with a smile. "You remember how to conjure your weapon and armor, don't you? How to make it disappear and then reappear when you need it?"

"I was taught by the best." Poros turned to Hestie. "I used to practice with Athena's shield and a sword my mother stole from Zeus."

The gifts from Hephaestus disappeared. It was a cool trick. Hestie was anxious to learn how to do it, too, but she had no weapon or armor of her own.

"Good," Prometheus said. "Ready, kids?"

"Can I go, too?" Hestie asked, trying to hide the eagerness in her voice. Telepathically, she prayed to Prometheus, *Please say yes. I won't look conspicuous to Athena, like the others, and maybe I can help.*

Mina jumped up. "That would be awesome, Captain! Maybe Hermie come, too?"

"Where is Hermie?" Jen asked.

"We don't know," Hestie said. "Could he be with my parents?"

"We don't have time to wait," Prometheus said.

"You go on," Hip said. "I'll look for Hermie."

"We better go by chariot," Prometheus said. "I don't mind risking god-travel when it's just me, but I won't risk everyone else's safety."

"Good point," Hip said. "I'll take you in my father's chariot and return before nightfall to bring Poros and Hestie back."

Hestie smiled at Poros, excited that they were going on another adventure together for the sake of the rebellion.

"If we succeed in getting Athena, our chances of success increase dramatically," Hip added.

"Let's hope for the best," Prometheus said, as they headed toward the stables.

CHAPTER SIX

Hard Choices

Hermie stared at the tall wooden doors of the dungeon. If he was right, and he had somehow entered his favorite video game, he knew what lay in store for him on the other side of the doors. But what if he was wrong? Gods couldn't travel into digital worlds, could they? The similarity to the game had to be a coincidence.

On quivering legs, he crossed the room and cracked one of the two doors open just far enough to peek inside. As he'd feared, the dragon was there, waiting for him.

He pushed the door closed and quietly lowered the iron latch, knowing it wouldn't hold for long.

So, he really was in a video game. What did that mean for him? Could he be injured or killed? Was he trapped? How could he get out?

Except for the Dreamworld, his parents had never told him stories about gods traveling to virtual worlds. If it were possible, they would have mentioned it. Educating him about the gods had been their obsession.

What if he was in the game because he had declared himself to be the god of technology? Maybe this ability was a gift, like his mother's gift with the bow and arrow.

If so, cool—so long as he was immune to pain and death and could come and go as he pleased. So long as that dragon in the next room couldn't actually eat him.

Right now, he had to get out of the game and back to the Underworld.

Before he could think of what to do next, the tall wooden doors burst open, and the dragon glared down at him before spitting out a stream of smoke and fire.

Hermie ran beneath the dragon between its huge legs and entered the great hall. As he hid behind a column, he groaned when a twenty-sided die appeared. In his game, he would use his controller to "roll" the die. He supposed he was expected to pick it up and roll it in the digital world. But he had no time for this. He needed to get out now.

As the dragon turned toward him, Hermie closed his eyes and thought again of Mina and Jinsoo in Tartarus. Maybe if he focused on his friends, and not on his destination, he'd have a better chance of success.

His mind wandered to *The Marcella* and how much fun he'd had with his friends there. Before he knew he'd done it, he was god traveling again.

***

Hestie flinched when Hermie appeared between her and Mina on board the upper deck of *The Marcella*.

"Hermie?" she shouted in surprise. "Did you god travel here, on your own?"

"That was risky," Prometheus said. "And not very smart."

"Hermie!" Mina threw her arms around his neck. Then she stepped back, awkwardly. "You okay?"

To Mina he said, "I'm fine." To Prometheus, he said, "It was an accident. I was trying to get back to the Underworld."

"*To* the Underworld?" Hestie asked. "From where?"

Hermie told them about overhearing Hermes and Hecate's conversation, accidentally traveling to their Colorado home, finding their animals gone, and ending up in a video game.

"No way!" Jinsoo said. "You in a video game?"

"I think so," Hermie said. "I don't know where else I could have been."

"That's interesting," Prometheus said. "I've never heard of such a thing."

"Do you think it happened because he's the god of technology?" Hestie asked Prometheus.

"That's the only explanation I can think of," the Titan replied.

"But how did you end up *here*?" Poros asked Hermie.

Hermie shrugged.

Hestie put a hand on her brother's shoulder. "Mom made the rest of our animals immortal and took them to the Underworld. They're safe."

"Chidori want to come here with me," Jinsoo said, laughing. "I like bird."

"Good," Hermie said, obviously glad to change the subject and the focus. "Did Lynn say anything about her dream while you were there with Grammie and Grampie?"

Hestie dropped her hand from his shoulder and averted her eyes, not sure what to say.

Hermie raised his palms in the air. "I can tell when you're hiding something. Just tell me."

"We'll have to finish this conversation later," Prometheus said. "Our guest has finally arrived."

Hestie turned and was stunned to see the beautiful, gray-eyed Athena in full armor descending from the sky to land beside Prometheus on the upper deck of the ship. The goddess was staring at Poros with wonder. Hestie soon realized it was the first time the goddess had ever laid eyes on her brother.

"Poros?" she asked.

"Hello, Athena," Poros said. "It's nice to finally meet you."

"Likewise." Athena glanced at Hestie and Hermie. "These children are gods. How is that possible?"

Poros made to answer, but Prometheus interrupted him. "We have our ways."

"It's against Zeus's decree," Athena said sharply.

"And we are at war," Prometheus pointed out.

After staring at Poros for a few more moments in awkward silence, Athena turned to Prometheus. "Thank you for arranging this meeting, though I wonder why it didn't happen years ago."

Prometheus cleared his throat, appearing embarrassed, before saying, "Your brother has something to give you, don't you, Poros?"

Poros conjured a shield. Hestie recognized it as the one that had hung over his bed.

"Your shield," Poros said, presenting it to Athena. "I believe our mother took it from you when she was pregnant with me. I'd like to give it back."

Athena turned the shield over in her hands and studied it. "I wondered where it had gone. I tried to conjure it many times, unsuccessfully. Did our mother ever say why she stole it from me?"

A woman with long, dark hair, a lavender gown, and gray eyes, like those belonging to Athena and Poros, emerged from the water and hovered above the sea about twenty yards away from the stern of the ship. She was dripping with sea water and surrounded by a purple aura. Hestie noticed two other faces in the sea below, one silver and the other gold. The faces belonged to the goddesses that had helped Hestie during the attack by the Harpies. They were Prometheus's mother, Clymene, and her sister, Dione.

"Mother!" Athena cried. "Is it really you?"

"I took your shield because I wanted something of yours to remember you by," the purple goddess said. "Will you forgive me?"

"Where have you been?" Athena demanded. "Why did you abandon me? For centuries, I begged my father to release you, and, not long after I finally succeeded in getting you free, you left! Don't you care about me?"

"I care very much," Metis said, still hovering over the sea, which was beginning to swell. "But I sacrificed my desire to be with you for a higher purpose."

Athena glanced at Poros with a face full of jealousy. "You've made that very clear."

"Please hear your mother out," Prometheus intervened. "She doesn't love your brother more than you."

"You can't speak for her," Athena said. "And you have no right to make excuses for her when you have none of your own."

Hestie glanced at Hermie and said telepathically, *This isn't going very well.*

Obviously, Hermie replied. *But what do we do?*

Be ready to help Mina and Jinsoo, Hestie said. *We can take them back to Tartarus.*

I suck at god travel, Hermie said. *You better do it.*

"This isn't about love," Metis declared. "I love you and your brother equally. This is about justice and wisdom, things your father cares little about."

Athena gawked. "Wisdom? How is yet one more son overthrowing his father an instance of wisdom? Why exchange one power-monger for another when history shows us that this is as good as it gets?"

"I'm not a power-monger," Poros insisted. "I don't want to rule the gods."

Athena's dark brows bent over her stunning gray eyes. "Then what do you want?"

"A better world," Poros said.

"Then why not appeal to our father?" Athena asked. "Why wage war?"

"Because if history has shown us anything," Metis said, "it's that your father will never change. He cannot be the one to lead us."

"Then who can?" Athena scoffed. "Prometheus?"

"I don't want to lead, either," Prometheus said gently.

"Then who?" Athena asked.

"Why not *you*?" Metis implored her, moving closer to the ship.

Athena glared at her mother. "You want *me* to overthrow my own father?"

Hestie took Mina and Jinsoo by the hands, pulling them a few steps back from the group, ready to flee if needed.

"We want the gods to vote on a leader, as they do in most of the countries of the modern world," Poros explained.

"Why should the gods follow the lead of mortals?" Athena challenged.

"Because, regardless of its origins, democracy is wise," her mother said. "And you know this to be true. Why are you fighting it?"

Athena blinked and shook her head.

"Take some time to think about it, Athena," Prometheus said. "Please?"

"You have no right to ask anything of me after what you did to me," Athena said angrily. "Neither of you do," she added, glaring at her mother. "Both of you abandoned me when I needed you, but my father has been at my side. Why should I turn my back on the one who has never left me?"

"He turned you to stone," Metis reminded her. "He convinced Poseidon to take you as a prisoner."

"Because he knew I wanted to release *you*," Athena said. "And now I understand why he resisted me."

Without another word, Athena vanished.

Hestie tried to read the faces of Poros and Prometheus.

"I'm sorry that didn't go better," Prometheus said to Metis.

"She'll come around," Metis said. "Give her time."

"How can you be so sure?" Poros asked his mother.

"Because no one is wiser than my daughter; but, right now, her emotions are getting the best of her. Once her emotions have a chance to settle down, she'll see that we're on the side of right."

Dione flew from the water to hover in the air beside Metis. "My sister speaks the truth. Athena needs time."

Clymene joined her sisters in the air above the sea. They were only a few feet from the stern of the ship. Hestie moved toward the rail of the back upper deck to get a better look at them.

"Son," Clymene said, "You are the key to winning her over."

"What can I do?" Prometheus asked.

"Mend her broken heart," Metis said.

"I tried to tell you," Clymene added. "For centuries, I tried to tell you. She still cares for you. She's never been with another."

"Metis must do the same," Dione said. "Both of you need to find a way to make amends with her, or the rebellion will be lost."

***

Morpheus left Mount Olympus beneath the helm of invisibility and god traveled to Lemon Reservoir in Colorado, just outside of Durango, to his cousins' grandparents' house. He felt sick to his stomach, realizing he had made another mistake in the face of hopelessness and desperation. He wanted Iris free, but not at the cost of another's freedom.

Why had he offered to bring Zeus another seer?

The only thing he could do now was to warn Lynn that she could be in danger. If Zeus and his followers discovered that she was the seer Morpheus had been talking about, they would take her to Mount Olympus to use her for their own ends.

He'd never forgive himself if something happened to her. She could be killed, and it would be his fault. Hermie and Hestie and Than and Therese would never forgive him. He'd be an outcast in his own family.

When he landed on the gravel drive leading up to the house beneath the late afternoon sun, Hecate appeared beside him.

"What are you doing here?' she asked him.

"I need to warn Lynn," he said. "Why are *you* here?"

"Does Zeus know of her gifts?" Hecate asked.

"How do you know of them?" Morpheus asked.

"Than asked me to have a word with Hermes."

"Great." Morpheus wished he hadn't told anyone. If Hermes knew…

"Why have you come to warn her?" Hecate asked. "Does Zeus know?"

"Not yet. But he knows another seer exists, and that she's a mortal from Colorado. It might not be long before he figures out who she is."

Hecate sighed. "How did Zeus come to know that? Was it Hermes who said something?"

Morpheus hung his head in shame. "No. No, it was me."

She looked at him with wide eyes.

"I made a mistake," he added. "If you could see how frightened Iris is…I just want to rescue her. I'm such an idiot."

"You're young," she said. "You've made mistakes. We all have."

Morpheus wished her words could make him feel better. "What can I do? I was going to warn Lynn. But what can she do, anyway? If Hermes tells Zeus, she's screwed."

Hecate scratched her head and took a few steps toward the street, as if she was going to walk away.

"Hecate?" Morpheus asked.

"I don't think Hermes will say anything," she said, "especially if you give him someone more valuable than Lynn."

Morpheus lifted his chin. "Who?"

Hecate smiled. "Me."

"What?"

"Tell Zeus he can have me if he promises to free Iris, Demeter, *and* Persephone."

"I doubt he'll give up all three."

"Just go back and make the offer. Come to my rooms when you have an answer."

Morpheus threw up his hands. "But if he has you, won't that be bad for the rebellion?"

"Trust me, will you? And before you go, tell me everything you saw in Lynn's dream."

<u>CHAPTER SEVEN</u>

Prisoner Exchange

Thanatos sat across the table from Artemis, Apollo, and Hades in one of his parents' meeting rooms, where the light from the Phlegethon flickered, as if they were sitting around a campfire. Hip was there, too, with Hecate between them. Therese and Jen were carrying out their duties elsewhere but were on their way. His sisters and Pete had remained in Tartarus to interrogate a mortal warrior whom they believed was a son of Ares. The Furies had heard the warrior was beloved by their father and might know something about the loyalists' plans. Poseidon had returned to his palace to defend it against potential attacks by Zeus.

As Hecate told them about her proposition, Than was glad his kids weren't there to hear the gory details. He'd just finished checking on them on the Mediterranean, where they were safely aboard *The Marcella* with Prometheus.

"I don't like it," Hades said to Hecate. "Zeus will make you swear an oath."

"You'll be forced to lie or, worse, to tell the truth," Apollo added.

"And if you refuse, they'll torture you," Artemis said.

Hecate stood from her chair. "You saw what they did to me in the Pit. I will not be broken."

Than shuddered at the memory of Hecate's injuries, given to her by the imprisoned Titans.

"I appreciate what you're willing to do for us, Hecate," Hades said as he tugged at his beard. "But I can't let you endure more torment. You've barely recovered."

"Shouldn't that be my choice?" Hecate challenged.

"There's no way Zeus will exchange three for one," Hip said.

Than sat up in his chair. "Demeter would make a powerful ally, though."

"She won't help us," Hades said.

"She would do anything to rescue her daughter," Hecate said to Hades. "Even align herself with you."

"Zeus knows that," Apollo said. "He'd give us Persephone before he'd let Demeter go."

"I might agree to those terms," Hecate said. "But I didn't want to start there."

Hades frowned.

"Zeus needs a seer," Artemis said. "And the fact that she's also a witch sweetens the deal. I think he might go for it."

"We'll find out soon enough," Hecate said, taking her seat once more. "I've sent Morpheus to Mount Olympus to make the offer."

Hades jumped to his feet. "Without consulting me?"

"I knew what you'd say, Lord Hades. You'd try to talk me out of it, even though you'd know this was our best shot."

"This might be a good thing for Morpheus," Hip said. "With Hecate on Mount Olympus, I'd feel better, anyway."

Than knew his brother hated the role Morpheus had been forced to play in this dangerous conflict. He wished he could shield the young god from the treacheries of war. If Lynn's dream was truly a prediction, then none of the young gods were immune to them. It made Than eager to act.

"What can I do?" he asked his father. "Maybe I could use the helm to spy."

"We do need a spy," Hades said, "but it would be best to send someone without your power of disintegration, since the helm prevents it."

"I agree," Artemis said. "You never know when you or Hypnos might be needed to amass an army."

"In fact," Hades continued, "one of you should join Poseidon at his palace. His spies have heard whispers of possible attacks by sea."

"A distraction, no doubt," Apollo said.

Than knew how much his brother hated water. "I'll do it."

Hip gave him a grateful grin. "Thanks, bro'. I'll keep an eye on things down here."

Therese appeared and asked Than telepathically what she'd missed as she took the empty seat at the end of the table, next to Artemis. Than filled her in. Before he could stop her, she was volunteering to join him in defending Poseidon's palace.

Then she added, telepathically to Than, *Jen and Scylla are spying on Keto and Phorcys. Scylla suspects Zeus is recruiting them. We're not to tell anyone.*

Than replied that it was a bad idea for the two goddesses to go without backup, but their telepathic conversation was interrupted by Apollo.

"I should be the spy on Mount Olympus," Apollo said. "It might provoke a vision, and I'll know whom to trust."

"We can't afford to lose you," Hades said. "No one is disposable, but your special skills are particularly useful when brothers wage war against brothers."

"I'll do it, then" Artemis said.

"Let's first wait and hear from Morpheus," Hades said. "We'll amend our plans from there."

"I'm here," Morpheus said, removing the helm and stepping into the room. "Zeus has agreed to Hecate's terms."

"To *all* of them?" Hecate asked.

Morpheus grinned. "To all of them."

Than scrutinized their expressions, having the feeling that there were other terms Hecate had failed to mention.

****

Hestie followed Poros from the upper deck to the salon, where the broken windows had been replaced, and there was no sign of the attack that had nearly killed her and Mina and Jinsoo. The others had remained above with Prometheus, but Hestie could tell that something was upsetting Poros, and she didn't want him to be alone.

"Are you okay?" she asked him.

He stood near the kitchen, staring at nothing. "I guess so."

"What's wrong?" She crossed the room and sat on the long couch that stretched beneath the starboard bank of windows.

"I thought it would be different. What a letdown."

"What are you talking about?"

"Meeting my sister. I imagined it differently. I saw her giving me a hug, kissing my cheek, or, at least, mussing my hair, like Prometheus always does. I thought she'd be as glad to see me as I was her."

"I'm sure she was glad to see you."

"She was jealous. She thought our mother loved me more. What a disappointment." He swiped at his eyes, made even more stunning by the well of tears threatening to drop to his cheeks.

Hestie climbed to her feet and went to him. She put her hand on his shoulder and met his beautiful gray eyes: soulful, kind, but troubled. She couldn't get over how stunning they were—even more so than Athena's. "There's a lot going on right now. Under different circumstances…"

"That's what I keep telling myself. But it's still a disappointment, nonetheless."

She didn't know what to say.

"I waited a long time for that moment," he said, "and now I'll never have it back."

"There will be other moments."

"I knew it wouldn't live up to my expectations, but I didn't think it would go that badly."

Hestie squeezed his shoulder. "Give her another chance to show she cares."

"She seemed cold, didn't she?"

"The strategist in her is being cautious. For centuries, she's only had her father."

"I didn't know there was a history between her and Prometheus," he said. "He never told me about it."

"Maybe he would, if you asked him."

Poros gave her a half-smile. "Maybe."

She suddenly realized she'd been clutching his shoulder for too long, and now he was gazing down at her, his face close to hers, as if he might kiss her. And to her own annoyance, she couldn't stop looking at his mouth—those perfectly formed lips. As much as she wanted to comfort him, she didn't think a relationship was a good idea—not while the entire pantheon was in jeopardy and they were on the brink of war.

She cleared her throat, dropped her hand from his shoulder to her side, and looked away, trying to distract herself with the view through the windows. "Maybe we should rejoin the others."

Angrily, he muttered, "Athena isn't the only cold one today," as he brushed past her toward the steps to the upper deck.

"Poros," she said as she followed him. "I didn't mean to hurt your feelings."

He stopped on the bottom step and looked down at her with narrowed eyes. "I may have been raised on a ship away from most people, but I know I'm not imagining this thing between us."

Hestie's mouth dropped open. She resisted covering her cheeks, which were hot with embarrassment. She tried to speak, but no words came out.

Still angry—whether at Athena or Hestie or both—Poros stomped up the steps and didn't look back.

Hestie followed him to the upper deck, where the others were still gathered. Clymene, Dione, and Metis had left shortly after Athena. Prometheus now sat at the helm with Jinsoo beside him in the swivel chairs, turned to face the couch, where Mina and Hermie were sitting.

They looked up at Poros and Hestie as they approached.

Jinsoo jumped from the chair that everyone knew belonged to Poros and scooted onto the couch beside his sister.

Poros took his seat and once more wiped his eyes with the back of his hand.

Hestie squeezed onto the couch beside her brother. There wasn't adequate room for all four of them, but none of them seemed to mind being pinned together like packaged sausages.

"Captain was telling us about Athena," Mina said.

Poros looked up at Prometheus. "What about her?"

"I'm sorry she wasn't herself today," Prometheus said. "She's hurt and conflicted."

"You haven't seen her in centuries," Poros said. "How can you be sure she hasn't changed since you knew her?"

"I'm sure she has," Prometheus said. "But some things about a person never change. I knew Athena better than anyone, and, from what I've heard, no one has managed to get close to her since I left the gods behind."

"Why did you never reach out to her over the years?" Hestie asked, and then immediately regretted it. This wasn't her business, and she hadn't meant to pry.

"For her safety, as well as mine," he said. "As Zeus's number-one enemy, I couldn't afford to risk her father's wrath. And I couldn't very well be an advocate for the human race from the Titan Pit."

"Do you still love her?" Mina asked.

"Mina!" Jinsoo complained.

"It's okay, Jinsoo," Prometheus said kindly. "As I said, some things about a person never change."

"You should ask her to marry you!" Mina said with a smile that split her face in half.

Everyone laughed.

"I'd like nothing more," Prometheus said with a smile.

Hestie noticed a movement at the top of the mast. It was a bird of some kind. It must have been perched there before flying off. She pointed. "What kind of bird is that? It's huge."

"An owl," Poros said.

Hestie looked from Poros to Prometheus and back again. Had the owl been Athena?

***

Full of excitement over his upcoming reunion with Iris, Morpheus followed Hecate and Artemis through the rainbow arch from the Underworld to Mount Olympus. The rainbow was barely visible in the evening sky, and Artemis was completely invisible to him beneath Hades's helm. She was going to spy on the prisoner exchange, and, if Morpheus understood the plan correctly, she would stay to ensure Hecate's safety and to learn all she could about Zeus's plans.

Zeus and Hera were waiting for them with extra security. In addition to Ares and Hermes, Phobos and Deimos—the twin sons of Ares and Aphrodite—were stationed near the bird cages holding Iris and Demeter. Phobos and Deimos stood like lions with their red manes and fierce brows and jutting jaws. Aphrodite, Hestia, Rhea, and Hephaestus were also there.

"Where's Persephone?" Hecate asked before anyone had been greeted.

"Rest assured I will deliver her," Zeus said from where he stood before his throne.

Hera climbed to her feet beside him. "But not until we have you secured."

"Release Demeter and Iris," Hecate demanded. "Then you can cough up the Queen of Hades after you've taken me."

Ares's face turned red with rage. "No one makes demands of my father!"

Zeus lifted his hand to silence his son. "I honor my agreements."

To Morpheus's surprise, the doors to both bird cages opened. Iris stumbled out, weakened from the psychological terror she'd suffered. Morpheus rushed to her side and glared at Phobos, who stood too close.

"Thank you," Iris whispered to Morpheus through her parched lips.

He held her up, grateful to have her in his arms again. It took every ounce of self-control for him not to god travel to the Underworld. He'd be happy to never set foot on Mount Olympus again.

Demeter stepped out of her cage, gave a hateful look to Deimos, and then took a few strides to stand before Zeus. With her arms crossed and her eyes narrowed, she said, "I shall never forgive you for what you've done to our daughter."

Without hesitation, Zeus said, "Secure Hecate."

Before Morpheus had blinked, swift Hermes had cuffed Hecate in rings of gold around her wrists and ankles. The rings weren't tethered to anything, so he assumed they were magical.

"As was agreed," Zeus said, "Hecate will remain a prisoner here under the care of Hermes."

Morpheus noticed a tender look between Hecate and Hermes. This made him hope that her sacrifice would be made more bearable by her love for her jailer.

He wasn't the only one to notice it. Aphrodite wore a smile on her face, apparently pleased by the arrangement. Morpheus hoped the goddess didn't have something foul planned for the couple.

"Now give me my daughter back," Demeter said coldly.

Hephaestus stepped forward with his axe. "I'm happy to serve."

"That won't be necessary, Hephaestus," Zeus said.

Then Zeus opened his great mouth and retched and gagged until Persephone, pale and damp and weak, slid from his throat and landed in a heap on the marble floor. Demeter picked her up in her arms and whisked her away. They both vanished without a word.

"You agreed to one more term," Hecate reminded Zeus.

"Watch your tone," Ares warned Hecate.

Zeus lifted both hands in the air. Within seconds, Morpheus felt a tingling sensation up and down his back. At the same time, he felt lighter. Joy filled his heart as he realized what had happened. Zeus had restored his wings!

He smiled across the room at Hecate, thanking her telepathically. Then he looked down at Iris, who managed to smile back at him before he covered her lips with his.

Suddenly, he was aware that all were watching them. He glanced around the room, embarrassed.

"True love," Aphrodite said. "What a wonderful reprieve from these hard times."

Iris turned to Hera. "Am I really free to go, my Lady?"

"If you must," the queen replied, but not without kindness. "I wish it hadn't come to this."

"You no more than I," Iris said.

"Go, then!" Zeus said, his rage returning.

Morpheus took Iris by the hand, and, together, they flew across the rainbow arch to the Underworld.

CHAPTER EIGHT

Persephone's Plan

Therese sat in the air chamber of Poseidon's palace across the table from Amphitrite and the queen's daughter, Rhode. Because an antechamber magically drained the water from the room, Therese didn't have to worry about remembering that she could breathe beneath the sea.

A nymph, whose name Therese did not know, served them each a cup of tea.

"Thank you," Therese said.

After taking a sip, Rhode, the wife of the sun god Helios, said, "Have you heard back from Jen and Scylla yet? Helios is concerned for them."

"Not yet," Therese admitted. "I wish they hadn't gone to Phorcys's castle without backup, but Jen is stubborn and willful and won't ever listen to me."

"I've heard the same has been said of you," Amphitrite said with a smile.

Therese grinned. "Maybe so, but Jen is worse than I am."

The tea was warm and spicy. Therese took another sip, trying not to worry about Jen, even though night was falling, and her friend had been gone for hours. She also tried not to worry about an attack on Poseidon and Amphitrite's palace. The rumors of a pending attack had become widespread among the mer-people. Than was with Poseidon, reinforcing the perimeter. Therese and her companions were the first line of defense against anyone who might breach the front door.

Even though she was on her guard, she enjoyed the tea, needing a moment of respite to calm her nerves. One thing she did allow herself to worry about was the plight of her children.

For sixteen years, she'd wanted nothing more than to find a way to make them immortal, and, now that they were, she feared they were worse off. An eternity of misery as a prisoner would be worse than a short and happy life as a human.

And even if the rebellion was a complete success, she worried about other aspects of immortality. Although Hermie had figured out his purpose, how difficult would it be to achieve his goals? Would he become a slave to them? And what about Hestie? Smart and multi-talented, Hestie had many interests, and they could obscure her one true calling. What if she couldn't figure out her purpose in time?

Just then, Thanatos appeared. "Demeter and Persephone are back. I thought you'd want to know."

Therese jumped up.

"Wonderful news!" Amphitrite said.

"What a relief!" Rhode added.

"I can't believe Zeus released them," Therese said.

Therese doubted Zeus would free the prisoners in exchange for Hecate without something else up his sleeve. She was happy for Persephone and Demeter but worried that there was a catch that might be worse than any of them suspected.

"I'm with them now," Than said. "Mother's weak but more determined than ever."

"Can I come?" Therese asked, eager to see her mother-in-law. She turned to Amphitrite. "Would you mind? I'll be back shortly."

"I don't mind," the queen of the sea said. "You should go. We'll talk more when you return."

Therese took Thanatos by the hand, and, together, they god traveled to the Underworld, to the throne room, where Persephone was laid out on a chaise lounge. Hades was hanging over her and onto her every word, reminding Therese of how capable Hades could sometimes be of tenderness. It didn't often show through his iron façade, but it was showing now as he caressed Persephone's face and pushed her corn-yellow hair from her eyes.

Demeter sat nearby on a cushioned chair drinking from a goblet. Both prisoners appeared worn out from the ordeal.

"I'm telling you, that woman is mad," Persephone was saying.

"What woman?" Therese asked.

"Hera," Demeter said. "Persephone is telling us what we already know."

"To make a point, Mother," Persephone said. "Hello, Therese. I'm so relieved to see you back in your godly form. I can't tell you how happy I am for you—for all of you. It's the one light in this dark time."

Therese went to Persephone's side and squeezed her hand before releasing it. "That's sweet of you to say. We're glad to be back, aren't we, Than?"

Than gave Persephone a wink before saying, "And even more glad to have you back, Mother. Please go on. What is it you wanted to say about Hera?"

"She's the key to everything," Persephone said.

***

Hip drove his father's chariot across the evening sky. As Helios was sinking to the west, Hip spotted *The Marcella* below and directed Swift and Sure down to meet it.

The chariot hovered above the surface of the water a few yards away from the ship.

"Time to go, kids!" Hip called out.

Hip heard Poros ask Prometheus, "Can't I stay here with you?"

"Not this time," the Titan replied. "But one day."

Hip was concerned to find Hermie with them. He must have god traveled on his own, without any concern for safety. But that was very unlike his nephew. Hermie was the most cautious person Hip had ever known.

Hip waited while the kids hugged each other and said their goodbyes, and once the three young gods were boarded, he drove the chariot up into the sky before steering it into the nearest chasm to the Underworld.

Once he'd parked the chariot, Hermie turned to him and asked, "Do you know anything about a prophetic dream my cousin Lynn had about me?"

"Yes. Why?"

"What was it?" Hermie asked.

Don't tell him, came Hestie's telepathic message. *It will only paralyze him with fear.*

"Poros, why don't you and Hestie go on to the palace, and we'll catch up with you?" Hip said.

Poros and Hestie didn't need to be told twice. They flew away from the stables.

Alone with Hermie, Hip said, "Why don't you tell me why you god traveled to *The Marcella* all by yourself?"

"It was an accident."

"You need to be more careful." Hip began to unbridle the horses.

"I know that, Uncle Hip. Will you tell me about the dream? I heard Hermes talking to Hecate. Is he going to hurt me?"

Even though his niece and nephew now looked nearly the same age as he, he still felt a paternal feeling toward them. He patted Hermie on the head and said, "Hermes would never do anything to hurt you. He loves you. He saved your life. That's why your parents gave you his name."

"But…"

"It won't do you any good to know the details of the dream," Hip said. "Have you ever heard of a self-fulling prophecy?"

Hermie nodded.

"That's what happens when people hear prophecies," Hip explained. "In trying to avoid them, they make them come true. Trust me. It's best you don't know." Then he added. "Now follow me. I have some awesome news."

Hip led Hermie to the throne room, where Persephone and Demeter were still recovering. Than, Therese, Pete, and all three Furies were there, too, as were Poros and Hestie.

"Grandma!" Hermie cried, as he rushed to Persephone's side, where Hestie was already embracing the queen of the Underworld.

"Hello, darling," Persephone said.

"Thank the gods," Hermie said.

"Thank Hecate," Hades said. "She's the one who arranged this."

Just then, Morpheus arrived with Iris in tow. Hip couldn't believe his eyes. His son's beautiful silver wings had been restored.

"Your wings!" Tizzie said with glee.

"You look fabulous!" Meg added.

"What a relief!" Therese said, giving Morpheus a hug.

Hestie and Hermie did the same.

"Looking good, cuz," Hermie said.

"Thanks, everyone," Morpheus said. "Y'all remember Iris?"

"Get her a drink, would you Than?" Persephone asked.

Than left and returned with another goblet of ambrosia and gave it to Iris as Hip cupped his son's cheek, grateful to have him in one piece again.

Hey, Pops," Morpheus said with a smile. "Where's Mom?"

"She and Scylla haven't returned from Phorcys and Keto's castle," Therese said.

"They've been at it all day," Than said. "I think we should go looking for them."

"What?" Hades jumped to his feet. "I'm growing tired of people acting independently. Why was I not told of this?"

"And you wonder why no one on Mount Olympus likes you," Demeter said. "Calm down."

"Mother, please!" Persephone cried.

Hades glared at Demeter.

Hip turned to Than. "Why didn't you tell me?"

"I told him not to," Therese said. "Jen asked me not to tell anyone."

"You should know better," Hades said to her. "This tells me that you don't truly grasp the danger we're all in."

Hip was surprised to see Therese stand up to Hades. "I grasp it, all right. Jen knew the risk, too."

"You tell him," Demeter prodded.

"Wait a minute," Persephone covered her mouth.

"What is it?" Hades was at her side in an instant.

"Zeus has been planning something with Phorcys," Persephone said. "Jen and Scylla are in danger. Someone needs to go get them and bring them back right away."

"I'll go," Hip said.

"I'll go with you, Pops," Morpheus offered.

"You stay with Iris," Than said. "I'll go."

"Morpheus, why don't you take Iris to your room to rest?" Persephone suggested.

"Pops?"

"Go rest," Hip said. "Than and I will handle this."

"Well, okay," Morpheus said before he and Iris flew off.

"Where's Apollo?" Hip asked.

"Meeting with Helios," Hades answered. "Swing by and pick him up. Take him with you."

Hip gave his brother a nod, and the two of them took off.

***

Than disintegrated with Hip, and they took their father's chariot to the western side of the world, where Helios was preparing to descend. From a distance, the sunset looked more brilliant than usual, full of reds and oranges, because of Apollo's shining chariot hovering alongside Helios's golden cup.

"We'll find them," Than reassured his brother, meaning Jen and Scylla.

"And then I'll kill them for going in the first place," Hip said angrily.

When they reached Helios, Apollo sat up in his chariot, his horses as bright as flames.

"Has something happened?" he asked them.

"We think Jen and Scylla are in trouble," Hip said. "They went to spy on Phorcys and Keto."

"They've been down there too long," Helios added from his golden cup, as his golden hair and beard blew in the wind. "I told Rhode the same thing not long ago."

"Will you come with us to investigate?" Than asked Apollo.

"Lead the way," Apollo said.

As Than and his brother took the chariot down into the Ionian Sea, just west of the mainland of Greece, they also listened to Persephone in the throne room as she explained why Hera was the key to overthrowing Zeus.

"All day long, Hera badgered Zeus about Metis," Persephone was explaining. "She's paranoid that he'll be deceived by her again."

"With Poros birthed and raised, there's no reason for Metis to try such a thing," Hades pointed out.

"Zeus told Hera the very same thing," Persephone said, "but she can think of nothing else."

"I don't understand how this makes Hera the key," Tizzie said.

"It drove me half mad listening to her," Persephone said. "She wanted him to recount everything he'd done every minute of the day that he was away from her."

"And was he truthful with her?" Hades asked.

"No," Persephone said. "It's the funniest thing, really, because he lied about the most insignificant things, like where he went to have his bath, or under what tree he took his nap. By reading his thoughts, I came to understand that Zeus tells such lies to Hera every day."

"That's strange," Pete said.

Meg nodded. "Not to mention rude."

"No wonder Hera's mad," Alecto put in.

"He does it because he's a control freak," Hades said.

Demeter scoffed. "Talk about the pot calling the kettle black."

"Mother, please!" Persephone said again.

"My dear goddess," Hades said to Demeter. "I can easily have you removed."

"You forget that it's by my good graces that my daughter is here at all," Demeter said through gritted teeth. "It's still my rightful time with her. I could have taken her to my winter cabin."

"Where I'm sure it's much safer," Hades said sarcastically.

Than realized that today was the first time in his life that his mother was home during springtime.

"Please, both of you," Persephone pleaded. Turning to Hades, she asked, "How does Zeus being a control freak have anything to do with his little white lies?"

"He doesn't want Hera to micromanage his life, so he deceives her in small ways to feel in control."

"That's awfully preceptive of you, darling," Persephone said.

"I still don't understand how any of this helps us," Tizzie repeated.

"Don't you see?" Persephone began. "We need to trick Hera into thinking Zeus is meeting with Metis."

"You want to create a trap for Hera," Than said.

Persephone smiled. "Exactly."

"And then we can use Hera as leverage against Zeus," Hip surmised.

"Unless Zeus is happy to have her gone," Demeter said.

"Don't be rude, Grandmama," Meg said.

"Zeus loves her," Persephone said. "I could see it. He's amused by her badgering—flattered by it. She feeds his ego, I think. He would be lost without her."

"So, we trap her and use her," Hades said.

"First, we have to get Hecate back," Persephone said. "But, yes. Once Hecate is safely home, we can use Hera."

"And how do we rescue Hecate?" Tizzie wanted to know.

"We don't," Persephone said with a look of mischief in her eyes. "Hecate will rescue herself."

Suddenly Hecate appeared. "And, so I have."

Demeter stood up. "Thank goodness!"

Than furled his brows. "How did you manage it so quickly?"

"Amazing!" Meg cried.

"Absolutely brilliant!" Alecto echoed.

"Hecate," Hades said. "Tell us what happened."

"It was easy," Hecate said. "The first thing Zeus demanded of me was a locator spell. He wants Metis."

"Did you perform the spell?" Therese asked with a frown.

"I told him I couldn't perform magic with the cuffs on," she said.

Hades cocked his head to the side. "I can't believe he would remove them."

Hecate grinned. "He did, entrusting Hermes to act should I attempt to escape."

"Hermes is faster than you," Pete pointed out. "How did you escape?"

"With a kiss," Hecate said. "Hermes was taken by surprise, and I god traveled here before he could recover."

"Well done!" Persephone said. "I never doubted you. Not for a minute."

Hades pulled at his beard. "Needless to say, I'm sure my brother's throwing a fit about now."

"I doubt he's very happy," Hecate agreed.

"And Hermes probably isn't too pleased, either," Than said.

Hip gave Than a worried glance. "Let's just hope Zeus hasn't got Jen."

Than had a bad feeling as he and Hip reached the quiet castle belonging to the Old Man of the Sea.

CHAPTER NINE

Attack by Sea

Morpheus lay beside Iris on the couch in his room. He didn't have a proper bed, because whenever he slept, he went to the field of asphodel, and because he needed space for the collection of toys, games, and books he'd acquired over the years. Not having had anything of his own except a plastic toothbrush for the first four years of his life, he'd overcompensated, with the help of his parents' need to indulge him. He was spoiled, and he liked it that way. And now that he had his Iris back, he couldn't be happier.

Her right golden wing gently caressed his left side as his left silver wing encased them, like a cocoon.

"Are you sure you don't want more to eat?" he asked her.

"I'm stuffed," she said. "Are you trying to get me fat?"

He laughed. "Dang. You caught me out."

She laughed too. "Oh, Morpheus, thank you for saving me. I was so afraid."

"I'm sorry I got you into that."

"It wasn't your fault."

"Sure, it was."

She stroked his cheek. "You can't be blamed for what Zeus does. I can't believe I ever loved him."

"But you still love Hera. I can tell you do."

Tears dropped from the corners of her eyes as she nodded. "I can't believe she let him treat me like that."

"I don't think she has much control over him."

"More than you think."

"But you love her anyway?" He pushed a golden lock behind her ear.

"I do. She's been my mistress for centuries. It's hard to let go of what we had."

"Maybe it's time for a new chapter." That was something his parents had told him when Zeus had transformed Morpheus into a god fifteen years ago. They told him that he'd been a victim, and it was time to take charge of his own story. "You can write the next chapter how you want it to be."

"I want it to be with you," she said.

He leaned in and kissed her. A sigh escaped her lips, and he wanted nothing more than to ravish her, but he knew she needed more time to recover from her recent ordeal.

She surprised him by pinning his back to the couch, straddling him, and kissing him hard on the mouth. So much for needing time to recover, he thought gleefully. Iris had never been this passionate with him before. It made him happy, thrilled, but also nervous. He wasn't sure how far they should go before marriage. Would they come to a point where he couldn't hold back?

He responded to her kisses, relishing in the sweet taste of her lips, before cupping her cheeks and saying, "Slow down, sweet pea."

She laughed. "And why should I?"

He returned her mischievous gaze with a look of seriousness. "I'm not ready for that, yet."

Iris blushed. "I forget how much younger you are."

She looked hurt. And he was embarrassed. Why did he have to say anything? He should have just gone with the flow. He wasn't a baby.

He caressed her shoulder and said, "I'd like nothing more than to marry you, Iris."

"Then why don't you?"

His heart hammered with excitement. He imagined a huge ceremony, someplace beautiful, like Mount Olympus, where all the gods watched as he and Iris declared their undying love for one another.

"Seriously?" he asked.

"Why not?" she said. "We've been best friends for fifteen years. You're of age, almost twenty years old. Why shouldn't we?"

He laced his fingers through hers. "When this is all over, even if we're trapped forever in the Titan Pit or in the belly of Zeus, as long as we're together, let's get hitched, okay?"

"Sounds like a plan," she said softly. "Like a very good plan, indeed."

***

Hip directed Swift and Sure to a large boulder covered in sea anemone at the bottom of the Ionian, about a mile away from Phorcys's castle. Apollo's shining chariot followed, illuminating the sea life around them, conspicuous in every way imaginable. Hip hoped they were far enough off not to draw attention. Their plan wasn't to charge the castle, but to investigate and, more importantly, to find Jen and Scylla.

He'd been attempting telepathic communication with Jen all day, without success, and he'd assumed it was because they were out of range of one another. Now, as he reached out to her and received no reply, he hoped it wasn't because she'd been swallowed.

I'll go around back, Than said telepathically. *Apollo, why don't you check out the east wing, and Hip, you the west?*

Hip and Apollo each gave Than a nod, and they swam their separate ways.

As Hip maneuvered over the cracked and partially broken wall and approached the west wing, he searched for signs of Jen and Scylla. He was surprised to find no one guarding the castle. The Old Man of the Sea had fallen out of favor with the mer and sea populations in recent centuries, so he had only his children and a few sharks to protect what was left of his ancient and decrepit abode. Even so, Hip had expected that a new alliance with Zeus would mean extra reinforcements, but there were none to be found. In fact, the place seemed abandoned, haunted by old shadows and memories that gave the place an eerie feel.

Hip tried the side door and, finding it locked, peered through a window to the inside. The place seemed deserted, so he decided to risk god travel inside. He landed in what appeared to be someone's bed chamber. There was a huge bed of sand and seaweed in its center, a side table made of rock and shiny stones, a collection of treasure inside an opened wooden chest, and a shelf lined with interesting seashells.

He swam from the room to a dark corridor, sensing no sign of anyone. Worried that Jen could be imprisoned in a room or dungeon, he decided he should look behind every door. As he came upon the next one, made of ancient, petrified wood and, like the others, warded so no god could see through it, he turned the handle and pulled it open.

A mass of tangled snakes leapt out and hissed at him. He conjured his sword and lopped off their heads. Black blood oozed around him, making him feel queasy. The water was bad enough, without snakes and their blood.

He looked around the room. It seemed to be a lounging area full of strange objects—a beheaded statue stood in one corner. A golden trough lay half-hidden in the sand of the ocean floor, and it was filled with jewels and coins. Beside it on a stone table, sat a collection of busts. A shelf against the wall was filled with plates, bowls, and goblets. And hanging on the wall opposite it were very old swords, a pitchfork, and two shields. There was even a half-dozen paintings lining another— paintings of people Hip didn't recognize. Someone in this castle was a collector of ancient artifacts. Hip supposed the monsters needed something to pass the time when they weren't eating lost seamen.

He left the room and returned to the corridor in search of another door. He was about to open one, when he heard voices in another, more central area of the castle. He swam toward the sounds.

He followed the corridor and came upon the dining hall. The long table and half-broken chairs were empty. Hermes and Than floated at the end of the room. Hermes clutched the helm of invisibility.

"I followed you here," Hermes said to Than. "I have the helm, and we have Artemis."

Apollo emerged through another entrance. "Don't do this, brother."

"You took the words right out of my mouth," Hermes said. "You can end this. It doesn't have to be this way."

"Where's Jen?" Hip asked.

"Zeus took her as his prisoner," Hermes said. "With Echidna's help."

"Where? On Mount Olympus?" Than asked.

"I can't tell you that," Hermes answered.

"Please, cousin," Hip begged. "If you won't help me get her back, at least tell me where she is."

"I'm sorry," Hermes said. "But you brought this on yourself. I tried to stop you."

"How can you work with *Echidna*?" Than asked. "She nearly killed my twins. Or have you forgotten?"

"If I remember correctly, Scylla was in on that, too, and now she's *your* ally," Hermes said.

"Scylla changed," Apollo said. "Echidna is still the same cruel monster she's always been."

"And you've changed, brother," Hermes said. "You, like me, were once devoted to our father. Don't you remember all the adventures we've shared? I was just a babe when you took me under your wing. You pushed me to run faster. *You* are the reason I became the fastest god of all."

"I remember," Apollo said. "I still cherish the lyre you gave me all those years ago."

"Then how can you do this?" Hermes beseeched him. "How can you turn your back on your family?"

"Zeus's selfishness has grown worse with age," Apollo said.

"Who among us isn't selfish?" Hermes argued.

"Zeus is ruled by fear," Than said. "Selfishness, paranoia, and fear."

Hip nodded. "Fear of losing his throne, of being overthrown by his son, as Zeus did his father."

"What king doesn't fear losing his throne?" Hermes pointed out.

"They all do," Apollo said. "But how they handle that fear defines the kind of king they become."

"Our father is a good king," Hermes insisted. He turned to Thanatos. "Didn't it mean anything to you that he took your annual punishment from the Maenads? Hip, that helped you, as well, since you volunteered to take your brother's place while he was mortal."

Hip shook his head. "Zeus only did that because he could sense the unrest among the other gods. He wanted to regain our trust and favor."

"You wouldn't have your happy little family if it weren't for my father, Hypnos," Hermes said. "Admit it. He didn't have to make Morpheus a god."

"Yes, he did," Apollo said. "He made a deal, swore an oath."

"And have you forgotten that I nearly died while in the service of Zeus?" Hip pointed out.

"That was Uranus's doing," Hermes replied. "You can't blame my father."

"We can blame him for plenty of things," Than said.

"Like what he did to our mother," Hip added.

"She committed treason against him!" Hermes shouted.

"Not the night Melinoe was conceived," Than said.

"That's ancient history," Hermes said. "We've all made mistakes."

"Some worse than others," Hip said.

Hermes swam across the room, as if to leave, and then turned to face them again. "Let's work together to make things better, not split apart. Brother against brother and son against father isn't the way forward.

Please, I beg you to declare your loyalty to Zeus and end this before it's too late."

"It's already too late," Apollo said.

Hermes sighed. He was breathing fast, and his hands trembled as he held tightly to the helm of invisibility. Hip knew that none of them were fast enough to take it from him. Even if they all three attempted to descend upon him at once, Hermes would leave with the helm.

"I was hoping you wouldn't say so," Hermes said sadly. "You can't blame me for trying to keep the peace."

"Join us," Apollo said.

Hermes frowned. "I can't. I love all of you, but I love my father more."

With that, Hermes disappeared.

As they stood there, unsure of what to do next, they heard a loud shriek coming from below. A trap door burst open, and out popped Scylla, in her monster form. She was bleeding from where the center four of her six heads had been severed, along with three of the dog heads, that usually howled at her waist.

"Scylla?" Hip cried, swimming over to her aid. "What happened?"

"Zeus undid Circe's magic," she said. "He told me that if I joined him, he'd return me to my goddess form."

"We'll find a way to help you," Than said. "You won't be stuck like this forever."

"What can you do?" she asked. "Without Circe's potion, I'm stuck. Only the most powerful god…"

"Poros is the most powerful god," Apollo said. "He'll transform you back."

"But Zeus kept the bits he cut off," she said mournfully. "Without them, I don't know if I can change back."

"We'll find a way," Hip said. "Do you have any idea where Zeus took Jen?"

"He didn't say," she wailed. "But before you go looking for her, there's something else you should be worried about."

"What?" Than asked.

"Zeus is using my family to mount an attack on Poseidon as we speak."

***

Therese followed Than through the main corridor of Poseidon's castle into the throne room, having to remind herself more than once as she swam that she could breathe underwater.

"Did Hermes say where they're keeping them?" Therese asked him.

"No."

"Poor Jen." She felt bad for Artemis and Scylla, but she felt even worse for her best friend, whom she loved like a sister. "Where's Scylla now?"

"She swam to her old cave, to heal."

"The one near the Messina Straight?" Therese asked.

"That's the one. She wanted to come help, but she wouldn't have been any good to us in her condition. The four heads with eyes were all severed, leaving her blind."

"Poor thing."

As they entered, Poseidon was holding a boulder in one hand and his trident in another and was pacing the floor. Amphitrite sat on her throne, looking as though she'd rather be anywhere else.

Than said, "They're coming—Phorcys and his family are en route."

"Alert the guards," Poseidon said to a merman near the door, who quickly swam away with his orders.

"I've disintegrated around the perimeter," Than said. "Hypnos is with me, and Apollo is on his way. So are Phorcys and his crew. They're about a mile from here. I can see them."

"Who's with Phorcys?" Amphitrite asked.

"Keto, Chimera, Echidna, Nike, Phobos, Deimos, and…what the?"

"What?" Poseidon asked.

Than gave Poseidon a worried look. "Hera is there with Ladon."

"The one-hundred headed serpent?" Amphitrite asked.

"That's the one," Than said.

"No worries." Poseidon lifted his trident. "We've got them out-numbered."

Therese wanted to say, "but not out-matched," but she held her tongue. Ladon tipped the odds in their enemies' favor. Even though Than and Hip could disintegrate into the billions, if either of them suffered a life-threatening injury, he would be forced to reintegrate, and the army would be diminished, unlike Ladon, who could continue to fight with the loss of a few heads.

"They've got the helm now," Than warned. "And there could be another beneath its protection."

"Like Zeus and his thunderbolt," Poseidon said through gritted teeth. "Prepare yourselves."

Poseidon gave a backward glance to Amphitrite before joining Than and Hip outside the castle to await the attack. Therese treaded at the ready behind the front door. Amphitrite joined her. And, in another moment, Rhode and Helios did, too.

"Clymene and Dione are on their way," the bright sun god said.

As the entire castle shuddered, along with the ocean floor beneath it, Therese hoped the reinforcements would arrive in time to help.

CHAPTER TEN

The Marcella

Hestie knew she shouldn't be afraid of her Grandpa Hades, but she was. It wasn't because of anything he had ever said or done in her presence, but because of things she had read about online and in books. So, when she couldn't find her parents, or Uncle Hip, or Aunt Jen, or any of the Furies in the Underworld, and her Grandma Persephone was still recovering from having been swallowed by Zeus, she decided to go looking for Hecate.

Poros and Hermie, having nothing better to do, followed.

She'd already gone to ask Morpheus if he knew anything, but he seemed more interested in Iris than in what was going on between the gods. Besides, it was her opinion that he and Iris deserved a little down time, after what they'd just gone through.

Still adjusting to her new god senses, she was startled by the sound of Hecate's voice emanating through the walls of her chambers. The goddess of the crossroads and of witches was chanting in a language Hestie recognized as ancient Greek. Again and again, the goddess said, "Water, sky, rock, and sea, show me the helm of invisibility."

The helm was missing? Hestie turned to her companions.

The boys shrugged, apparently as clueless as she was.

In the next moment, Hecate said, "I see you there. Come inside."

The three teens obeyed, and when neither Poros nor Hermie offered Hecate any kind of explanation, Hestie took the lead. "We want to help the cause. What can we do?"

"Nothing for the moment," the goddess said.

"Is the helm really missing?" Hermie asked.

"I'm afraid so," Hecate admitted. "And Artemis has been taken. Your father gave me the news moments ago."

"Not swallowed," Hestie said, hoping she was right as her stomach tightened with worry.

Hecate shook her head. "We don't know where she is. My first priority is locating the helm so that I can use magic to retrieve it, then I'll look for her."

"Is that possible?" Hermie asked. "Using magic to retrieve the helm?"

"It's never been done before, but that doesn't mean it isn't possible," Hecate said.

"There's got to be something we can do," Poros said. "I'm stronger than my father. I should be helping."

Hecate put a hand on Poros's shoulder. "There will come a time when you'll be needed. But, for now, stay out of trouble. Be ready. Okay?"

Poros nodded.

"Can we hang out with you?" Hermie asked.

"Not now," she said. "I need to concentrate. Run along, okay?"

The teens left, aimlessly following the Phlegethon.

"I want to go home," Poros said.

"You mean to the ship?" Hermie asked.

"Yeah. I want to shower and change clothes and, …I don't know… I feel lost."

"But Prometheus said to stay here," Hestie pointed out.

"I can't."

"What? Why not?" Hermie asked.

"I just can't," he said simply.

Hestie wasn't sure what to say, but she didn't want Poros to go alone. "I'll come with you."

"No, Hestie," Hermie warned. "That's not a good idea. Both of you should stay here."

"I'm going crazy down here," Poros finally admitted. "I don't know how anyone can stand it. I miss the open sea and sky, not to mention my room and all my things."

Hestie kicked a loose pebble into the river of fire. "You're homesick. I am, too. I miss my house, my room, the forest, the lake."

"Let's go find our animals," Hermie said. "I miss Noodle and Kitty. They'll make us feel better."

"Go ahead," Poros said. "But I'm leaving."

Hestie sighed. "I can't let you go alone."

"Hestie, come on," Hermie insisted.

"Sorry," she said. "I'm going with Poros."

Hermie shook his head. "Then I guess I'm going, too."

Hestie took her brother's hand and then, rather awkwardly, took Poros's.

Poros smiled down at her, seeming to be aware of how his touch affected her. She wished more than ever that she could keep the blush from giving her away, but she failed. Abysmally.

"Let's go to my room," Poros suggested, before the pressure of god travel enveloped them all.

As soon as they'd arrived safely in Poros's bed chamber, they heard voices. They sounded like the voices of Prometheus and Athena, and they were coming from down the hall, near the bow of the ship— probably from the captain's quarters.

Poros put a finger to his lips and said, telepathically, *Prometheus has excellent hearing. Don't say anything. Just listen.*

"Do you really believe I wouldn't have risked my wellbeing to be with you?" Athena was saying.

"No," Prometheus replied. "I know you would have. And that's the point."

"So, you decided for me," Athena said bitterly. "I hate you for that, Prometheus. I doubt I can ever forgive you."

"I'd rather see you free and angry than imprisoned for all eternity," Prometheus said gently.

"Is that what your visions foretold? That if you came back for me, I'd be imprisoned?"

"I had no vision of our future," Prometheus replied.

Athena said nothing for a long moment, and then she said, "My father might have forgiven you, in time, if you'd asked."

"I didn't want his forgiveness. And if you think I had anything to be sorry for—except for leaving you—then you don't know me as well as I thought. Mortals could not have survived without fire. I will never regret giving it to them."

"In time, he might have come to admire your devotion to humanity," Athena insisted.

"He's a jealous god. I doubt it."

"But we'll never know," Athena said. "We'll never know what might have been. You robbed us of that."

"Sweet Athena," Prometheus said softly. "Why focus on what might have been? Let the past stay in the past. You're here now. We might still be together, if you can find it in your heart to forgive me."

Just then, another voice, loud and shrill and female, cried out, "Prometheus! Poseidon is under attack!"

Then Prometheus said, "That's my mother. Did you know about this? Were you just a distraction this whole time?"

***

In front of Poseidon's palace, Than conjured his sword and plunged it into the heart of Phobos while he simultaneously threw a spear at Echidna. Phobos fell, but the snake woman evaded the spear and lashed back at him, gripping him with her serpent's tail. The pressure against his chest began to squeeze the life out of him. He felt himself reintegrating into the one helpless version of himself, trapped and on the verge of death.

Poseidon came to his rescue, paralyzing the monstrous half-woman, half-snake with a jolt from his trident. Than watched with relief as Echidna, as stiff as a statue, began to sink to the bottom of the sea, with only her eyes, fearful and angry, showing any signs of movement. As soon as Than had wriggled free of her slimy coils, he disintegrated again. He noticed Hip making headway with Keto, and, across from him, he saw Poseidon throwing bursts from his trident at Ares, Deimos, and Nike. But Phorcys charged past them and breached the doors to the palace, and on his heels were Hera and the one-hundred-headed serpent, Ladon.

Thanatos followed them into the palace, where Therese, Amphitrite, Helios, and Rhode attempted to hold the line. Apollo appeared from behind, shooting arrows at each of Ladon's heads. The beast went wild with fear and rage, thrashing his many heads through the water. As Than attacked Hera from behind, Therese and Apollo took down Ladon. But then Than noticed Hip in Chimera's lion-footed clutches, where he integrated into one. Than swung his sword at Chimera and missed. He charged again but was attacked from behind. Someone's spear pierced his back. He stared at the spearhead jutting from his chest, covered in his blood.

Before he reintegrated, he saw it had been Hermes who'd attacked him.

Unable to believe that his beloved cousin could do such a thing, he paused for a split second, in shock. It was just enough of a pause for Ares to swoop in and cuff Than from behind with adamantine chains.

As he was carried off with the spearhead still jutting from his chest, Than heard his father's shouts. In the distance, he saw his father in his chariot, coming toward him through the sea. The chariot was still miles away when Thanatos spied Zeus in his own chariot, trailing behind

Hades with a lightning bolt in his hand. Before Than could warn his father, Ares flew into the sky with the helm of invisibility.

Now, Than was lost to his father and to the rest of the rebel alliance. While the helm hid Ares, it hid all he touched. No one knew where Than's captor was taking him.

Then the pressure of god travel enveloped him, and suddenly, he was dropped from the sky into a throng of outreached arms belonging to the Cyclopes.

***

Hermie followed Hestie and Poros to the salon of *The Marcella*, where they'd overheard Prometheus order Jinsoo and Mina to stay while he flew to the upper deck. Hermie was surprised to find that night had fallen.

"Athena!" they heard Clymene wail. "Why are you here? To distract us from the attack?"

"I knew nothing about it," Athena said. "I swear on the River Styx."

"Are you with us, or against us?" Clymene asked.

"I, I…" Athena didn't finish her reply.

Hermie was shocked when Poros revealed himself by leaving the salon and taking the steps to the upper deck of the ship. Hestie followed before Hermie could stop her.

"What happening?' Mina asked Hermie with wide eyes.

"There's been an attack on Poseidon's palace, I think," he said. "But don't worry. We'll be fine. Wait here."

"We must go immediately," Dione insisted from above.

"I can't abandon the ship and leave the kids behind," Prometheus said.

As he climbed the steps to the upper deck, Hermie heard Poros say, "I'll watch the ship. You go."

Prometheus did not look happy when he said, "I told you to stay put."

"I know," Poros said. "I'm sorry. I couldn't. I'm the most powerful god. Shouldn't I be helping?"

"What does he mean, he's the most powerful god?" Athena asked.

"Whose side are you on?" Dione asked the goddess of wisdom.

"Are you with us, or against us?" Clymene asked again.

"Where's my mother?" Athena asked.

"Hidden," Prometheus answered. "As you should be, Poros."

"I said I want to help," Poros said.

Prometheus pointed a finger at Poros. "You're also your father's number-one enemy, his greatest threat. You're exposed here. You were safe in the Underworld. I can't protect you and defend Poseidon's palace at the same time."

"I can protect myself," Poros insisted.

"There's no time to waste," Clymene urged them. "Declare yourself, Athena!"

"Are you our friend or foe?" Dione asked.

"I don't know," Athena said, before she disappeared.

"I'm going to fight, son," Clymene said to Prometheus. "With or without you."

Clymene and Dione vanished.

Prometheus looked at all three of the teens with more anger on his face than Hermie had ever seen on the Titan before. "You put yourselves in jeopardy coming here, against my wishes."

"Poros is right," Hestie said. "We should be helping. We're gods now, too."

"Barely gods," the Titan said. "And as soon as our enemies learn of your whereabouts, you'll become their leverage."

"Give me more credit," Poros said.

Prometheus frowned. "I need to go, but I can't leave you here, out in the open. We have Mina and Jinsoo to consider. I'm taking the whole ship to the Aegean. I know a quiet cove not far from the palace. I'll hide you there while I help defend the rebels."

Hermie was scared but was glad he had come. He couldn't imagine how frightened Mina and Jinsoo would have been if Prometheus had left them alone on the ship, even if it was well hidden. At least now, they had gods to defend them, and one of them was the most powerful of all.

The pressure of god travel enveloped them, and suddenly the ship was on a different sea altogether.

"Be on your guard and don't leave the ship," Prometheus said, before he disappeared.

Hermie turned to his sister. Poros flew up in the air to have a look around. Hestie followed.

"Wait!" Hermie said. "That's not safe."

Thankfully, they returned to his side.

"We need a plan," Poros said.

"Prometheus said to wait here," Hermie said. "We need to protect Mina and Jinsoo."

"Protect us from what?" Jinsoo asked, as he reached the upper deck.

"The gods are at war," Hestie explained.

"Where are we?" Mina asked, as she appeared behind her brother and glanced at their new surroundings. "And how we get here?"

"Don't worry," Hermie said. "You're safe with us."

Mina took Hermie's hand. "You protect me."

Hermie smiled bashfully and gave her an awkward nod.

His embarrassment didn't last long, however. The overcast sky was suddenly alight with electricity.

"Is that a storm?" Jinsoo asked. "Or gods?"

"Both," Poros said. "We better go below deck."

"I'm hungry," Mina said.

"We still got kimchi," Jinsoo said.

Hermie rolled his eyes. He had hoped he'd never have to see or smell kimchi again. But, he supposed if tolerating it was the bravest thing he'd have to do that day, then he'd survive.

CHAPTER ELEVEN

Cyclopes Island

Therese opened her eyes and squinted against the light. Her arms were chained above her head, and she hung from them, kneeling with her back against a wall of rock in the middle of a jungle with her knees deep in sand. She was still half-dazed, trying to figure out where she was and how she'd gotten here.

The last thing she could recall was Aphrodite beckoning to her after Hera and Phorcys had breached the castle door. Therese and Amphitrite, along with Rhode and Helios, had put up a good fight, until Zeus had struck the palace with his lightning bolt and had scattered them in different directions. Therese had hit her head on the palace wall but had opened her eyes in time to see Aphrodite beckoning to her to come. With her allies scattered, Therese had decided to trust Aphrodite. She had used her fastest free-style to swim to the goddess of love awaiting in her chariot, and the next thing she knew, Therese had awakened here, in the middle of who-knew-where.

"Therese."

She turned her head but couldn't see another living soul.

"Therese, it's Helios. I'm in chains, too, in a cave behind you. Thanatos is on the floor at my feet, unconscious."

"Than? Is he breathing?" She wasn't sure if she was breathing herself.

"Yes. But he has a spear through his chest, and I have no way of pulling it out."

Tears pricked her eyes. She wondered what was happening back at Poseidon's palace. Whether it had been taken or defended, how many had been harmed or imprisoned…or worse?

"How did you get here?" she asked the sun god.

"Chimera bit off my arms and swallowed them," he said. "Before I could escape, Ares scooped me up in his chariot and chained me here. You and Than were already here when I arrived."

"Where are we?" Therese asked.

"Cyclopes Island."

Therese knew this place. She'd come here years ago—once to take the eye of Polyphemus, and a second time to question Polyphemus when Amphitrite and the trident had gone missing.

"Hopefully our rescuers are on their way," she said.

"No one knows we're here," Helios said. "Ares wore the helm. I haven't been able to make telepathic contact with anyone. I'm not even sure if Selene will be able to notice us beneath these thick trees and with me stuck in here."

"Some of your light is shining from the cave," Therese pointed out. "Maybe someone will notice it."

"Like I said, these trees are thick."

"If you're down here," Therese asked, "does that mean the earth is in darkness?"

"My chariot is still making the rounds. It's not as bright without me in it. The days will be overcast and dark, but not as dark as night."

Therese pulled at her chains, to no avail. "I can't believe Aphrodite tricked me. Or that I trusted her to begin with."

"How did she capture you?" Helios asked.

"By pretending to be my friend. As soon as I climbed into her chariot, she stuck me with a needle, and I passed out. I woke up here, just now."

"Therese?" another voice called out to her from a short distance across the jungle.

"Jen?" Therese stood up and leaned toward the sound of the voice, pulling her chains taut. "Is that you?"

"Yes! I'm here in a cage with Hip and Artemis. Can you break us out?"

Therese groaned. "No. I'm chained to the outside of a cave. Helios and Than are imprisoned inside. Are you guys okay?"

"I'm okay, but Artemis is paralyzed," Jen said. "She hasn't been able to speak. Zeus the dick probably struck her with a lightning bolt."

"Oh, no!" Therese shouted. "What about Hip?"

"I'm here," Hip said. "What about Than and Helios?"

"Here," Helios said. "My arms were swallowed by Chimera, and Than's out cold with a spear in his chest."

"Great," Hip said.

"Hip has been trying to find Morpheus in the Dreamworld," Jen said. "To get him a message."

"I haven't had any luck finding him," Hip said.

"But you're the god of slumber," Therese said. "Can't you put us all into the deep boon of sleep, so we can look for Morpheus, too?"

"Than's there looking for him," Hip said. "We should come up with another plan, in case Morpheus isn't there."

"What kind of cage are you in?" Helios asked.

"Electric bars," Jen replied. "We get zapped every time we touch it."

"We're in adamantine chains and cuffs," Therese said. "But I still have my quiver and bow. Maybe one of our allies would notice if I shot an arrow into the sky."

"It's worth a try," Helios said. "And I just might be close enough to light it on fire with my rays as you shoot it."

Therese removed an arrow from her quiver and fit it into her bow. The chains didn't allow her to pull the bow back as far as she could, but it would be enough to breach the treetops.

"Ready?" she asked Helios. "On the count of three."

"Ready."

"One, two, three." She let the arrow fly.

Helios blew a ray of sunshine but missed the arrow by a few inches.

"Let's try that again," Therese said. "This time, shine a ray, and I'll shoot the arrow through it."

She worried the arrow would fly through the ray too quickly to catch fire. She would shoot with less speed, even if it meant it would barely breach the canopy above them.

Helios blew a ray of sunshine, and Therese launched the arrow. With luck, the arrow caught fire and disappeared above the trees. Therese suspected it would start a fire and create an even better signal than the single arrow.

"Now we wait," she said, hoping it was an ally, and not an enemy, that noticed the signal first.

***

Morpheus stopped kissing Iris and sat up on the couch.

"What's wrong?" Iris asked.

"My Uncle Than found me in the Dreamworld. He's a prisoner, along with my parents and Artemis."

"Oh, no!" Iris flew up from the couch and scurried about the room. "What should we do? Alert the others?"

"Yes. Let's go."

They flew together to the throne room, but no one was there. After finding the meeting rooms empty and Tartarus all but deserted, they knocked on the door of Hecate's chambers. When they received no answer, they flew to the Furies' abode. No answer there, either.

"Where is everybody?" Iris said anxiously, as they followed the Phlegethon to the River Styx, where Charon ferried his skiff toward the gates.

They flew to the boat.

Hovering above the ferryman, Morpheus asked, "Do you know where everybody went?"

"The dead cannot die," Charon said.

Morpheus scratched his head. "Why not?"

"The duty of death cannot fall upon anyone," the old god said.

Morpheus had known the most decrepit god was one of few words, but this was ridiculous. "Come on," he said to Iris. "This isn't helping."

Remembering that his grandmother was still recovering from having been swallowed by Zeus, he led Iris to Persephone's chambers.

Morpheus knocked on the door. "Please be there. Anybody."

Demeter answered. "How dare you disturb us? Don't you know what my daughter has been through?"

"I'm sorry, but I can't find anyone else," Morpheus explained. "Do you know where they've gone?"

Demeter scoffed. "How should I know what goes on in this dastardly place?"

She was about to slam the door in his face, but he stopped her with his hand. "Can I please talk to my grandmother?"

"She's sleeping and needs her rest," Demeter said.

This time, she did slam the door. Morpheus was surprised the noise wasn't enough to wake Persephone, much less the dead.

"What an obstinate woman!" Iris said under her breath.

Morpheus was sure Demeter heard it. "I'm going to look for Persephone in the Dreamworld. I don't know what else to do."

He and Iris flew to the field of asphodel, so it would be easier for Morpheus to concentrate. They lay side by side, holding hands. Once he was completely asleep, he focused all his attention on seeking out his grandmother. She would know what to do, he thought.

He ran through the colorful prism, from one sleeper's dream to another, seeking out Persephone. He called out to her, shouting until his throat hurt; then, realizing he might wake her, he turned into a butterfly and flew to a field of jonquils—his grandmother's favorite flowers.

Sure enough, he saw her there, with a basket, picking the golden flowers in a sparkling meadow.

"Grandma Persephone," he said, still in butterfly form. "It's Morpheus."

"Don't you look lovely," she said with a smile.

"I need your help."

"What can I do for you, darling?"

"My parents and Than and Artemis are trapped on Cyclopes Island, and I can't find Lord Hades, or Hecate, or my Aunt Therese, or the Furies, or anyone else. Charon even said there's no one left to be death."

"Oh, dear!"

"Demeter won't let me into your room to talk to you. What should I do?"

"My mother sure is a piece of work, isn't she?"

"Tell me what to do. Iris is with me. I don't know where my cousins went."

"Take Iris's rainbow to Mount Olympus and see if you can find any of our people there. Then report back to me. I'll tell my mother to let you in."

"What about my parents?"

"We need to find the others if we're to have any hope of rescuing them," Persephone said.

Morpheus sat up in the field of asphodel and nudged Iris awake. "We need to go to Mount Olympus. Come on."

***

Than woke up to the sight of Polyphemus hovering over him. Without warning, the Cyclops yanked the spear from Than's chest. The pain seared through his body. The weapon had obviously been tainted with poison. It hurt like hell.

"What's going on?" Than asked the giant.

"Zeus ordered the others to guard yer," Polyphemus said. "But I'm loyal to me father. I've been runnin' like a chicken with its head cut off, tryin' to keep hidden. We better go, yer idiots."

"Than?" It was Therese.

Than was still healing, or he'd disintegrate and go to her at once.

"Help Therese," he told Polyphemus. Then he noticed Helios. The Titan's arms were missing, and at each shoulder were thick globs of blood. "And the sun god, too."

"Jen and Hip and Artemis are in a cage on the other side of those trees," Therese said as Polyphemus yanked the adamantine chains from the rock wall.

"I know," Than said, trying to climb to his feet. "I talked to Hip in the Dreamworld. I saw Morpheus. He's getting help."

"We better hurry, yer idiots," Polyphemus said as he ripped the sun god's chains. He couldn't crack open the cuffs, but at least they were free. "I ain't the only 'un who saw yer signal."

Therese was soon beside Than, helping him to his feet.

"Are you hurt?" Than asked her.

"I'm okay. I shot an arrow of fire into the air."

"Not the brightest idear," Polyphemus said. "We better run."

With Therese helping him along, Than followed Polyphemus and the armless sun god across the jungle to the prison holding Hip and Jen. Artemis lay on the floor, but her eyes were open.

"She's paralyzed," Therese said to him.

"We can't get 'em out," Polyphemus said of the others. "Let's leave 'em and go."

"We can't leave them," Than said.

He was afraid the other Cyclopes would take out their anger on the remaining prisoners, or worse, move them to a new location, without anyone else knowing what it was.

"I done me part," Polyphemus said before he ran into the jungle. "Good luck to yer, yer idiots."

"I need to find Chimera," Helios said. "I'm no help without my arms."

"Go," Than told him. "But first recruit a rescue team. Therese and I will hide in the jungle and keep an eye on the others."

"Someone's coming," Hip warned though the electric bars of his cage. "Hide."

Therese helped Than to a cluster of low-growing shrubs in the undergrowth of the thick-leaved loquat trees that dominated the jungle canopy. The ground shook from the weight of the heavy giants making their way to this part of the island. Soon the area was filled with at least a dozen half-naked Cyclopes, most carrying primitive tools, such as clubs and axes. Than squeezed Therese's hand, trying to comfort her, even though he knew they were in trouble.

One of the giants cried out from the cave where Than had awakened. "They're escaped! They're escaped!"

"That'll be the end of us," another wailed.

"If we don't find 'em first!" another shouted.

"Yer go that a way, and I'll go this a way!" someone said.

"No, yer idiot! Yer go that a way, and I'll go this a way!" another said.

"Scatter, yer idiots!" another said. "Or I'll eat yer alive!"

The Cyclopes bumbled about, bumping into each other before deciding on a direction to run. Than observed that they were as quick with their feet as they were with their wits.

Than's feelings of superiority diminished when a crowd of them stumbled upon the undergrowth where he and Therese were hiding.

Therese had an arrow fitted to her bow, ready to launch. Than was shocked when, instead of directing it into the Cyclopes, she shot it at Than. Once he got over the shock of being shot by his own wife, he was surprised that the arrow did not hurt his already opened wound. When he gazed back at her with a lifted brow, he saw her take another arrow and pierce her own heart before turning into a…gibbon?

"Lookie here," one of the Cyclopes said. "It's a pair o' monkeys!"

"Ain't they cute!" another said, lifting the leaves beneath which Than and Therese were hidden.

"Come lookie," the first said to his cohorts. "I ain't never seen monkeys on this here island."

"Two little monkeys a sittin' in a tree," one sang. "K-i-s-s…er, I forget the rest."

"Yer idiot!" the first one said. "Yer forget everything."

"I do not!"

"Yer do, too!"

While the Cyclopes argued, Therese led Than through the leaves and up to the highest branches of the loquat tree, higher than even the giants could reach. Because their monkey hands were too small for the cuffs, they were free of the adamantine chains, which they left behind.

"Where'd they go?" the first one said.

"Lookie there! Ain't they cute! Up in that there tree!"

"Those ain't monkeys, yer idiot!" another said. "Look! The chains!"

Than followed Therese from one branch to the next, running and jumping. The pain of his wound slowed him down. The poison from the spear had severely inhibited his ability to heal.

Once they were free from the thick of the jungle, they came upon the rolling hills, where the sheep grazed. Therese returned to her godly form, so Than followed suit.

"What do we do now?" she asked him.

"We can't leave the others."

Therese's face transformed into a look of terror as she gazed overhead. Than followed her eyes to the sky where three ugly Harpies were descending on them.

"Run!" Than said.

CHAPTER TWELVE

The Rainbow Arch

Hestie sat beside Jinsoo on Jinsoo's twin bed watching *Naruto* with him on her phone, which they'd plugged in. Mina sat beside Hermie on Mina's bed watching the same episode on Hermie's phone. Poros had gone to take a shower and put on a fresh set of clothes. Hestie planned to do the same when he was finished but was waiting because the water pressure on the ship was poorly affected by two people showering at once.

Unless, of course, they were in the same shower.

Hestie blushed, hoping she hadn't accidentally prayed that thought to Poros. It was something to get used to, the difference between thinking about someone and praying to them.

It wasn't long before Poros rejoined them. She could smell his clean hair, still wet and a little curly where it hung over his ears and at the nape of his neck. The wetness of his hair made it appear darker than its usual blond and made his stunning gray eyes even that much more spectacular. Without realizing it, she was thinking, *You are one fine specimen, Poros.*

I think the very same of you, Hestie.

She averted her eyes and cursed herself for not being more careful.

Let's go to my quarters, he said to her telepathically. *I want to talk to you.*

Nervously, she handed her phone over to Jinsoo and followed Poros from the room.

"I need to take a shower," she said, once they were in the hall and entering Poros's room. She felt self-conscious, even though she'd come to realize that gods can go much longer without showering before they smell.

Poros closed the door behind them and sat on his bed. "I just want to say something to you first."

He patted the bed beside him, indicating to her that he wanted her to sit.

She hoped he couldn't hear her heartbeat speed up as she sat next to him. "I know what you're going to say."

"Does that mean you're a seer?" He laughed.

"No." She thought of Lynn. "Of course not."

"Then hear me out."

"It's just that now's not the time."

He shook his head. "And why is that?"

"Um, because, hello, we're at war."

"The gods are always in conflict with one another," Poros said. "That's one of the reasons Prometheus keeps to himself."

"We can't just keep to ourselves."

"That's not what I meant."

"This is your destiny," she reminded him.

"I know that."

"Then what are you trying to say?"

He took her hand. "If you make me wait until the conflicts are over, I may never get to kiss you."

She pulled her hand away, overwhelmed by his touch and his words. She stood up and fidgeted near the door. She'd never been in a relationship before. Kissing a boy was no small thing to her.

"What's wrong?" he asked her.

She turned to face him "I need time. I've had a lot to take in, lately."

He grinned. "No worries. I can wait."

She heaved a sigh of relief.

"But you do want to kiss me," he said, still grinning. "Even if you don't know it yet."

It was true. She did. But she was scared. She'd rather rush into battle with a million monsters than kiss a boy.

"I'm going to take my shower now, smartie pants," she said bravely, even though his words had left her trembling.

***

Morpheus followed Iris through her rainbow arch from the Underworld to Mount Olympus, but when they reached the end of it, they found it blocked.

"Someone has sealed it shut with wards," Iris said.

"Can you unseal it?"

"I don't think so." Then she added, "This could be a trap."

Morpheus's stomach clenched. "They knew we'd come back to spy on them."

"We should go."

"Wait," Morpheus said. "I can hear them talking. Listen."

Zeus's loud voice exploded from the great hall of the palace below. "You of all people should know that I never lose, Hades!"

"It's not over yet," came the voice of Poseidon.

Zeus laughed a horrendous, arrogant, and malignant laugh. "Oh, I'd say it's over. I've got the trident and the helm and the two of you trapped. All I need now is a seer."

Morpheus gave Iris a worried look. "We're doomed."

"Don't say that. Let's get out of here before someone catches us."

As they turned to go, Morpheus felt a presence emerge near the sealed end of the arch. He turned back to see Nike grinning at him.

"Go!" he shouted to Iris as he flew through the arch toward the Underworld.

He stopped short when Deimos appeared and blocked the path.

Morpheus grabbed Iris's hand and was about to god travel away, when Nike struck him with her spear and threw adamantine cuffs around Iris's wrists.

"You're coming with us," Deimos said haughtily.

Deimos cuffed Morpheus before he could remove the spear, and then he and Iris were hauled through the arch down to Mount Olympus, to the great hall, where many of the gods were gathered. Morpheus gaped at the troubling spectacle of the great Lord Hades in one bird cage and the formidable Poseidon in the other. Without those two powerful gods, the rebellion was surely lost.

"Ah, Morpheus," Zeus said coolly. "Just the person I was hoping to find."

"You set me free, remember?"

"Well, yes," Zeus said. "But, you see, now I've captured you again."

Morpheus glanced at Iris.

"Morpheus," Zeus continued. "You never told me the name of that seer you found in Colorado."

"I can't remember her name," Morpheus lied.

"Tsk, tsk, tsk," Zeus taunted with his tongue. "That's too bad. I suppose I could rip the wings from your girlfriend, to see if that jogs your memory."

Iris broke into tears. "Please my Lord." Then to Hera, she said, "My Lady, please don't let him take my wings."

"Let her go," Morpheus said. "Let her go, and I'll tell you anything you want to know."

"Keep your mouth shut!" Hades growled from his cage.

As much as Morpheus wanted to obey Lord Hades, he couldn't allow Iris to undergo the same excruciating pain as he had a few days ago. And there was a chance she'd never get her wings back.

"Ares," Zeus said. "Pull off one of Iris's wings. Just one."

As Ares moved toward Iris, Morpheus shouted, "I'll talk!"

"Then quit stalling!" Ares shouted back.

Full of desperation and self-loathing, Morpheus said, "Her name is Lynn. She's Therese's little sister."

Through his tears, Morpheus was mortified by the smiles that crossed the faces of Zeus, Hera, and Ares.

Ares turned to Phobos and Deimos. "You boys know what to do."

***

Hermie laughed at the scene from *Naruto* playing on his phone. Mina did, too.

"You're cute when you laugh," he said.

"Only when I laugh?"

"Get a room," Jinsoo teased.

Hermie *did* wish he and Mina were alone. Now that things were relatively calm, he wanted to kiss her.

"*You* get a room!" Mina said to her brother.

Jinsoo was about to get up and leave when Hermie's phone rang. It was Lynn calling, so he answered it.

"Thank goodness," Lynn said. "Hestie didn't answer."

"Oh, I think she's taking a shower," he said into the phone.

"I just had the weirdest vision," Lynn said. "It was *so real*, and I was *awake* this time."

"What was it?" Hermie asked.

"Your parents turned into monkeys and ran through a jungle."

Hermie laughed. "Are you sure you were awake when you saw that?"

"I'm sure," Lynn said. "They were being chased by a herd of giant Cyclops."

"It's Cyclopeez," Hermie said.

"Huh?"

"The plural for Cyclops is Cyclopeez."

"Hermie, I'm trying to be serious here. I think your parents are in danger. It's a very strong feeling. Even stronger than the dream I had of you getting your head chopped off."

Hermie stopped breathing.

"Hermie? You there?"

"Uh, huh," he said, dazed. "So, I get beheaded? That was your dream?"

"Oh, I don't think I was supposed to tell you that," Lynn said. "Oops."

"No," Hermie agreed, his throat and chest suddenly tight. "I don't think you were."

"What's wrong?" Mina asked.

"Listen, Hermie," Lynn said over the phone. "You need to find those Cyclops—uh, Cyclo*peez* and save your parents. I have a really bad feeling about this."

"And exactly how am I supposed to do that?" Hermie asked.

"Wait," Lynn said. "It sounds like someone's here…Who is it?"

Over the phone, Hermie heard the muffled sounds of a skirmish, followed by screams.

"Lynn?" he said into the phone. "Lynn, are you there?"

The call ended. Hermie called Lynn back but got no answer. The phone rang six times and then went to voicemail. Then he tried his Grammie's phone. No answer. It was the same when he tried calling his Grampie.

"Something's wrong," he said to Mina and Jinsoo.

"What happen?" Jinsoo asked.

"I don't know." Then Hermie shouted, "Poros! Hestie, come here!"

Poros arrived first. "What's wrong?"

"It's Lynn," Hermie began, just as Hestie arrived in nothing but a white towel, with her wet hair plastered down her face, neck, and shoulders.

"What *about* Lynn?" Hestie asked.

Hermie told them why Lynn had called—about the vision of their parents running from the Cyclopes—and then about the skirmish and screams. "And now she's not answering. Neither are Grammie and Grampie."

"We have to do something," Hestie said to Poros.

"I know where Cyclopes Island is," Poros said. "But Prometheus will kill me if I leave the ship."

"God travel isn't safe right now anyway," Hermie added. "Especially to a place we've never been to before."

"Then we won't leave it," Hestie said. "Let's set sail. We know how to do it."

"I don't think that's a good idea," Hermie said, thinking of Mina and Jinsoo. "Plus, if we're going to go into danger, shouldn't we check on Grammie and Grampie and Lynn, too?"

"Maybe we should split up," Hestie said.

"Also not a good idea," Hermie complained.

"I don't think we have a choice," Hestie said. "What do you think, Poros?"

"It'll a take a few hours to get to Cyclopes Island. While Hermie and the twins man the ship, you and I can pop over to your grandparents' place."

Hermie didn't like that idea either. "And if you get taken? What will I do about Mom and Dad?"

"We won't get taken," Hestie insisted. "We'll be extra careful."

Hermie sighed, resigned to the truth that nothing was safe anymore, and they had to do something.

Poros turned to Jinsoo and Mina. "Are y'all okay with sailing across the sea?"

"Sure!" Jinsoo said.

Mina smiled up at Hermie. "Let's go!"

Hermie followed Mina and Jinsoo to the rigging to check the lines and hoist the sails, while Hestie followed Poros to the cockpit to pull up the anchor and start the engine. Once Poros turned the boat into the wind, he and the twins hoisted.

The sky was overcast, and the wind was strong. Hermie hoped they could manage the ship without Prometheus. He sent out a prayer to the Titan, asking why he hadn't yet returned, but he received nothing but silence in reply.

As Hermie worked, he also worried about his parents. They hadn't been gods in fifteen years. What if they'd lost their groove?

"Break the main!" Poros shouted from the cockpit.

Mina and Jinsoo went to work, looking happy to be doing something they knew how to do. Hermie just hoped he and the other gods weren't leading them into danger.

Once the ship was stabilized and moving in the right direction, Hermie and the twins joined Hestie and Poros on the upper deck, in the cockpit.

"We need a plan," Hermie said as he scooted onto the couch beside Mina across from where Poros and Hestie were sitting in the swivel chairs. "If we sail straight up to the island, the Cyclopes will see us coming. We should anchor a few miles away and take the dinghy."

"Good idea." Poros took a pen and pad from a compartment in the dashboard and drew a map. "Once you get past the Cyclades here," he pointed to his map, "look for a cove near the tip of the mainland, like the one we just left, somewhere around here. It's just a few miles away from Cyclopes Island, which is here." Poros drew an *x*. "Meanwhile, Hestie and I will go see what's going on at your grandparents' house."

"Shouldn't I come with you?" Hermie asked. "The twins can sail the ship."

"We shouldn't leave them without protection," Poros said.

"We'll text you with updates," Hestie added.

"That is, if we can't reach you telepathically," Poros added.

Hermie nodded, feeling conflicted about staying. He wanted to stay. He was afraid to go into danger. But was it really the right thing to do?

CHAPTER THIRTEEN

Rescue Mission

Hip looked up in horror as a squawking Harpy inserted a key into the top of the cage before opening it, just long enough for two other Harpies to drop Than and Therese into the cage with him and the others.

The Harpy with the key slammed the cage shut before Hip or Jen could attempt to god travel out.

"You'll pay for this!" Jen shouted with a raised fist. "I'll get every last one of you nasty creatures!"

The half-woman, half-bird with the key shrieked a throaty laugh and said, "Dream on." Then she and her companions flew off.

Hip knelt in the sand beside his brother and Therese, as they recovered from their fall. "Are you guys okay?"

Than laid a palm across his chest. "Still healing from my spear wound. Though I guess, as long as I'm trapped in here, there's no hope of disintegrating, anyway."

"Nope," Hip confirmed.

Therese knocked the sand off her legs and stood up. "Why hasn't anyone come for us yet? It's been hours, hasn't it?"

"At least three or four since Hip got here," Jen, crouched on the ground beside Artemis, said. "Artemis and I have been here much longer—nearly a full day now."

"That's too long," Therese said. "How can no one have found us by now?"

"Did either of you see what happened to the others?" Than asked Hip and Therese. "My father? Poseidon? Apollo?"

"I think Apollo got away," Hip said. "But our father was overtaken by Zeus. I saw it just before Ares knocked me out."

"That's not good," Than said grimly.

"And Poseidon and Amphitrite?" Therese asked.

Hip shrugged.

"At least our kids are safe in the Underworld," Therese said.

"And Helios or Morpheus should have already given a message to someone," Than added.

Jen nodded. "It can't be long now."

Therese inspected their cage. "I guess you've already felt around for weak spots."

"Trust me," Jen said. "You don't want to touch those bars."

"It's like they're imbued with electricity from one of Zeus's lightning bolts," Hip explained.

"The first thing I did when I was stuck in here was to try to pry them open," Jen said. "I was zapped so hard, that it took me over an hour to regain the use of my hands."

Hip glanced over at Artemis, where she lay on the ground. She could blink, but not much else. She needed Apollo to help her heal. The sooner they escaped, the better, or her condition could become permanent.

"I can't believe Hermes stabbed me in the back," Than said.

Therese crossed her arms. "And Aphrodite tricked me. I really thought she was secretly our ally."

"I thought so, too," Hip said.

"Do you think the rebellion still has a chance?" Jen asked.

"It's not looking good," Than said. "But there's always a chance. And we have the prophesy on our side."

Hip clung to his brother's optimism and continued to reach out in prayer to every ally he knew. No one had responded, but that didn't mean they couldn't hear *him*. Maybe the electric cage prevented him from hearing their replies.

A moan from Artemis brought Hip from his thoughts and prayers. He and the others crouched over her, watching and waiting.

"Water," Artemis mumbled.

The others looked at one another in frustration. There was no water.

Then Therese fitted an arrow to her bow and shot it through the bars of the cage up into a loquat tree, piercing one of its fruits. But the arrow hung from the tree because the fruit wouldn't fall.

Jen startled Hip by ripping the hem from her shirt.

"What are you doing?" he asked her.

"We need to make a rope," she said, "so we can pull the arrow back down. Rip off a piece of your shirt. We can knot them together."

All four of them ripped from their sleeves and hems and made tiny knots to secure them together.

"This might not be long enough," Therese said. "Take some from Artemis."

Jen reached down and ripped a strip from the bottom of Artemis's leather skirt.

Hip still wasn't sure if they had enough, as Therese tied the string of cloth to an arrow and tried again. The arrow struck another fruit, but the makeshift rope hung above the cage at least a foot out of their reach.

Therese took another arrow from her quiver, flew to the top of the cage, and thrust the arrow through the bars, looping the rope around the arrowhead. Then she tugged, and the fruit, along with the other arrow, fell, falling onto the top of the cage with a cacophony of electric zaps.

Hip reached through the bars with his fingers, trying not to scream from the pain, and pulled the half-fried fruit into the cage before handing it over to Jen. Two of his fingers would no longer move.

Jen squeezed the juice of the fruit into Artemis's mouth. The goddess of the wild had trouble swallowing it down, but she managed, and soon she could move her head.

"Thank you," she muttered. "That helped."

Hip felt a sense of accomplishment and began to think of ways they might use Therese's arrows to help them to escape. Could an arrowhead be used to pick the lock?

Before he could try out his new idea, the ground beneath them shuddered as a group of Cyclopes surrounded the cage.

"No funny business, yer idiots!" one of them hollered.

"We got our eyes on yer!" another said.

Hip looked at his brother and sighed. Was there no way out?

Come on, Morpheus, Hip prayed. *We really need you, buddy.*

***

"Ready?" Hestie asked Poros on the upper deck of *The Marcella*.

"Wait. Hold on." Poros conjured a weapon—a sword, but not the one Hephaestus had recently given to him. Handing it over to Hermie, he said, "Take this. Just in case."

Hermie's face paled.

"You probably won't need it," Hestie said. "As soon as you anchor, the three of you can hide in the hull. Okay?"

Hermie and the twins nodded.

"No worries," Jinsoo said. "We got this."

"Keep praying to the others," Hestie added. "Especially to Hecate. She could do a cloaking spell on the ship."

"Will do," Hermie said.

Poros took Hestie's hand.

She tried to act naturally and to not let on how thrilled she was to be touching him as she said, "We'll be right back."

Then she imagined the woods outside her Grammie's house in the San Juan Mountains of Colorado, and, in the next instant, she and Poros were there.

Whereas dusk had arrived in Greece, it was still the late morning of the previous day in the San Juan Mountains. The sky wasn't overcast, like it had been on the sea. Helios was ascending in his cup toward high noon.

Without saying a word, Hestie led Poros down the hill toward the cabin, listening with her goddess ears for anything unusual. She approached the garage, finding the side door unlocked, as usual. She opened it and was surprised to see both of her grandparents' cars. If they were home, there would be a television or a radio playing. It was too quiet.

She led Poros through the basement and upstairs to the main level, to the kitchen. She was startled by the whistling sound of a teapot on the stove. She turned off the burner and then looked around the living room.

Grammie's laptop lay, opened, on the floor near her chair. Grampie's newspaper was covered in milk beside an overturned bowl. Hestie's heart danced with fear as she crossed the room to search their bedroom. Finding no one there, she took the stairs to Lynn's room. Lynn's phone lay on the floor near her opened door.

"Someone took them," Hestie said.

"Zeus," Poros said. "He must have learned that she's a seer."

"What do we do?"

"Let's go find your parents."

He took her hand, and they were enveloped by the pressure of god travel before they landed in his cabin in the hull of *The Marcella*. They went looking for the others and, finding them on the upper deck, still navigating toward the tip of Greece, Hestie filled them in on what they had seen.

"You think Zeus has them?" Hermie asked.

Hestie and Poros nodded.

"But we'll get them back," Poros added.

"First, we're going to look for Mom and Dad," Hestie said. "We better go."

The others followed Hestie and Poros to the lower deck, where the dinghy was stored.

"Be careful," Mina said.

"We'll see you soon," Jinsoo added.

Hestie felt as if she'd lost her tongue as she and Poros climbed into the dinghy and took off.

After more than twenty minutes, the island came into view. Hestie could make out the rocky beach, rolling hills, and thick jungle toward the island's center. Her parents could be anywhere on the island—in any number of possible caves, huts, or trees. Since her telepathic prayers continued to go unanswered, there was only one thing they could do: search every square inch of it.

They docked near a large rock jutting from the island but had to be careful that the wind didn't bash their little boat to bits. Once they were on land, they hauled the boat out of the water and tucked it between two boulders.

To be less conspicuous, they climbed on foot over the rocky embankment until they reached smooth sand that stretched into rolling hills, where dozens of sheep were grazing. That's when Hestie saw her very first Cyclops, sitting with his back against a lone tree. He appeared to be sharpening a stick.

The giant was much larger than she'd expected, with harry legs and arms and a bare chest and round belly. All but his privates, covered by a primitive cloth, were exposed. His head was bald, and his one eye, in the center of his forehead, was huge.

Seeing no sign of prisoners, Hestie and Poros crept along the side of a hill, away from the Cyclops, toward the jungle. They were so busy keeping watch on the one, that they failed to see the three carrying armfuls of chopped wood and ambling down a path straight toward them, until it was too late.

The three Cyclopes dropped their wood and shouted, "Trespassers! Trespassers!"

Poros took Hestie's hand and god traveled with her to the jungle. The canopy was so heavy and the undergrowth so thick, that very little of the remaining daylight made its way into the area. Hestie used her god vision to lead Poros through the brush and foliage until they came upon a wide path.

As she followed the path, with Poros behind her, she reached out in prayer to her parents and to her Uncle Hip and Aunt Jen but got no answer.

I sense someone coming, Poros said to her telepathically. *We better get off the trail and hide.*

The ground shook beneath their feet as they slipped into the brush and crept through the trees toward a rocky slope.

I see a cave, Hestie prayed to Poros. *Follow me.*

Halfway up a rocky slope was an entrance to a cave. Embedded on both the outside and inside were bits of severed chain, as if prisoners had once been kept here.

As the sound of the approaching Cyclopes grew nearer, Hestie suggested to Poros that they hideout in the cave and hope the herd of giants would eventually move on. He nodded in silence. She turned and led the way, past the first open chamber into a narrow tunnel too small for a Cyclops. The tunnel came to a dead end, so she squatted on the ground in a little niche. Poros crouched beside her.

It sounds like they're right outside, Poros said to her.

Hestie held her breath as she listened to the Cyclopes snooping around the entrance to the cave. It seemed like several minutes had passed before the herd moved on and she felt safe enough to breathe.

Wait here, Poros said, before he crept back toward the mouth of the cave. He returned in an instant and said, *They're waiting outside to ambush us. I think they can smell us.*

Just great. What do we do?

Wait it out, I guess—at least until we can come up with a better plan.

Hestie sighed and scooted onto her bottom, trying to get comfortable. Poros did the same. It was impossible for them not to touch in such a tight space. The feel of his leg against her leg, his elbow against her elbow, and his shoulder near her cheek was almost too much to bear. Why was being so close to Poros as scary as Cyclopes lying in wait?

So, what's your favorite color? He asked her.

Yellow. Yours?

Blue. The color of the sky.

She gave him an awkward grin.

What about your favorite food? he asked.

Definitely those nachos we shared at Mr. Burger.

Same.

She giggled, but then quickly covered her mouth, nearly forgetting that there were giants outside the cave that wanted to eat them.

Then he said, *I know I said I could wait, but since we're trying to pass the time, mind if I kiss you?*

She tried to stay cool and not freak out. She supposed a first kiss in a dark cave on an island of flesh-eating Cyclopes would be memorable. As she struggled with her answer, he leaned in, but didn't make his move. He just smiled down at her, waiting for her consent. His breath smelled fresh and hot, and his lips looked so touchable. She really did want to kiss him but was scared he wouldn't like the way she did it. She supposed leaving him hanging would be worse.

She nodded, and before she could breathe again, he went for it.

***

Hermie sat on the couch of the upper deck across from Mina and Jinsoo, who seemed pleased to be in the captain and Poros's swivel chairs at the helm. Even though the ship had been anchored for hours, the twins seemed to have a feeling of responsibility for the ship. Hermie, on the other hand, was feeling responsible for his sister.

He should have gone with them.

He'd spent the past few hours creating powerful weapons out of swords and taser guns he found in the captain's quarters. Each sword now had a taser gun attached to its hilt with electrical tape and a circuit of copper wire running along the blade. The swords could now be used to cut and electrocute their enemies. He'd wanted to arm the twins and himself in case they were attacked.

But, as they sat beneath the night sky, a feeling in the pit of Hermie's stomach confirmed that he'd been wrong to stay behind. Hestie and Poros had been gone for hours. What if something bad had happened to them? Hermie felt like he needed to do something. But what?

"I'm a god," he said out loud. "I should do something."

"What you going to do?" Mina asked him.

None of the other gods were answering his prayers. He'd texted Hestie a dozen times but had received no reply.

According to the map Poros had drawn earlier, Cyclopes Island was less than three miles from where *The Marcella* was anchored. Although Hermie couldn't risk god travel to a place he'd never been before, he could swim for it and, with his god speed, probably reach the island in less than thirty minutes. He hated swimming in anything but a chlorinated pool, because he didn't like sharing the water with the creepy unknown creatures of the deep. But, tonight, he felt he had no choice but to go to the island on his own to find out what had happened to his family and friends.

He handed his cell phone to Mina. "I'm going to swim for it."

"What?" Jinsoo stood up. "It way too dark."

"I have night vision now, remember?"

"Don't leave us, Hermie," Mina said. "What if monsters come?"

"I think they would have come by now. Don't worry. You'll be safe."

He spoke confidently, as if he knew what he was talking about. But the truth was, he'd never felt more insecure about a decision.

"I'll come right back," he promised. "Keep texting Hestie, and be sure not to let the phone die, okay?"

"You got it," Jinsoo said.

"Be careful," Mina said before she kissed his cheek.

"I always am," he said with a smile.

They followed him down to the lower deck where he used the ladder to ease into the cold water. He was grateful that his body was less sensitive to his environment and could tolerate extreme temperatures with ease. Since he hadn't yet tried to use his gift of breathing underwater, he practiced it there beside the ship while holding onto the ladder. It was strange how the water didn't burn his lungs. It entered and exited through his mouth and nose, just like air. It tickled a little, but it wasn't nearly as strange as he'd expected it to be.

However, he saw all manner of living things swimming at various depths within the hundreds of feet between him and the ocean floor. He shuddered at the thought of any one of them attacking him, or even brushing up against him. He hated slimy, slithering things, unlike his sister, who'd always defended them.

"They can't help what they are," she'd always say, just like their mother.

But Hermie couldn't help what *he* was either, and he was a natural born coward. He could admit it, because he'd always felt like his extreme intelligence, strength, and good looks made up for it. He'd never minded that he was a coward, until now. Tonight, he had to pretend to be brave because his family needed him.

CHAPTER FOURTEEN

Loss

Morpheus pulled against the straps holding him and Iris on Demeter and Persephone's double throne in the great hall of Mount Olympus. Galin and Cubie had come to whimper at his feet as Zeus continued to chastise his brothers for their betrayal. Still in the identical oversized bird cages in the center of the room, Hades and Poseidon glared at their brother, having grown tired of arguing with him hours ago.

Phobos and Deimos had returned to Mount Olympus with not only Lynn, but her parents, too. The sons of Ares were then ordered to go to the Underworld with a handful of others—Nike, Cupid, and Psyche—to attempt to breach the wards and take whatever prisoners they could find.

Lynn had been tied beside Morpheus on Artemis's empty throne. Her parents had been locked away behind them in Demeter's chambers, because their screams and shouts had become a nuisance to Zeus and to his loyalists. When Carol and Richard had refused to remain silent, Morpheus had feared for their lives. If Zeus meant to keep Lynn as his seer, the loss would be hard enough on Therese; Morpheus couldn't imagine her pain and outrage if she lost her aunt and uncle, too. He was hopeful when Zeus didn't kill them on the spot. Perhaps he meant to use them as leverage.

Trembling and with eyes full of tears, Lynn had already shared her vision of Than and Therese running from the Cyclopes, but this didn't interest Zeus as much as something else she had claimed to have seen: Poros.

"What about Poros?" Zeus now demanded.

"I had a dream last night," Lynn said. "In the dream, Poros was surrounded by lightning, or maybe he was filled with it."

Hera's brows lifted. "Perhaps this means Zeus strikes him down!"

"The prophecy has changed!" Ares said. "Zeus is the victor!"

"Did you see Poros fall?" Hermes asked.

"Not exactly," Lynn said. "He seemed to possess the lightning."

Zeus's face reddened. "You mean he stole it?"

"Impossible!" Hera screeched.

"His bolts are heavily guarded by both the Cyclopes and the Harpies," Hestia added.

"Tell us exactly what you saw!" Ares demanded. "Or we'll kill your parents!"

"I saw Poros in this room," Lynn said as tears ran down her cheeks. "But not as a prisoner."

Aphrodite gasped. Morpheus exchanged a hopeful glance with Iris.

"Did you see how he entered?" Hermes asked.

"Through there," Lynn pointed to the front entrance, by the dining hall and Hephaestus's forge.

"And the lightning?" Zeus asked. "Was he wielding it as he entered?"

Before Lynn could answer, Phobos and Deimos returned with the greatest seer of all: Apollo. The god of light and of prophecy, of truth, of healing, and of music now stood before the court in the great hall, captured by the loyalists. Morpheus felt his heart sink in his chest.

"Excellent work, boys!" Ares shouted at his grinning sons.

"My, my, my!" Zeus exclaimed gleefully. "Phoebus Apollo, my prodigal son, is returned!"

"How was he captured?" Hermes asked.

Without letting go of his prisoner, Deimos stepped forward and said, "We found him with Helios fighting Chimera in the Ionian Sea."

"They pried the sun god's arms from the belly of the beast," Phobos added. "But we captured both gods as they took to the sky."

"And where's Helios?" Zeus asked.

"Chained to his golden cup," Deimos replied. "Just as you asked us to do with Selene."

"Wonderful!" Hera exclaimed.

"Chain Apollo to his throne," Zeus commanded, and the sons of Ares obeyed. "Now go the Underworld and fetch me more prisoners."

Phobos and Deimos disappeared.

Morpheus found it difficult to look at Apollo. He must have fought one hell of a battle with Chimera to have been so easily captured by Phobos and Deimos. They got him when he'd been weakened. That was the only explanation Morpheus could accept.

"Dear Apollo," Zeus said. "I'd like you to meet my newest seer, Lynn. She was just describing a dream she had last night about Poros."

"Tell Apollo what you saw," Ares demanded.

Lynn's lips quivered as she said, "He came into this room through there." She pointed to the main entrance. "Then he stood before Zeus and called him *father.*"

Zeus's face changed from anger to bewilderment. "You saw this?"

Lynn nodded. "He begged you to accept him."

Gasps filled the room.

"Then what?" Hermes asked.

"Zeus threw a bolt of lightning directly at him, from just a few feet away," Lynn said.

"That would permanently paralyze him," Hera said, astonished.

"Indeed, the prophecy has changed, Father!" Ares cried.

"You're wrong," Apollo said.

"You refuse to admit defeat," Zeus said to Apollo. "Only the Fates know for certain what is to come. Even you have said so. Prophecies can be altered."

"Tell them what happens next," Apollo said to Lynn.

Lynn turned to Morpheus and prayed, *I'm scared he's going to kill me and my parents once I tell him all I know. Help me, Morpheus!*

***

Hermie swam his fastest freestyle across the surface of the sea, trying not to look at the creatures in the depths below him. The only way he could tell if he was going in the right direction was to stop every few hundred feet and look up at the night sky. If the north star remained to his right, then he knew he was still heading west.

The ocean floor became shallow, which meant he was getting close. Soon, he could stand and walk, and the island became visible to him. He only hoped it was the right island.

He crossed a rocky beach, and then his feet began to sink into softer sand. Hills spread out before him, and beyond them, the tops of trees. He headed for the trees.

As he crossed over the hills, he debated flying but was afraid he'd be easier to spot if the island was being watched. The island seemed lonely and uninhabited until he reached the thick jungle and heard the distinct hum of electricity running through a closed circuit.

He reached out in prayer to Hestie and Poros, to his parents, and to every ally he could think of, but no one replied.

Carefully, he crept through the trees and the undergrowth, glancing all around him as he made his way into the jungle. He still saw no sign of life, so he continued to hike toward the humming sound.

"Hermie?"

It was his mother's voice!

"Careful, son," his father said from the distance. "The Cyclopes are everywhere."

"And don't forget the Harpies," his Uncle Hip said.

Hermie crept toward them and discovered what had been causing the hum.

"I'm so happy to see you!" his mother said softly.

"Whatever you do, don't touch the cage," his Aunt Jen warned.

"Where's Hestie?" his father wanted to know.

"She and Poros should be somewhere on this island," he said. "They've been gone for hours. That's why I'm here."

His mother covered her mouth with both hands. "Oh, no."

"Go back for help," Artemis said from where she laid in the sand. "It's too dangerous for you to be here alone."

"What happened to you?" Hermie asked her.

"Zeus's lightning bolt," Hip explained.

"Artemis is right," his father said. "Go back for help."

"There is no help," Hermie said. "Prometheus is missing. No one's answering my prayers."

"Great," Jen said beneath her breath.

Hermie came up with an idea. If he could remember how to conjure his sword—the one he rigged with a taser gun—he could make a rechargeable battery to drain the electricity from the cage. He closed his eyes and summoned the weapon. He was shocked when it appeared in his hand.

"What are you doing?" his mother asked. "You can't fight an entire herd of Cyclopes by yourself."

"Your mother's right, son," his father said. "Get out of here, before you're stuck in here with us."

"I have an idea," Hermie said, as he stripped away the electrical tape from the hilt of his weapon. "I'm going to turn this sword into a battery cell."

First, he needed to drain the battery in the taser gun and use it in conjunction with the blade of the sword to create a larger holding cell for the electricity in the cage. He got to work, ignoring his family's pleas urging him to safety.

He hadn't been working long when the ground beneath him shook with the slow tread of something big. Hermie turned to see a Cyclops ambling toward him. The giant didn't seem to notice Hermie perched over his work near the cage—or, if he had, the Cyclops wasn't in a hurry to capture him. It occurred to Hermie that maybe the vision in the giant's one eye wasn't so good. Then, he realized a one-eyed being would have terrible depth perception and very little peripheral vision. The giant moved slowly because he couldn't see well. This would give Hermie and advantage.

Hermie could speed up the draining of the taser gun by using it to stun the giant. And now that Hermie knew the beast couldn't see well, he knew exactly how to do it. In fact, if Hermie played his cards right, the giant could help Hermie to drain the electricity from the cage and possibly deter the rest of the Cyclopes population.

For the plan to work, the giant would probably be paralyzed for all eternity. Hermie wasn't sure if he was capable of doing that to anyone, even a flesh-eating Cyclops.

***

As Poros ran his fingers though her hair and kissed her ear, her chin, her neck, Hestie had never felt such pleasure. She half-expected to wake up from an incredible dream. Somehow, her mind could accept that she'd become a god. It could accept that she was on an island surrounded by Cyclopes. It could accept that she was fighting in a war to overthrow Zeus, the strongest of the Olympians. What her mind could not accept, however, was that Poros was falling in love with her and that she was falling in love with him.

"Why not?" he whispered.

Dang it! she said to him telepathically. *I did it again! How do you separate your thoughts from your prayers?*

"I guess I've had more practice," he whispered before he kissed her again.

Then he lifted his head. "What was that?"

"What?" she whispered.

"Listen."

Sticks breaking, pebbles moving, and the quivering of the earth indicated that the Cyclopes were on the move.

"Let's follow them," she said.

She crept through the narrow cave into the larger one.

Slow down, Poros warned. *It could be a trick.*

Together, they crossed to the cave's mouth and peered into the dark jungle. The sound of the herd plodding away continued. Occasionally, Hestie could see the backs of the giants through the undergrowth.

"Come on," she whispered as she stepped from the cave.

They followed the giants through the trees until the herd came to a stop.

"What's that smell?" Hestie whispered.

It smells like burning flesh.

Hestie's heartbeat picked up speed as she imagined one of her loved ones being burned by their enemies.

Poros left Hestie's side to fly up to the treetops to get a better view. She followed.

A nearly blinding light, brighter than any god, shone from below. Hestie had to blink several times before her goddess eyes adjusted. Once she could see, she took in the scene. One of the Cyclopes lay on his side, unconscious, as smoke and light rose from his body. He was next to a cage that sparked with electricity. It seemed as if the cage was electrocuting him.

Hestie took a closer look at the cage and gasped.

I see my mom and dad and Jen and Hip, she said.

Artemis is there, too.

Oh my god, is that Hermie?

What's he doing? Poros asked.

I don't know. Why is the herd just standing there?

They're saying something. Listen.

"I'll go that a way! Yer go this a way!"

"I'm as blind as yer, yer idiot!"

"None of us can see!"

"Call the Harpies!"

Hestie gave Poros a worried glance.

Poros flew from the tree down to the cage and gripped the bars. His entire body became alight with electricity. Hestie covered her mouth, afraid to cry out, lest the Harpies might hear and come for them.

Poros pried the bars open, allowing her dad and uncle to fly free and disintegrate into a massive army. Hestie flew down to meet one of her fathers, who was helping Artemis from the cage.

"I'm taking Artemis home to the Underworld," her father said. "You kids come with me."

Poros, who seemed unhurt from the electricity flowing through his body, said, "I need to get back to the ship. Prometheus is gone, and the twins are alone."

Hermie flew up to meet them. "I'm going with Poros."

"Me, too," Hestie said. "Please, Dad? We'll come home as soon as we can."

"I'll go with them," their mother said. "But we need to go *now*. The Harpies."

***

Therese looked up in the night sky at the three ugly creatures flying toward them.

"This way," Poros said.

With her children on either side of her, Therese followed Poros through the jungle, hoping the trees hid them from the ugly beasts flying overhead. She held an arrow, ready to send it flying if any one of them attacked.

A loud, terrifying screech made her look up again. Through the leaves, she saw her husband form an army around the Harpies and strip them of their feathers until they fell, crashing through branches to the ground. One landed only a few feet behind her. The beast was still alive but badly injured.

"Keep going!" Therese hollered to the kids.

Poros led them to a small boat tucked between two boulders.

"We can fly faster than that boat can take us," Therese said.

"But is it safe?" Hermie asked.

"The sea is no safer than the sky," Therese said. "Poseidon's been captured, and, for all I know, Amphitrite may have been, too."

"Poseidon's been captured?" Hestie asked with wide eyes.

"And Hades, too," Therese told them. "Come on."

They took to the air, with Poros leading the way to the ship.

As they flew, Therese turned to each of her kids. "You okay?"

Hestie nodded. Hermie shrugged.

Therese knew her son. She knew paralyzing the Cyclops had been the hardest thing he'd ever had to do. She squeezed his hand. "You saved us back there. I'm so sorry it was up to you to do it, but I'm proud of you for coming through for us. I know it wasn't easy."

He looked at her with tears in his eyes. "I don't think I'm cut out to be a god."

"It's not always like this," she said. "I promise."

"Oh, no," Poros said, stopping midair. "No. Oh, my gods, no."

Therese looked down at the turbulent ocean to find *The Marcella* ripped to shreds.

"No!" Hermie shouted in a desperate cry—one unlike Therese had ever heard from him in all the sixteen years he'd been alive.

Hermie dove through the air like an eagle dropping to its death. Therese followed, with Hestie and Poros on her heels.

They searched through the wreckage, both the bits of ship still floating on the surface, and the larger parts that had submerged and were still sinking toward the ocean's depths. Throughout their search, Therese could hear Hestie's prayers: *Please let Mina and Jinsoo be alive. Please, oh, please, oh, please let Mina and Jinsoo be alive.*

Hermie's voice rang out through the dark night as he screamed Mina's name. It was then that Therese realized that her son was in love. Her heart ached for him, and she, too, began to pray harder for Mina and Jinsoo.

Then Poros emerged from the sea with Jinsoo in his arms. He laid the unconscious boy on a large piece of floating wreckage. While Poros attempted to resuscitate Jinsoo, the rest of them continued their desperate search for Mina.

When Than arrived, Therese assumed it was to help them in their search; however, the look on his face told her otherwise. The children noticed it, too.

Hestie hovered above the water beside Therese and said, "Dad, they're just kids."

"I'm not here for the boy," Than said.

Just then, another version of Than emerged from the depths with the girl in his arms.

Hermie flew to them. "Mina!" He looked at his father. "You found her!"

"Because her soul called to me," Thanatos said, and Therese's heart began to break in two.

The look on Hermie's face as he shook his head and pleaded with his father was enough to make Therese want to throw in the towel and give up on the fight—the rebellion, life, everything. But she had to be strong for her kids.

"Can't you make an exception, Dad?" Hestie asked. "Just this once?"

"I wish I could," Than replied. "I've never wished it more than I do right now."

Therese had once asked him the same thing. She'd just met him after her parents were killed by one of McAdams's men. A chill snaked up her spine at the memory of how all of this had begun. It had begun with death.

Then a giant claw thrust from the turbulent waves and threatened to overwhelm them.

"Back to the Underworld!" Therese shouted. "Poros, you bring Jinsoo. Hermie, take my hand."

Than took Hestie's hand, and they all risked god travel to escape the oncoming threat of Phorcys and his family.

Therese and Hestie landed in one of the meeting rooms. They heard Poros and Than in another room next door, so they flew down the hall to meet them. The bodies of Jinsoo and Mina were laid out, side by side, on the big meeting table. Jinsoo was still breathing; Mina was not.

"I need to go," Thanatos said, "so you can save the boy."

"Please, Dad!" Hermie cried. "I'll do anything! Please don't take Mina's soul! You're my father! You're Death! Can't you help me? I'll never ask you for anything ever again! Just please! Please don't take her!"

"I'm sorry, son," Than said before he and the girl vanished.

"Poros!" Hermie shouted. "Can't you turn her into one of us? Can't you save her?"

Poros's eyes were also full of tears. "I think it's too late, Hermie."

Hermie turned to his mother with a look of agony on his face. Therese took him into her arms and held him close. "I'm so sorry. My sweet, sweet boy. I'm so sorry."

"Jinsoo's waking up," Poros said.

"Jinsoo?" Hestie cried, leaning over him. "Jinsoo, can you speak?"

Jinsoo coughed and coughed for many seconds, clearing his lungs of water. Hestie patted him on the back, trying to help him to expel it.

Once he'd finished coughing, the boy looked around the room. "Where's Mina?"

<u>CHAPTER FIFTEEN</u>

Mutiny in the Pit

Than took Mina's soul to meet Charon on his raft, and, together, the three of them journeyed to the Room of Judgment. Thanatos kept his hand on Mina's shoulder, to bring her comfort, and the waters of the Lethe brushed against her feet, helping her to forget.

But throughout the journey, the only thing he could see was his son's face, twisted in agony, begging him to let his girlfriend live.

The god of death had never felt so inept as a father. To take his son's first love, to be the cause of Hermie's first heartbreak, was almost too much to bear. He reminded himself that this wasn't his fault; the Fates had decreed this, not he; nevertheless, he felt responsible and couldn't shake off the feeling of guilt eating him up inside.

Hermie would get through this, Than told himself. Hermie would grieve, and then he'd move on, and one day, he'd fall in love with another.

Thanatos recalled the first time he'd ever laid eyes on Therese, over twenty years ago. She'd captured his interest with her power of lucid dreaming while in a coma after her parents' deaths. She'd thought she was merely dreaming and that he was a figment. She'd brazenly flirted with him like no other living soul had ever dared, and he'd been completely enamored of her.

His father had taken her away from him, too. Hades hadn't *killed* Therese, but he'd sabotaged her chances to be with Than by creating a series of challenges that he knew she couldn't overcome. Out of desperation, Than had found another way—a loophole. He broke an oath, accepting a lifetime punishment of being ripped apart by the Maenads. He'd done it to avoid losing his girl. He would have done anything. Than imagined that Hermie would do anything to get his girl back, too. Unfortunately, Than could think of no loophole this time. Apart from finding someone willing to trade fates with Mina—and since she was an orphan, there was no one to ask—there was nothing that could save her.

As they journeyed on Charon's raft from the Room of Judgment to the Elysian Fields, Than heard an earth-shattering boom.

He turned to the old ferryman. "What was that?"

The ferryman shrugged and continued steering the raft.

A few seconds later, the earth-shattering sound repeated itself. It sounded like it was coming from the Titan Pit. Than disintegrated to investigate.

As he neared the iron door to the Titan Pit, he found Hip already there, with Jen at his side.

"What's going on?" Than asked.

"We don't know," Jen said. "Hip wants to go in, but I think it's too dangerous."

"You're one to talk," Hip said to her.

"She's right," Than said. "Our father has said time and time again that we should never enter without him and one of his brothers, and since both Hades and Poseidon aren't here, we can't go in."

"But something's going on in there," Hip said. "Let me try to put the prisoners into the deep boon of sleep. You can close the door behind me, so no one escapes."

"Not happening," Jen insisted.

"You don't think I can do it," Hip accused.

Jen put her hands on her hips. "I don't want to take the chance."

"We've got to do something," Hip said. "Something's wrong."

"Maybe I can help," Poros said, appearing from around the bend. "I'm the most powerful god now, right?"

Than scratched his chin. "If we screw this up, we could ruin every-thing. Poros won't be able to fulfill his destiny if he's trapped by the Titans."

"This might seem hard to believe," Poros said, "but I think I sense Prometheus in there. I feel him calling to me."

"You hear his prayers?" Hip asked.

"Not exactly," Poros said. "I can't explain it, but I *feel* him."

"Why would Prometheus be in the Titan Pit?" Jen asked.

Than shook his head. "Maybe he's not the only ally trapped in there. Hecate, the Furies, and Pete are all missing."

"Do you think Zeus threw them into the Pit?" Hip asked.

"The protection wards should be holding," Than answered. "But I guess it's a possibility."

If Zeus had breached the wards protecting the Underworld, the war was over, and the rebellion squashed.

"Then we have no choice," Poros said. "Right?"

***

Hermie sat between Hestie and Jinsoo staring at Mina where she lay on the table in the meeting room of Hades's palace. His mother paced near the door. She'd finally stopped talking.

Clifford whined while he followed Hermie's mother around, back and forth. Noodle lay curled in Hestie's lap, while Kitty stood alone in the corner. Chidori, who had taken to Jinsoo, sat perched on Jinsoo's shoulder. Katniss and Prim were probably off exploring the Under-world, and Jewels was most likely in her tank in his mother's room.

The animals could probably sense that Hermie wanted to be left alone. He didn't want to talk to anyone. He just wanted to sit there qui-etly. *No more talking. Just let me sit here and look at her.*

If he hadn't left Mina and Jinsoo behind on the ship, he might have saved her. Why had he gone? The gods would have eventually saved themselves, but what hope did Mina and Jinsoo have against the monsters of the sea? It was Hermie's fault that Mina was gone. He shouldn't have left her.

He remembered what she'd said to him just before he'd left the ship: "Don't leave us, Hermie. What if monsters come?"

She'd begged him to stay, and he'd let her down.

He was being punished. Not only had he abandoned the twins on the ship, but he'd also destroyed a life. Had it really been necessary to paralyze the Cyclops? Might Hermie have found another way?

He couldn't let go of this idea that there had to be something the gods could do. They were the most powerful beings in existence. It was only logical that they could impact life and death. If his father had really wanted to save Mina, he should have been able to do it.

What good was it to be a god if you couldn't save the people you loved?

He recalled his parents telling him the story of how they'd gone to the Fates to learn how many children they would have, so they could bargain with Ares. The Fates told his parents that they would have two children, but none immortal. And here he and Hestie were—living proof that the Fates could be wrong.

His parents had tried to explain that it was all in the wording. They wouldn't *have* immortal children, but that hadn't meant their children wouldn't *become* immortal.

To Hermie, it sounded as if destiny could be twisted and changed at will. Maybe he would go to the Fates to see if there was a way to bring Mina back.

Just then, the ground shook, like it had on Cyclopes Island, and it was followed by a terrifying sound, like a bomb exploding underground.

Chidori squawked, and Clifford whined. Even Kitty left her corner to be closer to the others.

"What was that?" Hestie asked their mother.

"I don't know," their mother said. "Stay here. I'll be right back."

After his mother had gone, Hermie turned to his sister. "I'm going to see the Fates."

She lifted her brows in surprise. "Why? There's nothing…"

"There has to be."

"We've gone over this a million times with Mom. Weren't you listening?"

"There's nothing you can say to stop me," Hermie insisted.

Don't give Jinsoo false hope, she warned.

Without another word, Hermie left the room and headed toward the Fates' Abode.

***

Hip was terrified that, once he opened the door to the Pit, all the Titans who hated him and his family would ambush him, charge the door, and destroy whatever hope the rebellion had left. But if Poros was right, and Prometheus and possibly others were trapped in there, then Hip had to take the chance.

As he'd been investigating the unusual sounds emanating from the Titan Pit, he'd also been desperately searching for Morpheus. He was nowhere to be found in the Underworld, so Hip had gone to the Field of Asphodel, to seek him in the Dreamworld but hadn't found him yet.

He'd also gone to his mother's chambers to see if she knew where Morpheus was. Demeter had been reluctant to let him in, and when he finally convinced her, he'd been shocked to find his mother in the deep boon of sleep, brought on by a powerful herb Demeter had given her.

"Why would you do this in our time of need?" he'd asked Demeter.

"To keep my daughter safe and out of her husband's dastardly affairs."

Now Hip conjured all his powers of persuasion to convince Demeter to help him and the others with the Titans, and to allow his mother to help as well.

"There's a good chance Hecate's in there, being tortured again," Hip said, knowing how much his grandmother loved the goddess of witches.

Demeter refused to wake Persephone, but she agreed to go.

Since they couldn't risk the capture of the only two gods capable of disintegration, Than would stay behind. But he would amass an army outside the iron door to prevent the prisoners from escaping. Of course, if any version of Than were to be fatally wounded, the army would reintegrate into one, but Hip tried not to think about that.

"Ready?" Jen asked him.

Hip had tried to convince Jen to stay put, but, as usual, she refused to listen to him. Therese, who'd arrived just as he was preparing to open the door, had also insisted on going. There was nothing Hip or Than could say to keep their wives from going into danger; but, at least the most powerful god was at their side, and Demeter was as powerful as Hades and Poseidon.

Hip pulled the consecutive latches and bolts along the door and took a deep breath before pushing the door open. After Poros, Jen, and Therese had followed him inside, he filled the entrance with a dozen versions of himself. Demeter remained near the doorway, too.

Down below, the Titans stood in a huddle, shouting at one another with raised fists. Circe was huddled in a corner, her hair matted with blood, her eyes wide with a look of madness. The stench of blood permeated the air. Hypnos lifted his arms and focused on putting the prisoners into the deep boon of sleep. That's when the Titans sensed he was there.

They stopped shouting and gesticulating and turned to glare at him. At their center, on the ground, bound in rope, bleeding, with torn limbs and faces of agony, were his sisters, along with Pete, Hecate, and Prometheus. Also bound but not injured were Iapetus and Hyperion.

Arke, Iris's sister and the only female Titan imprisoned after the war, ran up to Hip and said, "I tried to stop them. They wouldn't listen. Please have mercy on me!"

Hip was struck by how much the little goddess resembled her sister in features and mannerisms, except for her coloring. Whereas Iris's hair was golden, Arke's was the color of ebony.

And, unlike Iris, Arke was without her wings, bearing the same horrible scab along her back that Morpheus had formed after his wings had been ripped away by Zeus.

Uranus shouted, "Silence, Arke, or you'll be next!"

Hip narrowed his eyes at Uranus, recalling how the sky god had nearly taken over Hip's body with dark magic while imprisoning him in Hephaestus's old trick chair. "Let them go, unless you want to suffer more torment than you can imagine."

Cronos stepped forward. "That's impossible, Hypnos. There is no torment we can't imagine, because, I assure you, we have experienced the worst."

Then Crius said, "Can you imagine an eternal life devoid of beauty, devoid of peace, devoid of hope? Can you imagine what we've endured down here for centuries? You can't, can you?"

"What are you getting at?" Hip shouted angrily.

Atlas pointed at their victims on the ground. "They came here to recruit an army to help you overthrow Zeus. I tried to do that very thing years ago, remember? And you stood against me and stuck me in here."

Hip swallowed hard.

"Don't you talk to him like that!" Jen hollered. "He's not anything like you!"

Menoetius lifted his chin. "What do you know of my brother?"

"He's evil!" Jen said. "Unlike my husband!"

"Anyone who allows endless torture to a group of people who happened to be on the other side of a war is evil," Atlas said.

"Your stay here has been brief compared to mine!" Perses shouted in Atlas's face.

Atlas pushed Perses. "I know that!"

Uranus got between the two Titans and pointed at Hip and his allies. "Direct your anger at them, brothers!"

Before Hip could stop them, all the angry Titans rushed at Hip's first line of defense. Down in the deepest recesses of the pit, the two one-hundred armed giants began to climb toward them.

Therese shot two of the Titans with her arrows. Jen lodged a spear in Menoetius's chest. And Hip sliced an arm off Uranus.

And it had felt good.

But the Titans kept coming at them.

Suddenly, a jolt of lightning flashed through the darkness. It originated from Poros.

Hip watched in astonishment as Poros pointed his finger at Cronos and shot him down with a bolt of lightning. It was as if Zeus himself had done so!

Cronos lay, paralyzed, on the floor of the pit.

How did you do that? Hip asked Poros.

I'm not sure, the boy replied.

The other Titans retreated to their huddle, where the Furies, Pete, Hecate, and Prometheus still lay, bound, beside Iapetus and Hyperion. Even the one-hundred armed giants crawled back down to their hole.

Poros raised his arms in the air. "You don't know me, but I'm Poros, Zeus's son, the one prophesied to unseat the king of the Olympians."

"I know who you are," Uranus said. "It's because of me that you exist!"

"You are here because you're an enemy of my father's," Poros continued. "Once I overthrow him, I promise the new leaders will hear each of you out, to give you a chance to defend yourselves. I promise you the opportunity to be free."

Hip was shocked—first by Poros's bold promise and then by the tears that formed in the eyes of the powerful Titans below.

"Let us join you!" Crius said. "We would happily make Zeus suffer for his crimes against us!"

"Now is not the time for blind clemency," Poros said. "I don't know you, and you don't know me. Your chance will come, though. I swear on the River Styx."

Therese gasped.

Jen whispered, "Poros, how can you promise such a thing?"

"Everyone deserves a chance to be redeemed," Poros said.

Hip glanced at Therese, recalling a time when she'd said the very same thing about Melinoe.

"Poros is right," Therese said, loud enough for the Titans to hear. "Everyone deserves a chance at redemption. No one should be sentenced to eternal damnation."

Hip could not believe his eyes. Uranus, Cronos, Crius—all of them were in tears, half-dazed, wanting to believe and yet unable to believe their ears.

"How can we trust that what you say is true?" Crius asked.

"This could be another trick," Uranus added.

"Poros has sworn an oath," Therese said. "You know as well as I that an oath is not something made lightly."

"That's all I can give you for now," Poros said.

Hyperion, still bound, said, "It's the best gift you could give us."

"Hope," Iapetus said. "There is beauty and peace in hope."

"Now set your victims free," Hip demanded. "We have a war to win."

CHAPTER SIXTEEN

Revelations

Hermie followed the Phlegethon past the Fields of Elysium, past his parents' chambers, past the asphodel—almost to the Dreamworld, until he came upon the door to the dwelling of the Fates.

His parents had told him all about the Fates. The oldest of beings, they hadn't always lived in the Underworld. Tired of being harassed by mortals and immortals alike—all wanting to know or to change their destiny—the Fates had found solace here in their own private arcade. The only futures they could not see were their own and one another's, so they enjoyed occupying themselves with games of chance in isolation. It stayed off the dreariness of their omniscience.

Under normal circumstances, no one would make it to the door of the Fates. Mortals would die if they managed to make it past Cerberus, and gods would be prevented by wards. Only the Underworld gods had access, and they'd sworn to guard—not to harass—the Fates. But Hermie hadn't sworn any such oath. He knew he was taking advantage of special circumstances, and he was okay with that.

When he reached the door, he took a deep breath and knocked. His fist had barely hit the wood when it opened.

An elderly-looking woman with white bangs, black spectacles, and a lavender velvet jacket poked her head through the door, allowing a cloud of cigarette smoke into the hall.

"Is it already time for this?" she asked in a throaty voice. "Oh, goodie. Please come in."

This was not the reaction he'd anticipated. His parents had told him that the Fates despised visitors.

He stepped through the door. "Are you really glad to see me? Or is that sarcasm?"

"We're delighted," one of the others said in an equally low and throaty voice. "Come in, Hermes, god of technology."

He crossed to the middle of the room, where two of the old ladies were sitting at a round table with a roulette wheel mounted to the top of it.

The one in the pink velvet pant suit with some of her white hair high in a bun and the rest of it hanging to her shoulders had been about to spin the wheel when she said, "Oh, no use spinning it now that he's here. I remember what happens."

"Then you know you must spin it anyway, Clotho," the one in the blue velvet outfit said. She had short curly hair and big eyes. "What's gotten into you?"

Clotho spun the wheel. "You *know* what, Lachesis. He's finally here."

Was Clotho talking about *him*?

The Fate in the lavender and spectacles, whose name Hermie deduced was Atropos, joined them at the table and said, "Have a seat, young Hermes."

"Everyone calls me Hermie," he said.

"Don't you think we know that?" Lachesis said before she took another puff from her cigarette.

"Why are you glad to see me?" he asked. "I thought you didn't like visitors."

"We don't, normally," Clotho explained. "But you're special."

"You see," Atropos began, "we know from having seen your future that you update this arcade for us and enrich our lives like never before."

"We are ever so excited to play new games!" Lachesis added.

Hermie smiled. "Awesome. I can do that. But first I came to ask you about my friend."

Lachesis frowned. "We know. I guess we still have to go through the motions, don't we, sisters?"

"Of course, we do, Lachesis!" Clotho chastised her. "You were just on my case about it. Have you no memory! Spin the wheel, you said. And, so, I've spun, and, look, you won."

Lachesis shrugged. "Of course, I did."

"Look," Hermie said, getting frustrated with their bickering. "My girlfriend Mina was killed by the sea monsters. It was my fault. I shouldn't have left her unprotected. It wasn't her time."

"Indeed, it was," Atropos said. "I'm sorry to say."

He wasn't sure if she meant, "Indeed, it was your fault," or if she was saying, "Indeed, it was her time."

"Isn't there anything I can do about it?" Hermie asked, his throat suddenly dry.

"You will visit Arke, sister to Iris," Lachesis said.

"She longs for death," Clotho explained.

"And you will ask her to volunteer, which she will," Atropos said.

Hermie's heartbeat drummed against his ribs. "Seriously? That's amazing! Thank you! You've made me so happy!"

Lachesis snubbed the butt of her cigarette into an ashtray. "Well, you shouldn't be."

Clotho nodded. "I'm sorry to say, you'll talk her out of it."

"You shouldn't have told him that part," Atropos scolded.

"You knew I would," Clotho argued. "So why argue?"

Atropos shrugged.

"Why would I talk Arke out of saving my girlfriend's life?" Hermie asked, the pain in his stomach returning.

"You'll have to find out for yourself," Atropos said.

"Now, while you're here, please give us a taste of what's to come," Atropos said.

Her sisters laughed, and Clotho explained, "We never get to say that."

Hermie was confused. "How can I give you a taste of what's to come?"

"By giving us our very first computer," Lachesis said.

Hermie didn't have time for that, and it wasn't safe for him to go shopping for computers. "How can I? We're in the middle of a war."

"You're the god of technology," Atropos reminded him. "You can conjure it at will."

"I can?" Hermie found that hard to believe. He just had to will a computer to appear, and it would?

"Go ahead!" Clotho said. "Try it! You'll like it!"

Hermie closed his eyes and imagined a computer, like the one he'd built at home—lots of power, multiple controllers, with plenty of games already installed.

He was shocked beyond belief when the computer appeared on a desk before him, exactly as he'd imagined it.

"Welcome to your power, god of technology," Lachesis said.

"Now, show us how to play," Clotho insisted.

He glanced around at their arcade, realizing their machines were powered by magic and not electricity. He used his new powers to bring electricity to the Underworld with modern copper wiring, because he wasn't sure how to use magic to power his computer. With his mind, he manipulated the wiring throughout the rock and grounded it before commanding it to seek the nearest transformers for harnessing energy. To be on the safe side, he imagined a generator, which he located in the bat cave, and ran his wiring throughout the entire realm. If they survived the rebellion, he hoped his parents and grandparents would be impressed. Sure, gods didn't need electricity to see in the dark or to cook food; however, wouldn't it be nice to watch Netflix down here from time to time?

He plugged in the computer, powered it up, and quickly figured out how to gain them wifi access. Then he searched for a fighting game they could play against one another. He handed them each a controller. "It might be more fun if you figure it out as you go. The reward system in this game is randomized, so you won't be able to predict who wins."

"Goodie!" Atropos cried, clutching her controller.

"Our time with you for now has come to an end," Clotho said without taking her eyes from the computer monitor.

"But you'll be back," Lachesis said. "And we can't wait!"

"Of course, we can," Clotho complained.

"Figure of speech!" Lachesis argued.

"How do I talk to Arke?" Hermie asked them. "Where can I find her?"

"The Titan Pit, of course," Atropos said, as she walked him to the door. "Now run along, little god of technology."

Atropos all but shoved him from the room, which seemed no way to treat someone who's just given you a gift. He hadn't even had the chance to ask them about Lynn's dream. But at least they had taught him something about his powers, and they had given him a tip about Mina, even if they predicted it would do him no good. He couldn't imagine talking Arke out of trading places with her. If Arke wanted to die and Mina wanted to live, what was the problem?

The problem was getting into the Titan Pit. As scared as he was to come face to face with the greatest enemies of the Olympians, he'd hate himself if he didn't try everything in his power to bring Mina back. He owed it to her, and to Jinsoo, since he was the one who'd abandoned them.

***

Hestie continued to sit with Jinsoo in the room with Mina's body, stroking Noodle in her lap, and Clifford, too, who lay at her feet, until she heard the gods talking in the meeting room next door—something about Poros paralyzing Cronos in the Titan Pit. Her curiosity piqued, she told Jinsoo she'd be back, and then, leaving the animals with him, she flew down the hall.

As soon as she had entered, she covered her mouth with both hands, unable to believe her eyes. Tizzie, Meg, Alecto, Hecate, Pete, and Prometheus sat in chairs at the center table with their arms folded, their heads down, weakened and bleeding.

The other gods were standing around them, including Poros.

"Why aren't you on the ship?" Prometheus asked Poros.

Poros told Prometheus what had happened. Hearing it all over again made Hestie cry. Her mother noticed and moved to her side to comfort her.

"Is Mina really gone?" Prometheus asked Hestie's father.

"I'm afraid so," he said.

Hestie noticed Prometheus wipe away a tear. She knew he loved Mina and Jinsoo, and this was hard on him—even harder than it was on her.

"I shouldn't have left them," Prometheus said.

"It wasn't your fault," Poros said. "It was mine."

"Don't say that, Poros," Hestie said. "We did what we thought was right."

"Has anyone heard from Athena?" Prometheus asked.

"No," Hip said.

"She must have returned to Mount Olympus," Meg said.

Hecate turned to Demeter. "I know you want to protect her. I do, too. But she's powerful, and we need her. Have faith in her abilities. Let her join us."

Hecate must have been referring to Persephone. Did Demeter have her locked away?

Alecto raised her bleeding hand. "Let's get back to Poros."

"Yes," Hestie's father agreed. "Where did that lightning come from?"

"I don't know," Poros said. "It's happened before, though."

What happened? Hestie asked Poros telepathically.

I struck down a Titan with lightning from my finger, Poros replied. *It was crazy.*

"Years ago," Prometheus said. "He was struck by lightning when he was a babe. I thought Zeus had found us."

Are you okay? Hestie asked Poros.

He gave her a nod and said, "When I was around five years old, I was frightened by a shark. I struck it and killed it."

"I remember that," Pete said. "I didn't understand how the shark could have died of electrocution."

"Is that the only time?" Hestie's mother asked Poros.

"I tried to do it again a few months later, and it didn't work," Poros said. "I don't know how I did it. I've never been able to replicate it, until today."

"Fear or anger could generate his power," Alecto said.

"I don't think so," Prometheus said. "There were plenty of times he could have shocked a shark or a pirate and didn't."

"We had to use taser guns on the pirates," Poros said.

"Maybe he absorbs the electricity," Hecate said. "Have you been struck, or nearly struck, recently?"

"It was the cage," Hestie said. "Poros absorbed the electricity from the cage on Cyclopes Island."

"That's why it didn't hurt him!" Jen exclaimed.

"That makes sense," Hip added.

"Poros doesn't *wield* a lightning bolt," Tizzie said. "He *becomes* it."

"But only after being struck, it seems," Prometheus said.

Hecate, still weak and trembling a little, slowly stood from her chair and took Demeter's hand in hers. "It's time to wake your daughter. We need her."

Demeter nodded at Hip, and, in another moment, Persephone appeared. Her eyes and mouth were wide open.

She seemed about to say something, when she noticed the Furies, Hecate, Pete, and Prometheus injured and recovering from their torment. She rushed to her daughters and cried, "My darlings! What happened?"

Meg told her about Prometheus's idea to get help from some of the Titans and how it had all gone wrong.

"I'm sorry, Persephone," Prometheus said. "We'd lost so many of our people. I thought it was a chance worth taking."

"I don't fault you," Persephone said to the Titan. "This is perhaps our darkest hour, and it may get worse, yet. I'm afraid I have more bad news."

Hestie braced herself and muttered, "Oh, no."

"I saw Morpheus in the Dreamworld, and you won't believe what he told me," Persephone said.

"Where is he?' Hip asked. "I've been looking everywhere for him."

"He and Iris are prisoners on the throne my mother and I usually sit upon," Persephone said.

"What?" Jen flew to Hip's side. "How did that happen? We told him to stay here."

Persephone broke into tears. "He came to me after Than found him in the Dreamworld and told him you were prisoners on Cyclopes Island. I suggested he use the rainbow arch to spy on Zeus. I'm so sorry, Hypnos! Please forgive me, darling Jen! Like Prometheus, I was desperate."

Hestie covered her mouth. Jen said nothing to Persephone, but Hestie could tell her aunt wanted to chew out the queen of the Underworld.

"I was on my way to help him, but I couldn't wake up," Persephone said.

Everyone looked at Demeter.

"I'm afraid that was my fault," the goddess of the harvest admitted. "I was trying to keep you out of it."

"Mother, how dare you?" Persephone cried. "That's *your* style. Not mine!"

"Did Morpheus tell you anything else?" Prometheus asked.

"Hades and Poseidon are being held prisoner in the bird cages," Persephone said through her tears. "I can only imagine how humiliating that is for those two formidable brothers. In *bird* cages!"

"What else did he say, Mother?" Hestie's father asked.

"They have Apollo, too!" she cried.

Everyone gasped.

"He'd been helping Helios fight Chimera, I think, when Phobos and Deimos took them by surprise. Helios was chained to his golden cup, as Selene is to her silver chariot!"

"We won't be able to heal Artemis without Apollo," Hecate said.

"What?" Persephone cried. "What's happened to Artemis?"

"Zeus paralyzed her with a direct hit after he took the helm from her," Hip explained.

"Did Morpheus say anything more?" Prometheus asked.

Persephone turned to Hestie's mother and put a hand on her shoulder. "Dear, darling Therese. I have some bad news."

Hestie flew to her mother's side and took her mother's hand. "What's happened, Grandma?"

"Before Zeus captured Apollo, he was obsessed with finding a seer," Persephone said.

Hestie's mother fell to her knees.

"He has Lynn," Hestie murmured.

"And Carol and Richard, too," Persephone said.

Hestie knelt on the floor beside her mother. "We'll save them. Somehow, we'll save them, Mom. It's going to be okay."

Hestie couldn't recall seeing her mother looking so distraught. It killed her to know her mother was suffering.

"I'm afraid that's not the worst of it," Persephone added, as she stroked Hestie's mother's hair. "Once he captured Apollo, Zeus no longer needed your sister."

Hestie's mother looked across the room at Hestie's father.

"They aren't dead," Hestie's father said.

"Worse," Persephone said. "Zeus paralyzed them and dumped them somewhere. Morpheus didn't know where."

***

Therese couldn't speak for many minutes, couldn't breathe. She was vaguely aware of Persephone stroking her hair and of Hestie squeezing her hand. Her mind was churning like a water wheel through sludge.

Her parents had given up their immortality to save her and her husband from death. Now her aunt and uncle—her second set of parents—along with her sweet little sister, Lynn, were casualties of a war they knew nothing about. Her family members were paralyzed and in danger of dying if they weren't found in time. How long could mortals survive without food or water? Days? Weeks?

Pete moved to her side. "We'll find them."

"Do you see it?" Tizzie asked.

Therese looked at Pete, who shook his head.

Finally, she found her tongue. "We have to search for them."

"Maybe they're on Cyclopes Island," Hestie suggested.

Therese hoped not. The flesh-eating Cyclopes may have already made a dinner of them.

"That's as good a place as any to start looking," Than said.

Therese climbed to her feet. "Let's go."

Than put his arms around her and said telepathically, *You should stay. You're too upset.*

You know I won't. I can't.

"I want to come," Hestie said.

"No way," Than said.

"Dad, it's Lynn and Grammie and Grampie!"

"Where's Hermie?" Therese asked Hestie.

"He went to see the Fates about Mina."

"What?" Therese couldn't take any more of this. It was all too much.

"Let him do what he must," Than said. "He's not in any danger. It will help him come to terms with it."

"You search Cyclopes Island," Hip said to Than. "I'll go see if Helios and Selene have noticed anything."

"Don't leave me," Jen, still weeping from the news of Morpheus, said to Hip.

"I won't," Hip said.

"I'll try a locator spell," Hecate offered.

"And I'll ask my mother to help with the search," Prometheus said.

"The chariots are still missing," Hip said. "So be careful."

"You, too, brother," Than said.

"I'm coming with you," Hestie said again.

Poros moved to Hestie's side. "Me, too."

Therese did not argue with them. Not only was Therese too upset and frightened to hold her ground against Hestie, but she remembered what it was like being a new god at a young age, determined to help.

"Come on then," Therese said to Hestie. She turned to Poros. "Let's go."

CHAPTER SEVENTEEN

Ideas

When Ares returned to Mount Olympus with his twin sons, Phobos and Deimos, Morpheus sat up straighter on Demeter's throne.

"The prisoners on Cyclopes Island have escaped," Ares said.

Morpheus exchanged smiles with Iris, who was still bound beside him. Thank goodness something was finally going their way.

Zeus stood from his throne. "And where are they now?"

"The Underworld, it seems," Ares replied.

Morpheus sighed with relief. He'd been worried about his family since he'd heard the news that they'd been captured.

This is a good sign, Iris said to him.

We needed one, he replied.

Zeus began to pace. "And no one's been able to break through the protection wards?"

"It's impossible," Hades said from his bird cage.

"Nothing's impossible," Hera jeered.

"I can think of a few things," Poseidon said from the cage next to the one holding Hades. "For example, you, my dear sister, will never be anything but dead to me. It would be *impossible* to believe otherwise."

Oh, burn, Morpheus said to Iris.

Although telepathy with Hades and Poseidon was made impossible by the cages, Poseidon seemed amused by Morpheus's reaction. The god of the sea winked at him.

Did you see that? he asked Iris. *Poseidon just winked at me!*

She tickled him with her wing. *Don't draw attention to yourself.*

Hestia turned to Zeus. "Is there nothing you can do to silence our brothers?"

"Enough," Zeus raged in frustration. He pointed to Hades and Poseidon. "You should be grateful that I haven't struck you both down with my lightning bolt. If you want to keep the use of your limbs, I suggest you stop irritating the hell out of me."

The glares given to Zeus by his two brothers sent a chill down Morpheus's spine. Morpheus couldn't believe that Ares and his sons had the audacity to laugh.

"We must think of a way to breach those wards," Zeus continued. "Hephaestus, you've been quiet these past few days. Have you no weapons that can break down their barriers?"

Morpheus knew Hephaestus was a sympathizer with the rebellion, but he wished the god of the forge would do more to help the cause than to make cool armor for Poros. He wanted to say to him, *Please don't help your dick of a father,* but he kept that thought to himself.

"None, Father," Hephaestus said. "Sorry to disappoint you."

"Perhaps you should return to your forge and see what you can come up with," Zeus suggested.

To Morpheus, it sounded more like a command.

Hephaestus gave his father a nod and left the room.

"Hermes," Zeus turned to his other son. "You've been in and out of that realm more than any of us. Can't you think of something?"

"The only way in is to be *invited* in," Hermes said.

Hera turned to Hermes. "Can't you make that happen? I imagine there's still some love between you and those degenerates."

Hera was really beginning to get on Morpheus's nerves. *What a be-yotch,* he said to Iris.

"You're forgetting the prophecy, dear," Zeus said to Hera. "Lynn's dream. Apollo saw it, too. Hermes is the last person the Underworld gods trust right now."

"I'll do it," Aphrodite said, stepping forward. "I have an idea that may get me in."

Morpheus did not like where this was going.

"My sweet Aphrodite." Zeus crossed the room and took her hands. "Please tell me what you have in mind."

***

Hermie stood before the iron door to the Titan Pit. He'd been standing there for at least an hour, debating. If he opened the door, the prisoners inside would likely overpower him and escape. This would not be good. The Titans hated his family and all of the Olympians, and their release might ruin whatever chance the rebellion still had of succeeding.

On the other hand, Zeus was the one responsible for their imprisonment. Perhaps the Titans could be persuaded to join the rebellion and increase its chances of success.

However, was Hermie the best person to convince them of this? They didn't know him, and they had no reason to trust him. Plus, his family would wring his neck for trying such a thing without their consent.

And if he tried to get that consent, they would most likely scold him for even asking.

But on the other hand, the Fates had seen him talking to Arke, so it must be his destiny to enter the pit. They also saw him upgrading their arcade, so he must survive, right? He couldn't upgrade their games if he was to be swallowed.

Unless…he becomes a prisoner and is ordered to make the upgrades as a slave.

Also, the Fates didn't indicate how soon in the future he was to make those upgrades. A hundred years to them was nothing. What if

Hermie and his family became prisoners because he opened this iron door? Years, decades, centuries could go by before he helped the Fates with their new games.

But didn't he owe it to Mina to try everything in his power to bring her back? It was his fault that she was gone. Why would the Fates mention Arke if there was no possibility of resurrecting his girlfriend?

He was the god of technology. There had to be something he could do.

He fingered the locks on the door. He had an idea.

He used his powers to conjure a state-of-the-art security system with an encrypted code that only he knew. Later, he would give it to his Grandpa Hades.

The trick would be to open and secure the door before any of the Titans could break free.

He had every confidence he could do it; but he wasn't so sure what the Titans would do to him once he was trapped inside the pit along with them. Maybe they would torture him for the code until he gave in and set them free.

He'd just have to resist, no matter what.

He shivered, wondering if he shouldn't tell someone where he was going, just in case he couldn't get out. He pulled out his phone and texted Hestie: *I'm going into the Titan Pit to talk to Arke. The Fates saw me do it, so it should be okay. But if I don't come out in an hour, could you send someone in to rescue me? The code to get in is our birthday (2 digits for month, 2 for day, and 4 for year) plus our zip code with no spaces or dashes between the digits.*

He had no idea if her phone was even charged. Eventually, she would get the message. He took a deep breath, entered the code to disarm the door, and rushed inside before securing it shut. Panting, sweating, and trembling a little, he stared down at the pit before him, terrified.

"Um, hello there," he said to the seven Titans standing in a ring around an eighth, who lay paralyzed on the ground. "My name is Hermie. I'm the god of technology. I came to offer you a deal."

***

Hestie followed her parents and Poros through the thick jungle of Cyclopes Island in their desperate search for Lynn and her Grammie and Grampie. They hiked in the direction of the cage that had once held her parents, aunt and uncle, and Artemis, just in case Zeus was using the giants to guard his newest prisoners. They saw no signs yet of either the Cyclopes or the Harpies, who were last seen plucked and flightless.

When they reached the center of the jungle, they found the cage in ruins, and the Cyclops Hermie had used to destroy it still lay paralyzed on the ground where they'd left him.

Because the giant was immortal, he was still alive. Hestie couldn't imagine what it must be like to lie there, unable to do anything but exist. She thought of her cousin and grandparents and shivered. Unlike the giant on the ground before her, Lynn and her Grammie and Grampie weren't immortal. She hoped with all her heart that her family members were still alive and would be found before it was too late.

Poor guy, Poros said to her telepathically as he touched the paralyzed giant, who lay at his feet like a stone statue. *This is no way for anyone to live, not even a Cyclops.*

"I wish there was something we could do to help him," Hestie said out loud.

As soon as she had spoken, the sound of twigs breaking, of pebbles rolling, and of the earth shaking beneath them alerted her that she had just made a giant mistake. The Cyclopes had heard her and were coming for them.

Her mother fitted an arrow to her bow.

"Let's get out of here," her father warned.

But Hestie and her parents hesitated when they noticed something happening to Poros. Still touching the paralyzed Cyclops, Poros was beginning to glow, just as he had when he'd pried open the bars of the cage.

"Poros?" her mother said. "What's happening?"

"We need to go," her father said again.

"He's absorbing the electricity from the Cyclops!" Hestie cried.

In the next moment, they were surrounded. At least a dozen big, fat, harry giants, wearing nothing but loin cloths and carrying clubs and axes, stared at them—each with his one eye—with looks that could kill. There was still time to get away, but this new discovery of Poros's abilities had Hestie and her family dumbfounded, especially when the giant at Poros's feet began to move.

"Back off!" Than said to the crowd as he disintegrated into twenty more, encircling Hestie, her mother, and Poros, along with the giant at their feet.

The previously paralyzed Cyclops suddenly sat up and said, "Huh?" He looked around with his one eye.

"Yer saved him," one of the Cyclopes closest to them said to Poros. "Why'd yer do that, yer idiot?"

Poros stared back at them blankly, still dazed by what he had done.

"Because he could!" Hestie shouted, flying up above her father, so she could be seen by the giants. "We mean yer no harm. It's Zeus yer should fear, not us."

"We do fear him, yer idiot!" another one of the Cyclopes said.

"Then turn against him, yer idiots, and join us!" Hestie said.

Hestie, what are you doing? her mother asked her telepathically as she flew beside her with her arrow at the ready.

Her father and Poros asked her the same thing.

Trying something different, Hestie told them.

"Yer can trust us, yer see," Hestie continued. "We just saved yer bud. Zeus were gonna leave 'em. He dudn't care for yer. Yer know that, don't yer, yer idiots!"

The Cyclopes looked at one another, each blinking his one eye.

Then the ground shook from somewhere in the distance, and the crowd of Cyclopes turned in fear to see what it was.

Polyphemus, the son of Poseidon, was making his way into the center of the group. "She speaks the truth, yer idiots! Join me and me father. Join the rebellion!"

"Freedom fer yer Cyclopes!" Hestie shouted as she lifted her fist into the air. "That's what yer get with the rebellion. Liberty! No more slavin' fer a king!"

"No more slavin' fer a king!" Polyphemus repeated.

"No more slavin' fer a king!" others in the crowd shouted.

Hestie smiled at her mother. "It's working."

Her mother smiled back. "Good job, Hestie!"

Then her mother, still hovering in the air beside her, addressed the giants. "We're looking for my little sister and…"

The Cyclopes were still shouting words of liberty to one another and didn't seem to care what Hestie's mother had to say. Hestie raised her voice and said, "Shut up, yer idiots! Shut up an' listen!"

A few looked up at her with their mouths hanging open.

"Yer want our help, dun't yer?" Hestie shouted. "Yer want the rebellion to free yer idiots?"

The crowd quieted down and listened to her.

"If yer want our help, yer gotta give us yers!" Hestie said. "That tyrant Zeus, yer slave driver, our enemy, he done hurt me cousin and me grandparents! The monster Zeus zapped 'em and paralyzed 'em! Help us find 'em, and we'll help yer get yer freedom!"

"Yer cousin and yer grandparents ain't on this island, yer idiot!" one of the Cyclopes hollered. "We'd know it, if they were, but they ain't."

"Go look somewheres else!" another shouted.

Tell them to destroy Zeus's lightning bolts, Hestie's father said to her telepathically. *Tell them they'll never have to make them again.*

Hestie smiled down at her father before shouting, "We're leavin', yer idiots! And when we're gone, yer can have some real fun! Yer can have a Break the Bolt Pardee all day long, okay yer idiots? And yer never have to make another bolt again! No more slavin' fer the king!"

"No more slavin' fer the king!" the Cyclopes repeated.

Hestie shouted, "Time fer a Break the Bolt Pardee!"

"Time fer a Break the Bolt Pardee!" they repeated.

That was amazing, Hestie's father prayed to her.

You're incredible, Poros said to her as he flew to her side.

Poros was glowing more brightly than usual, and his stunning gray eyes seemed to penetrate her soul. At that moment, she felt like telling him she loved him.

I feel the same way, he said with a grin.

Hestie blushed but no longer chastised herself for being unable to keep her thoughts separate from her prayers. She loved Poros, and he loved her. He could hear her thoughts however much he wished.

She gave him a warm smile.

"Let's go see how Hecate's coming along with that locator spell," Hestie's father said, bringing her from her reverie.

She took Poros's offered hand, and they followed her parents home.

CHAPTER EIGHTEEN

Visions

Each time a mortal soul called to Than, he half-expected to find Lynn or Carol or Richard to be the owner of it. So far, he'd been relieved, but the anxiety and the anticipation of what would be his wife's worst nightmare made him feel physically ill.

Hecate had said she needed something belonging to Therese's family members to perform a locator spell, so while he'd been helping with the search on Cyclopes Island, he'd also gone to Therese's childhood home in the San Juan Mountains of Colorado. He hadn't been there long—just long enough to collect Lynn's book, Carol's hairbrush, and Richard's robe—but it had been enough time to remember that this is where it had all begun.

He remembered the first time Therese had played her flute for him, the first time she had served him sweet, iced tea, and the first time he'd introduced her to his sisters. He remembered swimming with her in Lemon Reservoir, learning to dance at the Wildhorse Saloon, and comforting Therese after Dumbo's death. At first, she was only interested in him because she hoped to save her parents, but, eventually, they fell in love. He hadn't been able to believe that a girl so enamored of nature, animals, and life would choose darkness, caves, and Death. But she had.

He returned to the Underworld, to deliver the items from Colorado, to Hecate's chambers, where the Furies and Pete, still recovering from their abuse, sat in chairs around Hecate's table. His sister's familiars, upset by what had happened in the Pit, were especially clingy. The white wolf lay whimpering at Tizzie's feet, the falcon was perched on Meg's shoulder, kissing her ear lobe, and the snake lay coiled around Alecto's neck, ready to attack anyone who dared to bring harm to her mistress.

His mother and Demeter were there, too. Demeter was smearing Hecate's raw shoulder with an herbal paste. Persephone applied the same ointment to the others.

Back on Cyclopes Island, Thanatos watched with awe as his daughter used the language of the giants to convert them to the rebellion. She was a master at diplomacy and persuasion. Her ability to speak in their dialect with their cultural mannerisms was remarkable.

Hecate touched Lynn's book with the flame of her candle. Once the book was afire, the goddess then used it to set fire to a world map before dropping both burning items into a large silver basin. When the flames died, she used her finger to stir the water as she said, "Show me the location of Lynn Cameron."

"Did it work?" Than asked her.

While he'd searched the island and Therese's childhood home in Colorado, he'd also looked for Hermie. Hestie had said he'd gone to see the Fates, so he went there first.

"He left over an hour ago," Atropos told him at the door before slamming it in his face.

Next, Thanatos went to the meeting room where the boy, Jinsoo, had fallen asleep in a chair beside his sister's body. Chidori was perched on the arm of his chair, and Kitty lay in his lap. Clifford and Noodle greeted Than when he entered.

The god of death quickly and carefully moved the boy to a room with a comfortable bed with feather pillows and blankets, where he could finish his night of sleep. The animals curled on the bed around Jinsoo to keep him company. Hopefully Morpheus would bring him sweet dreams.

Thanatos continued to search the Underworld for his son but found no sign of him. As he flew through the sky from Cyclopes Island with his lovely wife and daughter and the most powerful god alive, he turned to Hestie and asked, "Did Hermie say where he was going after he visited the Fates?"

She shook her head.

"Well?" Meg asked, back in Hecate's room. "What do you see?"

Hecate bent over the silver basin studying a small scrap of the world map. "Northwest Athens, in Kerameikos, near the Eridanos River."

Than furrowed his brows. "There's an old cemetery near there."

"There's no time to lose," Pete said.

Tizzy leapt to her feet, and so did her wolf. "Let's go."

"We can't rush in without a plan," Hecate said, just as Therese, Hestie, and Poros entered with him from Cyclopes Island.

Hecate may have located your family, Than explained to Therese telepathically.

Alecto stroked the snake coiled around her neck. "Hecate's right. It could be a trap."

"But, unlike the rest of us," Therese said, her sweet face full of tears, "my family has an expiration date. We need to go *now*."

Hecate put a hand on Therese's shoulder. "Let me go alone beneath the protection of a cloaking spell. It won't be as powerful as the helm, but it should protect me long enough to get a read on the place, to make sure it's safe."

Therese frowned. "But…"

"I'll be right back," Hecate promised. "Give me ten minutes. Okay?"

Than rubbed his wife's back as she nodded and covered her face with her hands.

We'll bring them back safely, Thanatos said to Therese telepathically, though he knew his words were nothing more than a desperate attempt to comfort her.

***

Hypnos tried to pry the chains binding Helios to his golden cup, but to no avail.

"It's okay," Helios said to him. "My arms are still healing, anyway. I'm no good to the rebellion in this state."

"Are you kidding? You're our eyes, bro'. Have you seen anything?"

"As a matter of fact, I have," the sun god said. "As you know, Clymene and Dione have been guarding Metis in their hideout."

"Yeah?"

"An hour or so ago, I saw Prometheus go to them."

"He said he was going to touch base with his mom."

"Right. That wasn't the unusual part."

"Come on, Helios. You're killing me, bro'. What did you see?"

"Athena was following him."

"Uh-oh."

If Athena were to find her mother's hiding spot, it could mean the end of the rebellion.

Helios cocked his head to the side. "But here's what's also interesting: Prometheus *knew* she was following him. He led her to her mother."

"What?" Hip couldn't believe it. Prometheus would never betray the rebellion. "What was he thinking?"

"I suppose we have yet to find out," the sun god said.

While he was talking with Helios on one side of the earth, Hip was also talking to Selene on the other.

"Don't worry about the chains, Hypnos," Selene said, her long silver hair falling softly against her white luminous robe. "I've always been tethered to this chariot. I just wish I could be of more use."

The silver chariot glowed as brightly as her robe and silver eyes.

"You're right where we need you," Hip said. "Have you seen anything unusual?"

"Indeed," she replied. "A few hours ago, an entourage from Mount Olympus flew to Athens—at least two, maybe three, chariots."

"Did you see anything else?" Hip asked.

"No. Nor do I know why they were headed there or what they were planning," she said.

"That's okay, Selene. That's still useful info. I'll alert the others and check back with you again later."

While he was conversing with Helios and Selene on opposite sides of the earth, he was also with Jen, checking on Scylla in her old cave near the Messina Strait.

"You poor thing!" Jen cried when they'd first entered the dark cavern, where Scylla lay on the bank, half in and half out of the water. "Do you need anything?"

"Just my heads, the ones that are missing," she said, "if I'm to have any hope of returning to my goddess form."

"We'll find them," Hip said. "Are you hungry?"

"Always," she said. "But I can make it. Don't worry about me. I have some news for you."

Jen crouched on the bank beside the monster and lovingly stroked one of her long necks. "What is it?"

That was a sight Hip would have never expected to see—not in a million years. The girl who would shriek at a harmless snake, rat, or tiny bug was caressing the most terrifying-looking creature in existence.

"Charybdis came by to gloat a few hours ago," Scylla said.

"Thank goodness she didn't capture you," Hip said. "I wonder why."

"I suppose I'm no good to anyone like this, and my family thinks no one cares enough about me to bother with taking me as leverage."

"Well, they're wrong," Jen said. "You know you're like a sister to me, don't you?"

The only heads with eyes had been severed from Scylla, making her blind, so she used a tentacle to feel for Jen's face. "Yes. I've never felt loved by anyone as much as I do you."

Hip couldn't imagine what it would be like to grow up in a family of monsters that treated their children like crap, but he knew Jen had some insight into it. Her mother and brothers adored her, but her father had been a monster.

"So, what did Charybdis have to say?" Hip asked.

"My family took Amphitrite and her loyal subjects to the old castle and are holding them there for Zeus."

"Oh, no," Jen said. "We've got to rescue them, Hip. Who knows what torment those monsters are inflicting, just for kicks?"

Jen was right. They had to help Amphitrite and her subjects, because the Old Man of the Sea and his family were likely taking centuries' worth of resentment out on them in unimaginable ways.

Plus, with Poseidon, Hades, and Apollo taken, the rebellion needed Amphitrite and her subjects, along with all the help they could get, if they were to have any hope of victory.

But Hip had another concern weighing on his heart. He'd also found Morpheus in the Dreamworld.

"Pops!" Morpheus had cried when he'd first seen him across the prism of colors.

"Figment, I command you to show yourself," Hip had said, to be sure.

When Morpheus smiled back at him before wrapping his arms around his neck, Hip sighed with relief.

"You okay, son?" Hip asked.

"For now," Morpheus replied. "Hades and Poseidon are trapped in the giant bird cages in the middle of the great hall on Mount Olympus."

Morpheus was telling Hip what he already knew.

"Where's Apollo?" Hip asked.

"Tied to his throne," Morpheus said. "But, Pops, Lynn and…"

"I know. Persephone told us. Do you know where Zeus took them?"

Morpheus shook his head. "There's something else."

Hip's heart sank in his chest. What else could go wrong today?

"Zeus is trying to find a way to break into the Underworld," Morpheus explained. "The protection wards are holding, so they've come up with another plan."

"What?"

"Aphrodite is bringing me and Iris home," he said.

"That's great news. I thought…"

"No, you don't understand, Pops. She's going to pretend to be our ally. She's going to claim that she rescued us and that she needs protection from Zeus."

"We won't let her get away with that."

"Tell the others. We're on our way there now."

***

Hestie stood near Poros. He was bent over Artemis, who was laid out on a table in one of the meeting rooms in the Underworld. Callisto sat in a chair, her hand on Artemis's. She'd been sitting beside the goddess of the hunt, dripping ambrosia into Artemis's mouth, ever since Artemis had been rescued from Cyclopes Island.

Hestie had gone to check on Jinsoo and, finding him asleep with her animals, had returned to watch Poros work his magic. The Furies, Pete, Demeter, Persephone, Hip, and her parents were there as well. Hecate had just left for Athens and was due back at any minute.

As before, when he had touched the paralyzed Cyclops, Poros became illuminated from the inside out with a bright, stunning light—much brighter than a god's normal glow, equal to that of Helios. Hestie could detect the hum of electricity flowing from Artemis's body into his.

"Does it hurt?" Hestie asked Poros.

"No," he said. "I'm not sure how it feels for Artemis."

"Like relief," the goddess of the hunt murmured.

Everyone gasped and then cheered with glee when Artemis's body began to move. In another few moments, Artemis sat up and looked around the room. Callisto embraced Artemis and burst into tears of joy.

"Welcome back," Persephone said. "How do you feel?"

"Ready to fight," Artemis said. "You don't know how frustrated I've been."

"I can imagine," Hestie's father said. "I've been there."

"Thank goodness you're back!" Tizzie cried.

"Thank Poros," Hip said, before clapping Poros on the back.

"Yes," Hestie's father said. "Thank you, Poros."

Callisto had only just met Poros, but she threw her arms around him as if she'd known him for centuries. "Thank you, from the bottom of my heart."

Poros shrugged and smiled awkwardly.

You're one bad ass, Hestie said to him telepathically.

Awww, shucks, he replied with a smile.

"So glad to see you back to your normal self," Meg said to Artemis.

Alecto stood up. "And now that I'm feeling better, too, I should probably get back to work. Those evildoers in Tartarus aren't going to torture themselves."

"Hold on, sis," Hip said. "I'm afraid I have some bad news."

"*More* bad news?" Pete closed his eyes and shook his head.

"Can't we have one moment of celebration?" Persephone complained.

"Have you found Lynn and my aunt and uncle?" Hestie's mother asked Hip.

Hestie took her mother's hand and prepared herself for the worst.

"No," Hip said. "But I've gathered information from Helios, Selene, Scylla, and Morpheus, and none of it's good."

At that moment, Hestie heard a woman's voice calling in the distance.

"Someone's at the gate," Persephone said. "It sounds like Aphrodite."

<u>CHAPTER NINETEEN</u>

Confrontations

Hermie leaned against the iron door of the pit, his knees suddenly weak and unable to hold him up. In a flash, one of the Titans flew from the depths and wrapped his massive hand around Hermie's throat, pinning him against the door. The Titan pushed on the door with his free hand while he strangled Hermie with the other.

Frustrated that the door wouldn't budge, the Titan shouted, "What's to stop me from ripping your head off?"

Before Hermie could reply, the six other Titans, all whose names Hermie did not know, joined his fellow prisoner.

"Let him speak, Uranus," one of them said.

Hermie was relieved when the Titan released his grip on his throat and Hermie could breathe again. Then he nearly peed in his pants at the thought that Uranus, one of the first beings ever to exist, wanted to destroy him.

"Now answer my question!" Uranus said. "Why shouldn't I rip off your head and swallow it whole?"

"Um, because other than my sister, who's out there," Hermie pointed to the door, "I'm the only one who knows the code that releases the locks on the door."

"We'll torture it out of him," one of the others growled.

"I thought you might say that," Hermie said. "Which is why I told my sister to bring a rescue team if I'm not out in an hour."

"He won't last that long," another one said.

"Hold on," the most luminous among them said. "If Poros and the others find out that you tortured him, you can kiss your second chances goodbye."

"Shut up, Hyperion," Uranus said.

"Do you really think Poros was sincere?" one of them asked Hyperion.

"He swore an oath, Crius," Hyperion replied. "Why would a young god condemn himself to the Maenads?"

"I say we strangle him," one of the others said.

"What is Poros strikes us down, like he did Cronos?" another pointed out.

"I'm willing to take my chances," another said.

"Leave the boy alone, Menoetius," another, beside Hyperion, said.

"Shut up, Iapetus," Uranus said. "This will be fun."

Hermie cleared his throat. "Speaking of fun, how would you like me to install your very own media room down here, complete with games, movies, books in digital and audio, music…you name it?"

"Did he say games?" one of them asked.

"I heard books, too," another said.

"And music," another said.

Hermie realized that the Titans had been in the pit for so long, that they had no idea what movies, video games, and digital and audio books were. "I'm the god of technology. I'm here to make your stay a whole lot better."

It seemed to Hermie that if mortals in prison had access to games, movies, books, and recreational activities, it was only fair that immortals should have access to them, too. In fact, it seemed wrong to condemn the immortals to perpetual boredom for all of eternity—somehow inhumane. And it was only logical that happy prisoners would be less likely to revolt and more likely to be rehabilitated.

"Just let me show you," Hermie said. "And if you still want to torture me after that, go for it, deal?"

The Titans backed off and watched him go to work. He used his powers to bring electricity into the pit. Then he set up computers with keyboards and game controllers, big screen televisions with both satellite and Netflix access, and surround sound. He also conjured cell phones, ebook reading devices, earbuds, and headphones, so they wouldn't all have to listen to the same things. He spent at least an hour setting everything up and showing the Titans how to enjoy them.

He even showed a few of them how to take selfies and set up Facebook and Twitter profiles. Atlas went wild on Twitter. His favorite tweet? *Don't go through life holding the weight of the world on your shoulders.*

To Hermie, it wouldn't be an exaggeration to say that the Titans were eating it up.

While they continued to familiarize themselves with their new toys, Hermie found a small, melancholy goddess, who seemed disinterested in his gifts. "By any chance, are you Arke?"

"Yes. Why?" she asked.

"The Fates told me that you wish you could give up your immortality," Hermie said.

"It's true. I pray to them constantly. I just want to be at peace."

Hermie's hands twitched with excitement. "My girlfriend just died. Do you think you would switch fates with her so that she can come back to life as an immortal?"

Tears filled Arke's eyes. "That would be an answer to my prayers!"

Hermie's smile could not be bigger. Risking his life to come into the pit was definitely paying off. "I'm so glad to hear you say that."

"Well, my happiness ended the day Zeus took my wings," she said.

"Why did he do that?" Hermie asked, thinking of Morpheus.

"I fell in love with another Titan and switched sides during the war. Zeus captured me and took my wings before throwing me in here."

"And he never gave them back?" Hermie asked.

"I heard he gave them to another," she said sadly as more tears formed in her eyes. "I'm just not me without them."

"I wouldn't say that," Hermie said. "You're still you. Your wings aren't what define who you are."

"Yes, they are," she said.

"But you can still fly without them," Hermie said. "You can do almost anything you could do before. My greatest hero, Stephen Hawking, was a brilliant scientist who lost the use of his entire body, but he continued to do great things long after. And that's just one example. There have been marathon runners with only one leg, baseball players with only one arm, poets and musicians who've lost their vision, and the list goes on. You don't stop being you just because you lose one part of yourself."

"Well, it doesn't matter anyway," she said. "Not if I'm stuck in here."

Hermie realized he'd been doing the very thing the fates had predicted—trying to talk Arke into valuing her life. He hadn't meant to. His argument had come naturally, without thinking, as one living being who feels compassion for another. But, fortunately, she still seemed to want peace, and that was good for him and for Mina.

"So, I can tell the Fates that you'll switch with her?" he asked.

***

Morpheus sat beside Iris in Aphrodite's chariot at the gates to Hades, where Cerberus glared at him as if Morpheus had grown two more heads.

"Easy, boy," Morpheus said to his old friend.

"Persephone!" Aphrodite shouted again. "I know you hear me! Please hurry, before my father comes!"

Morpheus hoped his father had told the others about Aphrodite's deception in time. He prayed to everyone he knew in the Underworld, to warn them. For all he knew, one of their enemies could be sitting beside him beneath the helm of invisibility.

To Morpheus's surprise, Dionysus appeared in his chariot beside Aphrodite on the Acheron River.

"What are you doing here?" the goddess of love asked him.

"I've come to join the rebellion," Dionysus said. "Why are you here?"

"For the same reason," Aphrodite said. "I've just rescued Morpheus and Iris."

Don't trust her, Morpheus prayed to Dionysus. *It's just an act. She means to betray us to Zeus.*

Dionysus arched a brow and then did something Morpheus had not expected: He took Aphrodite's hand and kissed it.

"You're looking beautiful as always, my lady," Dionysus said. "It's nice that we finally have something in common."

"Indeed," Aphrodite said with a gleaming smile.

Morpheus rolled his eyes wondering what the hell was going on. Was Dionysus an enemy, too?

Soon Persephone was at the gate with Morpheus's father and Uncle Thanatos.

"Greetings, sister," Persephone said to Aphrodite. "And hello to you, too, Dionysus."

"We've come to join the fight," Dionysus said. "I've received reports that Ariadne and the Minotaur have been captured by Zeus and his followers. I need your help to rescue them."

Morpheus frowned. Ariadne and her brother had stayed out of the fight, because they rarely left the labyrinth. It was their duty to protect mortals from becoming lost in the maze that, over the centuries, had led to countless deaths, in spite of Asterion's efforts to frighten the mortals away.

"And I've rescued Morpheus and Iris," Aphrodite added. "Hurry and let us in. Zeus and the others are on my tail, and they aren't very happy with my change in loyalty."

"We'll let you enter," Thanatos began, "but not through these gates. And the chariots will have to remain outside."

"What?" Aphrodite complained. "Why?"

"We don't trust you yet," Morpheus's Pops explained.

Persephone crossed her arms at her chest. "And even if what you say is true, an enemy could be hiding beneath the helm, unbeknownst to you."

"So how will we enter?" Dionysus asked.

"Take your chariots along the Acheron to the Hydra's Sinkhole," Persephone said. "Leave your chariots and enter, one at a time."

She can't be serious, Morpheus said to Iris.

"The Furies are marking unique wards that will allow each of you in," Thanatos said. "You'll have to swim past the Hydra, but the Furies will be there to help you."

Morpheus did not like the sound of this. The Hydra had never grown to like him very much, unlike Cerberus, who was sometimes friendly, depending on how recently he'd eaten cakes.

To Iris, he said, *Don't worry. We've got this.*

Thanatos and Morpheus's father helped to guide the chariots around the winding river, where the Furies were waiting outside the Hydra's sinkhole. They were above ground, on a hillside, surrounded by ruins, the lights from the distant city miles away. Much to his annoyance, Morpheus was asked to enter first. He'd been hoping to go after Aphrodite and Dionysus, so the Hydra would be a little worn out by the time it was his turn. No such luck.

He god-traveled through the hillside to the underground caverns of the Hydra's lair, water up to his ankles. The Hydra could be anywhere in the winding tunnels that stretched and bent in the darkness. The only way into the Underworld from here was to swim down the sinkhole to the other side. Alecto appeared, waving him toward her.

Morpheus's first instinct was to go to her, but then he remembered Iris.

Telepathically, so as not to alert the Hydra to his presence, Morpheus said to Alecto, *I want to wait for Iris, to make sure she makes it in okay.*

It will be easier to sneak past one at a time, Alecto said.

I can't go on without Iris, Morpheus insisted.

They waited quietly in the darkness for another minute before Iris finally appeared. Morpheus took her hand and flew to Alecto.

Go, the Fury said, pointing to the body of water where the Hydra always slept.

Still holding onto Iris's hand, Morpheus jumped, and together, they swam down through the winding tunnel to the cave in the Underworld on the other side, where the Hydra, with her one ferocious head and eight hanging necks, was waiting.

Meg distracted the monster with cakes as Morpheus led Iris away, to the back entrance of Tartarus, where Pete was waiting.

Full of relief, Morpheus flew with Iris to the meeting room, where some of the other gods were gathered. He was happy to see Artemis back to herself, with Callisto by her side.

Hestie noticed him first. She wrapped her arms around his neck and said, "Boy, am I glad to see you."

Poros gave him a nod. "Glad to have you back."

"Where's Hermie?" Morpheus asked.

"I haven't seen him since he went to visit the Fates," Hestie said, taking out her phone.

"The Fates?" Morpheus asked her just before his Pops came and gave him a hug.

"Welcome home, son," his Pops said. "Your mom is with Scylla, but I've told her you're safe."

"Welcome, Iris," Thanatos said.

Demeter, Artemis, and Callisto gave them a wave.

"Oh, no!" Hestie cried. "Hermie went to the Titan Pit *alone*! And he's been in there for over an hour!"

Morpheus couldn't believe Hermie would do something so stupid.

With a much paler face than usual, Thanatos said, "Let's go."

***

Once Aphrodite and Dionysus had made it past the Hydra and into Tartarus, Thanatos cuffed them to his sisters' torture tables.

"What do you think you're doing?" Aphrodite asked as she struggled against her chains.

"I came to you for help!" Dionysus shouted angrily.

"This is just a precaution," Hip explained.

"We need to know if we can trust you before we let you roam free in our home," Meg explained.

"And how are you going to know if you can trust us?" Dionysus asked. "Make us swear? Well, I swear on the River Styx that you have nothing to fear from me."

"As do I!" Aphrodite said, though Than didn't believe her. Perhaps Zeus had the power to make such oaths meaningless. "I told Zeus I was helping him—that I'd damage your wards once I was in—but I lied. I'm telling you the truth! I can't stand my father's vile ways another minute! I want to join the rebellion!"

"Not so fast," Alecto warned, and the snake around her neck hissed.

"I swear on the River Styx!" Aphrodite said again.

Meg frowned. "People have been known to break oaths before."

Than felt his cheeks grow warm.

"Without Apollo, we can't know for sure if you're telling the truth," Tizzie said.

Tizzie's wolf howled her agreement.

"But how can we help the rebellion if you make us your prisoners?" Aphrodite asked through the tears running down her cheeks.

"I'll ask a seer," Than said, thinking of old Tiresias.

Hip gave them a smug grin. "Once the seer confirms your position, we'll let you go."

"Easy peasy," Meg said.

"And if the seer doesn't?" Aphrodite asked.

"That's up to our mother to decide," Than said.

"But it's likely the Titan Pit for you, in that case," Hip said, still grinning.

"They'll rip us to shreds in there!" Aphrodite cried.

Back in his father's meeting room, Thanatos turned pale. Hermie had gone to the Titan Pit? Alone?

"Leave the prisoners here," Than said to his brother and sisters in Tartarus. "We're needed at the Pit."

CHAPTER TWENTY

Reinforcements

Soon after learning that the sun god had seen Prometheus leading Athena to her mother's hiding place, Hip had decided to investigate. While he dealt with the problems back home in the Underworld—searching for Therese's family and the arrival of Aphrodite and Dionysus—he'd also gone to Metis's cave to spy on Prometheus.

Jen had been reluctant to leave Scylla alone and defenseless, so Hip stayed with them, too, near the Messina Strait in the dark cave, keeping them informed of everything else going on. Distraught over their son's capture, Jen had needed a chance to collect herself. Staying with Scylla had soothed Jen as much as it did her friend.

As Hip approached Metis's cave on the opposite side of the world in the South China Sea near the Philippines, he reported everything he saw to Jen and Scylla, in case anything should happen to him. Until Athena's loyalties were clear, she couldn't be trusted.

Hip avoided swimming because he felt claustrophobic while submerged in water, and today was no different. He'd disintegrated to an island near the Philippines, but the cave could not be reached by land or sky, so he swam.

He hid a few yards away from the mouth of the cave to listen. There was no use going closer; Clymene and Dione were fiercely protective of their sister, Metis, and would do everything in their power to protect her. Even from this distance, he could see the shimmering silver of Dione's skin and the flickering gold of Clymene's.

Fortunately for Hip, sound traveled well underwater, and he could hear what was being said inside the cave even if he couldn't get close enough to see it.

"You still haven't explained why you're here," Prometheus was saying.

"I'm on your side," Athena said. "There's no going back."

"How can we trust you?" Metis asked.

"Zeus left with Ares and Hermes and some of the others, so, while they were gone, I tried to free Apollo."

"What made you change sides?" Prometheus asked.

"What my father did to Therese's family is shameful. I thought with Apollo free, Zeus would let them go."

"Did you succeed?" Metis asked.

"No. I was nearly caught by Hestia," Athena said. "I flew away, in search of Prometheus and followed him here."

"Are you certain *you* weren't followed?" Metis asked.

"I was careful, though it's impossible to be sure."

"I believe she's telling the truth," Prometheus said.

"Make her swear it," Metis said. "It's the wise thing to do."

"I swear on the River Styx," Athena said, "that everything I've said is the truth."

Satisfied by what he'd heard, Hip decided to make himself known to Dione and Clymene.

"It's Hypnos," he said to them from a few feet away.

Clymene narrowed her golden eyes at him. "Did anyone follow you?"

"I disintegrated here, so no."

"Why have you come?" Dione asked. "It's risky. Someone may see you."

"It's about Amphitrite," he said.

Dione's silver brows lifted. "What about her?"

"Is our sister okay?" Clymene wanted to know.

"She's been captured by Phorcys, and she and some of her subjects are being held in his castle."

"We must go at once," Dione said. "Sister," she turned to Clymene. "You stay and guard Metis."

Athena appeared outside the cave. "We're going with you," she said of herself and Prometheus, who appeared beside her.

"It's a far swim," Hip said. "I'll disintegrate and meet you there."

"Normally, I'd advise against flight," Athena said to Prometheus. "But since my father and many of the others are occupied in Athens, I believe we should risk it."

"I agree," Prometheus said.

"I'm a fast swimmer," Dione said. "I'll meet you outside the castle."

Hip waited for them near the crumbling castle wall in the dark sea beneath Selene's shining chariot. Back in the cave in the Messina Strait, he told Jen and Scylla about his new recruits. Jen insisted on joining the effort to free Amphitrite. It wasn't long before Athena and Prometheus arrived. Dione wasn't long behind.

"We need a plan," Jen said.

"I say we storm in and take them by surprise," Dione said.

"Sounds good to me." Athena conjured her sword and shield. "Ready?"

***

While Thanatos flew with the other gods to the Titan Pit to rescue Hermie, he simultaneously went to visit two seers: Tiresias and Amphisbaena.

The Seers' Pit was rarely occupied these days since Tiresias spent much of his time in the Elysian Fields. Wanting to retain his memories, he often returned to the Pit until the effects of the Lethe wore off. Most souls were in a permanent state of oblivion after entering the Fields of Elysium, but seers had the ability to regain their memories over time once they returned to their Pit.

Cassandra, the seer no one believed, was there, but the others had moved on, thanks to Therese's advocacy for their redemption.

"Tiresias isn't here," Cassandra said.

As always, Than didn't believe her. But, as always, she'd told the truth, so, after a while, Than left to search the Elysian Fields until he found the old man, with the saggy breasts, smoking a pipe beneath a purple hemlock tree.

"Who are you?" Tiresias asked when Thanatos approached him.

Frustrated, he said, "The man in the moon," an idiom he'd picked up from Therese, and left.

Hopeful that he'd have better luck with the two-headed serpent dragon, Than continued his journey through the sacred caves in the underbelly of the acropolis. They smelled acrid and dank, reminding Thanatos of the last time he was there nearly twenty years ago.

He could sense Amphisbaena's presence but couldn't pinpoint her exact location as he stole silently over the rocky cavern floor. A thin ribbon of water, stagnant and foul, divided the ground in half. Than straddled it as he followed it to the back of the cave. The first chamber opened onto a second, larger one, the size of an auditorium. He unsheathed his sword as he glanced around the cliff edges above him, feeling the serpent dragon close. A billow of fire shot across the top of the cavern, and the residue of smoke lingered behind, spelling out the words, "I see you, Thanatos."

"Amphisbaena? I need your help," he said into the darkness.

Another flash of fire illuminated the cavern ceiling, and this time the smoke that remained spelled out, "Drop your sword."

Than recalled the last time she had asked it of him. As soon as he'd dropped it, she'd attacked him, and he might not have escaped without Athena's help. Athena had disguised herself as a spider and had woven a web around the beast. But today Athena wasn't there to help him.

"Can I trust you?" he asked the darkness.

The fire shot in a blaze above him, and the smoke read, "One says no. Two says yes."

Remembering that the second head was the one that told the truth, Thanatos dropped his sword, hoping for the best.

Then he asked, "Can you see the future of the rebellion?"

A blaze of fire shot from the darkness, and the smoke left behind spelled, "One says yes. Two says yes."

"Is the rebellion victorious?"

Another blaze shot out overhead and left smoke that spelled, "One says no. Two says yes."

Thanatos took that as a positive sign, a feeling of joy surging through him. Then, not wanting to get ahead of himself, he asked, "Will we suffer any casualties?"

Once again, the fire shot out overhead, leaving the words, "One says no. Two says yes."

Deflated, his throat suddenly tight with worry, he asked, "Who?"

He waited in the silence for many seconds, and then, realizing the serpent either couldn't or wouldn't reply, he asked, "Is Dionysus my enemy?"

Another hiss of fire, leaving the words, "One says no. Two says yes."

So, the god of wine wasn't to be trusted? Thanatos then realized that it was possible for Dionysus to be his enemy and yet still want to help the rebellion, so he asked, "Does Dionysus wish to help the rebellion?"

A flurry of fire shot overhead, but this time, the serpent dragon showed herself and leapt toward him. Thanatos grabbed his sword and fled from the cave. He supposed the two-headed serpent dragon had grown weary of his questions, but at least he'd gathered some helpful—albeit worrisome—information from her.

In the same moment that Than had entered the caves beneath the acropolis, he'd also gone to the iron door of the Pit with his sisters, his mother, his brother, his wife, his daughter, Artemis, Callisto, Demeter, and Poros. Feeling confident that there was enough power between them to subdue the Titans, he went to unbolt the door, only to find that he couldn't.

"What the…?"

"Hermie texted me the code," Hestie said from the back as she pushed her way through the other gods to the door. She pressed the numbers on a keypad, and, before pressing "Enter," asked, "Ready?"

"Get to the back," he told her. "I'll do it."

For once, she obeyed.

Than turned to his allies, noticing the look of worry on Therese's face. He could only imagine the pain Hermie had endured from the hands of the Titans over the hour or so in which he'd been their prisoner. Why had he gone in there alone? Thanatos thought his son was smarter than that.

"Ready?" Than asked them.

The other gods nodded, their weapons drawn.

Thanatos pressed "Enter," and the bolts turned, releasing the door. He rushed inside, only to find…

He stared in disbelief at the scene before him. Cronos remained paralyzed on the floor, but his head was positioned so that he could view the big screen television mounted on the wall. And the Titan, along with Perses and Crius, wore headphones, presumably through which they could hear the movie playing on the screen. Hyperion and Iapetus seemed to be playing a video game while Menoetius watched. Atlas was taking a selfie and—Than lifted his brows even higher—sharing it on social media?

He exchanged looks of bewilderment with Therese as Hermie, unharmed, flew up to greet them.

"I hope it's okay that I'm in here," he said.

With the door secured behind them, Artemis asked, "What's going on?"

Persephone flew to Hermie's side. "Did you do all of this?"

"The prisoners in the Upperworld get stuff like this," he said defensively. "Plus, look how content they are—less likely to cause a fuss."

Therese wrapped her arms around their son and kissed his cheek. "I'm so glad you're okay, god of technology. You had us worried sick. What possessed you to attempt this on your own?"

"I want to save Mina. The Fates gave me the idea. But now, Arke is having second thoughts about switching places with her."

Than sighed with relief at his son's safety but was immediately frustrated by his continual efforts to thwart Death.

"Mina's gone, son," he said. "And I'm sorry, but there's nothing to be done about it. Now, let's get back to the rebellion, shall we?"

At the word *rebellion*, Uranus looked up from his computer screen and shouted, "Let me help you!"

Suddenly, the Titans, who'd barely noticed the arrival of Than and his allies before, rushed toward them, promising their loyalty.

"We could use their help," Hermie said.

"That's enough, son," Thanatos said. "They're not to be trusted."

"I swear on the River Styx!" Hyperion cried out. "You have my loyalty!"

"Me, too!" Atlas shouted.

"Don't you remember what they did to us?" Meg said to Than and their allies as her serpentine hair hissed to life.

"And to Hecate?" Tizzie added, her wolf baring her teeth.

"We were bored," Menoetius said.

"We needed information," Perses said. "It wasn't personal."

"You tortured your own daughter!" Alecto cried, the snake around her neck hissing as her red hair flamed.

"I gave her a choice!" Perses growled.

"Not all participated in your torment," Iapetus pointed out.

"We now have a common enemy," Uranus said. "Let's work together to end Zeus's reign."

Hip turned to Than. "Are you with the seers now? Ask them if the Titans are to be trusted."

Alecto gawked at Hip. "Are you serious?"

"Tiresias is oblivious," Than said to Hip. "Amphisbaena has grown weary of me."

Demeter stepped closer to the door. "Let's leave this dreary place. It wreaks of piss and crap."

"And blood," Meg said.

"There was a time when an oath on the River Styx meant something," Crius said, probably aware that Thanatos was an oath breaker.

"We can't trust you, period," Tizzie said.

"Though I wish it were otherwise," Persephone said. "Tisiphone is right. How can we trust you, who were once our enemies?"

Suddenly Pete conjured two daggers, one in each hand.

"Pete?" Tizzie asked.

Without a reply, and before anyone could stop him, Pete used the daggers to gouge his eyes.

Everyone, even the Titans, gasped as blood spurt from Pete's face and he cried out in agony.

"What are you doing?" Therese rushed to her friend's side.

"Give me your blood," Pete said.

Thanatos realized what Pete had in mind. He took one of the daggers from Pete's hand, cut his wrist, and held it, dripping with blood, to Pete's lips.

Pete's body began to tremor. Then, his head bobbing, he muttered, "Hyperion of the heavenly light, Crius of the stars so bright, and Iapetus of the mortal spear—these three alone, we need not fear."

Pete's convulsions grew worse as he repeated himself.

"Pete!" Tizzie cried.

Pete finally stopped seizing and lay limp in Tizzie's arms.

In that moment, Than, also beside Cerberus guarding the gates, spotted Melinoe in the distance.

"Melinoe's at the gate," Than informed the others.

"Hecate's sent me a message," Melinoe said. "I've come to help."

To the others in the Pit, Than said, bring Hyperion, Crius, and Iapetus and leave the others."

"Are you sure?" Therese asked him.

"Pete endured horrific pain to give us this information," Persephone said. "Let's use it."

CHAPTER TWENTY-ONE

The Best Laid Plans

Therese sat beside Melinoe at the table with the other gods in the meeting room. Pete, whose gruesome empty sockets had finally been replaced by his beautiful regenerated brown eyes, sat between Tizzie and Meg. Artemis and Callisto had flown off to help Hip and his team rescue Amphitrite, but everyone else, except for Morpheus and Iris, who'd needed rest, was there, including Hip.

The three Titans from the Pit sat across the table from the Furies and Pete. Demeter sat, frowning, at one end of the table. Hermie stood in the corner of the room with Hestie and Poros. The teens seemed to be having a conversation of their own, but Therese couldn't concern herself with that right now. She was hunched over a piece of paper—a message from Hecate.

"Tell us again how you got this, my dear," Persephone, who sat on the other side of Melinoe, said. "You say it just appeared out of nowhere?"

Therese didn't see Melinoe often enough to be desensitized to the goddess's unusual appearance—the stark contrast between the two sides of the goddess's body, one black and the other white. The black side of her face contained a white eye, and the white a black eye. There were hairy moles on the white side that Aphrodite had once offered to remove but that Melinoe had wanted to keep. Melinoe had long white hair on the white side of her head and long black hair on the other. Unlike

Scylla, who'd wanted to change her appearance, Melinoe had embraced her startling features in her duties as the goddess of ghosts.

"That's right," Melinoe said in her scratchy voice. "I had just finished rounding up a lost soul and was about to summon Thanatos when this paper popped into my hand, as if I'd been carrying it all along."

Therese read the note, written in Hecate's handwriting, again:

Dear Melinoe,

Your family needs you.

Go to the Underworld and tell them a trap awaits them in Kerameikos, where the bodies of Lynn, Carol, and Richard, invisible to mortals, are on display in the ancient cemetery. At least ten gods lie in wait, including Zeus. Do not go without an army.

I'm hiding in Helios's chariot, where I can keep watch over Therese's family members. Helios recognizes the spot as the place where his son, Phaeton, was paralyzed and dropped by Zeus in the bottom of the river and where Helios's daughters, the Heliades, while sobbing over their brother's misfortune, were transformed into amber-teared poplar trees along the bank.

I'm working on a spell to free Helios. He desperately wants to help.

Gratefully Yours,

Hecate

"She says to bring an army," Crius said. "And now that you've freed us, you have one."

"We should wait for the others to return with Amphitrite," Persephone said.

"We have enough here to take down ten gods," Hyperion pointed out.

"But they have the lightning bolt, the trident, and the helm," Than argued.

"We have Poros," Hestie said from the corner. "He's as good as any lightning bolt."

"Hestie, please…" Therese snapped, not meaning to sound as rude as she did. She was anxious and taking it out on her sweet daughter. *I'm sorry*, she said to Hestie telepathically.

"It's not our numbers or our abilities that concern me," Persephone said. "I think we should take advantage of this opportunity."

"What do you mean, Mother?" Hip asked.

"No offense," Therese said to Persephone, "but my family is dying. This is hardly an *opportunity*."

The queen of the dead frowned. "I'm not suggesting that we leave them there to die."

"Then what are you suggesting?" Than asked.

Persephone stood up. "While we send one team to rescue Therese's family, we send another to Mount Olympus to bring Hades, Poseidon, and Apollo home."

Alecto stroked her snake. "You don't fear we'll be defeated if we divide ourselves?"

"We need to keep Zeus and his loyalists distracted in Kerameikos," Persephone explained. "Once the gods succeed in their mission on Mount Olympus, they *and* my dear husband and his brother and Apollo can help at Kerameikos, too."

Therese wasn't sure how much longer her family members would last.

"This sounds terribly risky, Mother," Tizzie said.

Her wolf whined, as if in agreement.

"Perhaps you should have freed more of us," Crius said with a grin.

"Pete," Therese said in desperation. "Can you see anything more? Can you offer us any counsel?"

Before she could stop him, Pete conjured daggers and thrust them into his eyes. He winced as blood sprayed across the table.

"Pete, no!" Tizzie shouted.

Therese hadn't meant for this to happen. "Pete, I…"

"Give me some of your blood," he said to her.

Trembling from the shock of it all, Therese took an arrow from her quiver, pricked her finger, and put it to his lips.

Pete sucked the blood from her fingertip and then began to tremor.

Just as Amphitrite walked in with her rescuers—save Dione, who returned to guard Metis's cave—Pete, with his head bobbing, muttered, "Send love to the potters dead and wine to the mountain stead. Let beauty find the clay, and the ram will lead the way."

Pete repeated the lines and then collapsed with his head on the table. Tizzie wrapped her arms around him, trying to console herself.

"What was that all about?" Artemis asked.

"Pete?" Jen rushed to her brother's side. "What the heck just happened?"

Therese looked from one god to another, as dumbfounded as any of them.

Persephone turned to Amphitrite. "Thank goodness you're okay."

"Thank Athena," Prometheus said. "We couldn't have done it without her."

"Glad to have you with us!" Meg said to the goddess of wisdom.

"As you can see," Persephone said to the newly arrived, "we're trying to solve an important riddle. Where are the others? Safe, I hope."

"In hiding, recuperating," Amphitrite said. "Phorcys and Keto were not kind to us."

"Come with me, dear," Demeter offered. "You should lie down."

Amphitrite, eyeing the Titans from the Pit, said, "I think I'll stay, thank you."

Alecto stood up with her snake and said to Amphitrite, "Take my seat."

"Thank you. I see we have some new…*allies.*"

From the corner, Poros said, "I'll go grab some refreshments for everyone."

"What was the riddle again?" Artemis asked after Poros had left.

Hip scratched his head. "Something about sending love to potters and wine to a mountain."

Suddenly, Hestie lifted her hand in the air. "I know what it means!"

Therese gasped. "Hestie?"

"Speak, child," Persephone prodded.

"Love and beauty refer to Aphrodite," Hestie said. "Wine and the ram are Dionysus."

"But what about them?" Hermie asked.

"Kerameikos means ceramic," Hestie said.

"Potters used to work the rich clay in the area, centuries ago," Hip pointed out.

"Send love to the potters dead," Persephone began, "means send Aphrodite to Kerameikos."

"Exactly!" Hestie said enthusiastically. "And the mountain stead is Mount Olympus."

Meg jumped from her chair, startling her falcon. "Dionysus should lead the rescue mission to save Father!"

"This is marvelous work," Persephone cried. "Thank you, Pete and Hestie."

"Now we just need a plan," Tizzie, a little less excited than her mother, said.

Therese still feared that the success of any plans the rebellion made would be at the cost of her family members. Not every plan had come to be—Persephone's idea of capturing Hera was just one example. Therese glanced across the room at Than, who seemed as apprehensive as she.

***

"I think I know what my purpose is," Hestie said to Poros as they followed the Phlegethon to Tartarus.

"It's about time," he teased.

"Hey." She nudged his arm. "Not all of us get theirs handed to them in a prophecy, god of sky."

"I just meant that I've known your purpose for a while now. It's pretty obvious."

"Why didn't you say anything?"

"Well, you almost bit my head off the last time I suggested something."

She nudged his arm again. "Stop exaggerating."

He laughed.

"So, tell me what you think it is," she said.

"Goddess of languages."

She beamed. "It wasn't clear to me at first because all gods can speak all languages. My gift didn't seem particularly special."

"Yeah, but your gift goes beyond fluency," he said. "You rocked on Cyclopes Island. And solving the riddle just now? That was amazing."

"Thanks." She smiled up at him. "I want to declare myself the goddess of languages and international diplomacy. Will that step on any toes?"

"Only one way to find out."

He stopped and grabbed her hand. "Come here."

She looked up at him as he asked, *Can I kiss you?*

I think we're past the point where you have to ask.

He laughed again and gave her a peck on the lips, but she held onto his neck and kissed him back—much more than a peck.

He grinned down at her, his stunning gray eyes sparkling with the reflection of the light from the Phlegethon.

You're so beautiful, she said, and this time, she'd meant for him to hear it.

"Come on, goddess of languages and international diplomacy." He took her hand and added, "That's a mouthful."

She nudged his arm again.

When they reached Tartarus, Hestie was troubled by the appearance of Aphrodite strapped to one of the Furies' torture tables like a condemned soul. Dionysus, whom Hestie had never met, was there, too.

"My father sent me to free you," she said to them as she pulled the key to their cuffs from her trouser pocket and removed their chains.

"It's a shame he was too much of a coward to do it himself," Aphrodite grumbled. "I wanted to thank him personally for chaining me here in the first place."

Dionysus rubbed his wrists where the cuffs had been. "Let it go, babe. We're free now."

"Where are the others?" the goddess of love and beauty asked.

"Making plans," Poros said. "Come on."

Hestie and Poros led the two gods to the meeting room, where the others were still discussing their next move. As much as Hestie wished she could announce her revelation about her purpose, she knew now was not the time, so she returned to the corner of the room with Poros, to stand beside Hermie.

Her brother looked down at her and frowned.

What's wrong? she asked Hermie telepathically.

Poros and Morpheus get to help, but you and I have to hide in Helios's cup.

That's not fair. We're gods, too.

Tell me about it. I just single-handedly reformed the Titan Pit, and now they're making me sit on the sidelines.

And I'm the one who solved Pete's riddle!

I tried to argue but was told to be quiet.

I wish I would have been here to argue with you, Hestie said.

Me, too.

Hestie crossed her arms at her chest, steamed. She might start out in Helios's cup, but no one, not even her parents, could force her to stay there.

***

Morpheus sat beside Iris in Aphrodite's chariot on the way to Kerameikos. The thought of ten angry gods lying in wait to destroy the rebellion made him more than a little afraid, especially since the rest of the gods had gone to Mount Olympus. He was counting on Hecate, Helios, Therese, and his mother, watching from the sun god's golden cup with Hermie and Hestie, to intervene if things went south.

As they neared the old cemetery, the area looked familiar to Morpheus, though he couldn't recall ever visiting. From above, he saw the ruins of stone walls near a mostly dry riverbed. There were few trees in the vicinity—just a small copse where the spring came up from the ground and disappeared again beneath a bridge. The ruins of ancient buildings and mausoleums spread out over what appeared to be an archaeological site. Fortunately for the gods, there were no mortals touring the ancient ruins—though plenty were driving past on a highway not far from there.

In the center of the barren ruins on the grass beneath the heat of the sun lay three bodies. Morpheus recognized them as Lynn, Carol, and Richard. Morpheus covered his mouth, both relieved to see them alive and horrified by how still they lay.

Where is everyone? Iris asked him.

Morpheus shrugged, fearing a trick. What if Zeus and his loyalists were waiting to ambush the other team, sent to Mount Olympus?

Aphrodite drove her chariot down to the cemetery and brought her mares to a halt a few yards from the paralyzed mortals.

Morpheus felt like a sitting duck, waiting to be attacked at any moment. He squeezed Iris's hand and held his breath.

"There you are, darling!" Aphrodite cried when Ares appeared with the helm of invisibility in his hands. "Oh, sweetheart, I've been looking for you everywhere!"

Ares eyed Morpheus and Iris as he rushed toward the chariot. "Love, what is it? Why have you come here?"

"They wouldn't let me in!" she said through her tears. "I tried everything I could think of to convince Persephone and her morbid brood to open the gates and let me in, but they refused! Even at the cost of these two!" Aphrodite waved her hand toward Morpheus and Iris.

"They must not care for him as much as we thought," Ares mumbled. "How does it feel to be expendable?" he said to Morpheus.

Tears filled Morpheus's eyes—not because there was any truth to what Ares had said, but because the god of dreams was terrified of being found out.

"Now look what you've done, darling!" Aphrodite teased. "You made him cry."

Iris glared at the goddess of love. Morpheus doubted she was acting.

"You can't stay here, love," Ares said. "I'm in the middle of something. Return to Mount Olympus and wait for me there."

"I went by there earlier and couldn't find anyone at home. I got scared and searched the world over at least three times before I saw these three lying here. I hoped you were nearby."

"Love, go home and wait for me," Ares said, before he kissed her hand. "I'll see you shortly."

"But why, darling? Can you believe that Persephone attacked my chariot? I haven't had it long. I'm so grateful to Hephaestus for making it for me. He wanted to thank me for all I've done for Cinny, you know. And to think it was almost destroyed."

The god of war was losing his patience. "You can tell me more about it later."

"What are you doing here, anyway?" Aphrodite asked. "And where are the others?"

Ares arched a brow. Morpheus feared the god of war had become suspicious of Aphrodite and her questions.

"Go home and wait for me, love," he said again. "I'll explain everything later."

Morpheus worried that if Aphrodite didn't do as the god of war said, she'd lose his trust forever.

Let's go, he said to her telepathically.

But we haven't distracted him long enough. And where are the others?

Just then, one of the trees by the small spring transformed into Zeus, and he flew to the chariot and raged, "Go home now, you dimwit! You've put my entire reign at risk!"

Frightened, Aphrodite commanded her mares to fly away. Morpheus doubted they'd distracted Ares and Zeus long enough for the other team to rescue Hades and the others. And he still worried that Hecate's warning about ten gods lying in wait had been wrong. He hoped and prayed that the rebellion hadn't walked into a trap on Mount Olympus.

Suddenly, his father appeared in the front seat beside Aphrodite.

"That wasn't enough time," he said, and, glancing back at Morpheus, added, "though I'm glad you're out of danger."

"What's happening on Mount Olympus?" Aphrodite asked. "Were they waiting for you? I didn't see them in Kerameikos—only Ares and Zeus."

"We've run into a complication," his Pops said.

"Pops, spill," Morpheus said from the back seat. "What's going on?"

When his father didn't answer right away, Morpheus leaned forward, grabbing his father's shoulder. Morpheus blanched when his father disappeared, leaving a spatter of blood on the bench.

"Pops?"

CHAPTER TWENTY-TWO

Death

Numb with fear and anticipation, Thanatos waited with the rest of his team a mile outside the gates of Mount Olympus, as Dionysus attempted to gain admission. Than was also in the Underworld with his mother, Amphitrite, Melinoe, and Demeter to defend it from attack, in case Zeus's plan had been to draw them out and overtake the palace, as they'd done with Poseidon's castle.

"Father! I'm home!" Dionysus shouted playfully at the gates of Mount Olympus. "Have you missed me?"

As soon as the clouds parted and the gates opened, Thanatos led the others in a flurry of panic past the god of wine, where they were met with—not an empty courtyard—but an army. At least twenty Curetes, led by Rhea, and fifty Amazons, led by Cupid, drew their weapons and charged.

The Curetes, gods of the wild mountainside of Crete, were known for protecting Zeus as an infant from his tyrannical father, Cronos. These male warriors were metal workers, shepherds, and beekeepers who spent their time practicing a strange war dance on the hillsides of Crete, not unlike the dance of the Maenads on Mount Kithairon.

The Amazons—so devoted were they to war that they cut and cauterized their right breasts so as not to interfere with the use of a bow—let their arrows fly. One pierced Hip's chest, causing the army he'd amassed to reintegrate as he fell to the ground. Than disintegrated and dispatched to Helios's cup to warn the others while he escorted Hip's soul to Tartarus to await his body's healing.

He couldn't persuade Therese to wait with their children in the cup. He should have known better than to try. Helios, Hecate, and Jen followed Therese across the sky to Mount Olympus, where the Titans from the Pit were barely able to keep the gates open, lest the allies be trapped inside.

Fearing that Zeus and the others would soon follow, Than shouted to his army on Mount Olympus, "Retreat!"

But Artemis and Callisto had breached the palace doors, and Prometheus and Athena followed them up the rainbow steps, forcing Than to shout, "Charge ahead! Do not retreat!"

Helios shone his rays on their enemies, blinding them long enough to give the Furies and Pete a momentary advantage as they cut the heads from six of their enemies. Therese shot arrows into the crowd and struck Cupid, who fell with a thud near Than's feet. Moments later, Athena, Prometheus, Artemis, and Callisto returned from the palace with Apollo, Poseidon, and Hades, along with Hestia as their prisoner.

Dionysus and his Maenads and Satyrs soon arrived to wreak havoc on the army of Mount Olympus, but even their savage ways weren't destructive enough to deter the mighty Amazons and Curetes as they attempted to take back the prisoners and rescue Hestia.

Poros, who had been told to remain outside the gates for his safety, flew into the courtyard in the beautiful armor made by Hephaestus and struck at least a dozen Amazons and Curetes to the ground, where they lay either paralyzed or twitching. This gave Jen the opportunity to move Hip's body out of harm's way as it healed.

Suddenly, Apollo went wild with his bow, shooting down one enemy after another. Hades and Poseidon rescued their chariots from Zeus's garage, and Apollo was soon behind them with his, yelling, "Jump in! Retreat!"

While Than swung his sword at enemies on Mount Olympus, he disintegrated back to Kerameikos, hoping to rescue Therese's family members and take them to the Underworld; but, when he arrived, he received a shock that stopped him in his tracks.

Hovering in the sky above the ancient cemetery, Thanatos saw Hermie with his taser sword talking to Ares near the dry riverbed, while Zeus hung back in the shadow of a copse of trees. In the cemetery, Hestie stood talking to Phobos and Deimos near the paralyzed bodies of Lynn, Carol, and Richard.

Before Thanatos could react, Ares growled at Hermie and opened his giant mouth.

***

Hestie knelt on the floor of Helios's golden cup, beside her brother and mother, peeking down at the ancient cemetery in Kerameikos, when her father arrived with bad news from Mount Olympus.

"Stay put," their mother said just before flying off with Helios and Hecate.

Great, Hermie said to her. *First Aphrodite fails, and now the team at Olympus is failing.*

No one's failed yet.

We're about to lose our view, he said. *The cup is moving too far west. Soon we won't be able to see the cemetery.*

I hope Ares isn't suspicious, Hestie said to Hermie. *How long do you suppose they'll wait down there for someone from the rebellion to come?*

Hermie shrugged. *Let's hope it's long enough.*

I want to move in closer, Hestie said.

Hermie shook his head. *Mom said to stay put.*

At this rate, we'd be better off in Selene's *chariot*, Hestie complained. *I wish we could hear if anything was being said down there.*

Hermie's face lit up. *We can!*

Huh?

I'm the god of technology, remember? I can conjure technology at will.

What are you doing?

Dropping mics in those trees and setting them up to transmit to my cell phone.

He pulled his phone from his pocket.

Dang it. It's dead, he said. *Oh, wait.*

He conjured another phone and grinned.

Wow, Hermie. You can enter video games and conjure technology, Hestie said. *I wish I had cool abilities.*

You can fly, speak telepathically, run at lightning speed, and pick up a train, sis. I'd say you have cool abilities.

I mean special *abilities.*

Wait. Listen. I'm picking something up.

"No one's coming," Ares's voice said over the cell phone. "Let's head back."

"They'll come," Zeus said. "Those Underworld gods won't leave their mortal friends to die. Trust me."

"We should give them water," Hermes said. "They won't be any good to us dead."

"They'll make it to nightfall," Zeus said. "Then they can die, for all I care. We'll have to try a new strategy."

Hestie gave Hermie a worried look.

"We're bored," Phobos or Deimos, Hestie didn't know which, said. "We want some action."

"What if the rebellion is attacking Mount Olympus?" the other twin asked.

"It's well protected," Zeus said. "And hopefully Hera and Ladon are making progress at Cerberus's gate."

Hermie gawked. "She's attacking the Underworld?"

"I agree with the others. I think we should call it a day," Hephaestus said to Zeus.

"I'll tell you what," Zeus said. "Night is an hour off. We'll split the difference and leave in thirty minutes."

We have to do something, Hestie said. *We have to distract them.*

How?

They listened for several more minutes, but no one said anything more. Afraid that they'd give up early, Hestie leapt from the golden cup. *Come on.*

Hestie, no!

Hestie flew down to Kerameikos, to the place where Ares had last been seen talking to Aphrodite, near the dry riverbed and wall of ruins. She couldn't see Ares in the dusk, even with her goddess vision. The cemetery seemed abandoned, except for her three mortal family members lying in the grass.

Then he appeared, the god of war, holding the helm of invisibility.

Hermie flew to her side. *I can't believe you're doing this.*

"I wasn't expecting children," Ares said.

Hestie put her hands on her hips. She hated being called a child. "Sorry to disappoint you."

"Everyone else is trapped in the Titan Pit," Hermie said. Then, telepathically to Hestie, he added, *Follow my lead.*

"I don't think you're supposed to tell him that, Hermie," Hestie said, understanding her brother's new strategy.

"Who's trapped in the pit, and why?" the god of war wanted to know.

"Well," Hermie began, "when our parents, aunt, uncle, and Artemis were trapped on Cyclopes Island, and Hades, Poseidon, and Apollo were stuck on Mount Olympus, and Demeter had given Persephone an herb to make her sleep, so she'd stay out of the conflict..."

Ares laughed. "Good ol' Demeter."

"Anyway," Hermie continued, "Prometheus took Hecate, Pete, and the Furies into the Titan Pit to recruit reinforcements."

Ares narrowed his eyes. "If they're trapped in the Pit, how do you know why they went inside in the first place? It's impossible to hear prayers from the Pit."

"Prometheus left a note," Hestie said.

"So, there's not much of a rebellion left," Hermie said. "Clymene and Dione won't leave Metis's side, and Morpheus and Iris are Aphrodite's prisoners."

"Aphrodite said Persephone wouldn't let her in," Ares said suspiciously. "But you said Persephone was asleep because of an herb."

"That was Demeter pretending to be Persephone," Hermie said quickly. "I guess she'll do anything to keep her daughter out of it."

"So, it's just us," Hestie said.

"But your parents escaped the Cyclopes," Ares said with furrowed brows. "Where are they now?"

"After they escaped, they went to rescue Amphitrite," Hermie said.

"And now they're trying to figure out a way to save Prometheus, Hecate, the Furies, and Pete from the Pit."

Ares lifted a brow. "That still doesn't explain why *you're* here, or how you found us. We could have been anywhere."

"We used a locator spell to find Lynn," Hermie said. "We didn't know you'd be here, too."

"Hecate taught us, remember?" Hestie added. "When you wanted us to find Prometheus?"

"I remember," Ares said, disgusted. "Well, this was a colossal waste of time."

"Not entirely," Zeus said from somewhere in the trees. "We gained some valuable information."

Hermie conjured his taser sword.

"Hermie," Hestie said. "What are you doing? We can't fight them."

"I just want to show them my creation," Hermie said. "Especially Ares. As the god of war, he'll appreciate it."

"Hermie is the god of technology," Hestie explained, hoping to keep Ares's interest.

Ares laughed. "What do you call that thing?"

"Can we go yet?" either Phobos or Deimos called from the cemetery, where the mortals lay in the grass.

Hestie flew over to talk to them, but fear and panic overcame her. "Get away from my family!"

The sons of Ares smirked at her. "You wish."

"There's a reason why gods don't use modern weaponry," she heard Ares say to Hermie.

"Oh?" Hermie asked. "Why?"

Hestie froze, still overcome by panic and fear, as she watched, in what seemed like slow motion, Ares, the god of war, open his giant mouth.

***

Morpheus clung to the side of Aphrodite's chariot as the goddess of love and beauty drove like a maniac from their hiding place in the bright hue of Selene's silver chariot toward the ancient cemetery in Kerameikos, where Hermie and Hestie had gone to confront Ares.

"Those stupid children!" Aphrodite grumbled. "What do they think they're doing?"

Morpheus squeezed Iris's hand and watched helplessly as Hermie conjured his taser sword. Was he really going to try and fight the god of war?

Then Hestie left her brother's side to what? Confront Phobos and Deimos?

"Can't these horses fly any faster?" Morpheus asked the goddess of love and beauty.

Then, to his great horror, Ares stretched his mouth wide open and leaned over Hermie, ready to swallow him.

Morpheus didn't want to look, but he couldn't peel his eyes away. In a flash, Hermes, faster than any god Morpheus had ever seen, flew to Ares and swung his blade.

Iris screamed. Aphrodite gasped. Morpheus's breath caught in his throat.

Ares leapt from Hermes's reach, and the blade caught Hermie on the neck.

Morpheus watched in horror as blood sprayed against a tree. Then Hermie's head fell to the grass and his body dropped beside it, just like in Lynn's dream.

Something moved in the grass near Hermie's head. It was a tortoise, covered in Hermie's blood.

Aphrodite brought the chariot so close to the scene that Morpheus thought she was going to grab Hermie's body; instead, she lifted Ares, who'd been momentarily stunned, into the chariot and into her arms.

"Darling!" she cried. "Are you okay? That was close!"

Morpheus was confused.

Then he noticed Aphrodite cuff a set of adamantine chains around the wrists of the god of war before tethering him to her chariot.

"Love?' he asked, gaping in disbelief. "What have you done?"

"What I should have done days ago."

She took the reins in both hands and led her mares to the nearest chasm to the Underworld. Persephone was waiting for them at Cerberus's gate.

"Splendid!" the queen of the dead cried, as they neared her and the three-headed dog. Ladon lay on the riverbank, his hundred heads limp. "Take Ares to Tartarus. I'll be right behind you."

Morpheus didn't know how to feel as Aphrodite parked the chariot and led Ares to Tartarus.

"Come on, you two," she said to him and Iris, beckoning them to follow. "Help me strap him to one of sweet Meg's tables."

Morpheus had never heard anyone refer to the Fury as "sweet Meg," but he said nothing as he followed.

Already waiting in Tartarus were his Uncle Than and the soul of Hermie.

"Than?" Morpheus rushed to his uncle. "Is Hermie going to be okay?"

"Where am I?" Hermie asked, looking confused.

Thanatos clapped Morpheus on the arm and smiled wide. "He's going to be just fine."

CHAPTER TWENTY-THREE

Preparations

Therese sat in a chair beside Hermie, where he lay on a bed in one of her old rooms in the Underworld, with Noodle curled beside him. She stroked Hermie's dark hair from his face. His soul had returned to his body. He was breathing. The color had returned to his skin. Therese was just waiting for him to wake up.

Hermes had saved her son's life—again. Although the swiftest god had meant to strike Ares and had missed, Hermes had provided enough of a distraction for Aphrodite to swoop in and capture her lover. Then Thanatos had been able to recover Hermie's remains and the helm of invisibility, which had been dropped when Ares had eluded Hermes's blade.

Therese supposed she could forgive Aphrodite for capturing her during the attack on Poseidon earlier in the week.

Hermie began to stir. He blinked and met her gaze. "Mom?"

She stroked his cheek. "Hello, my sweet boy. How do you feel?"

"Where's Hestie?"

"Resting with Poros."

"And Jinsoo?"

"With Prometheus."

"What about Lynn and Grammie and Grampie?"

"Healed by Apollo. Grammie and Grampie are sleeping in the next room. Lynn is talking with Pete."

"With Pete? Why?"

"He's helping her work through a vision she's had of Poros."

"Oh." Then he asked, "What about everyone else? Did Grampa Hades make it out okay?"

"Yes." She smiled down at Hermie and stroked his sweet cheek again. "He's home with your father and the other gods, planning our next move."

"What about Mina?"

Therese frowned. "Mina?"

"I want to bring her back."

Therese kissed Hermie's cheek. "Don't think about that right now, sweet boy. What you did last night was very brave, but it took a lot out of you. Try to rest and get some sleep."

Hermie closed his eyes and pulled his covers up to his chin. She stroked his hair, recalling the many times throughout his life that she'd sat and watched him sleep after she'd read him and Hestie a bedtime story. Tears filled her eyes. Her tears weren't of sadness or of joy but of a mix of overwhelming emotions. She hoped and prayed that her sweet children would have good and happy lives and that sorrow and conflict wouldn't follow them for all eternity.

***

Hestie curled against Poros on the bed. Her mom was with Hermie just a few doors down from them.

"I can't believe my parents let me be in my room alone with you," she said.

"Is this *your* room now?" Poros asked her sleepily.

His stunning gray eyes were hooded, and his voice husky.

"I called dibs on it. It's the coolest of the three we had to choose from."

He stroked her hair. "So, you're going to live here?"

She shrugged. "I guess so."

He licked his lips, and she was momentarily distracted by his tongue.

"Hestie, I know we've only known each other for a few months, but…"

"But what?" She searched his eyes—those beautiful mirrors to her soul. She could never gaze at them often enough.

He smiled. "Your mind is an open book."

"I don't care. Why should I?"

He laughed and pulled her close. "Because you're driving me wild with your lusty thoughts."

She hit his bicep with her fist. "I don't have lusty thoughts!"

"Owe! That hurt, you maniac," he teased.

She tickled his ribs. "Does this hurt, too, you baby?"

He giggled like a little girl. "Stop! Stop!"

He fell on his back, and she climbed on top of him. She stopped tickling him and looked down into those gorgeous, brilliant eyes before she kissed him.

Suddenly, he flipped her over on her back and had his revenge by tickling her ribs, her armpits, her belly. She screeched hysterically. "Enough! Enough!"

"We're even," he said, falling over on his back.

She lay there beside him smiling, recovering from the laughter, wishing they could lay there together all day.

"We're supposed to be sleeping," he reminded her.

She nuzzled up against him, curling her legs over his.

He wrapped his arm around her legs and held her.

She sighed and closed her eyes.

"Hestie?" he said in that husky voice.

"Hmm?"

"Prometheus is going to get another ship when this is over."

"I figured as much."

"I'm going with him, like I said."

She opened her eyes and gazed up at him.

"I want you to come with me," he said. "Hermie's going, you know."

"That was before Mina…" She was still unable to believe that their friend was dead.

"Would you come with me?" he asked her. "When this is all over? You can visit the Underworld anytime."

Chills of pleasure coursed through her as she smiled up at him. "Poros, god of the sky, I'd go anywhere with you."

***

Hip watched his father, who was standing at the head of the table, and admired how he had so seamlessly returned to his role as leader of the rebellion. Persephone stood beside him, more fearless and determined than ever. Most of the other gods were there as well—even Demeter, who seemed to have embraced the rebellion now that its victory was imminent.

Hip was reminded of a time, not long ago, when the gods of Olympus rarely spoke to one from the Underworld; and now, most of them were gathered around his parents' table.

Hephaestus had shown up at Cerberus's gate with his wife and daughters late last night. The Charities had gone to rest, but Hephaestus was here in the meeting room with Hades.

Ares and Hestia were chained up in Tartarus. And although Hera and a few of her allies had escaped last night, Persephone, Melinoe, and Amphitrite had captured Ladon. They'd been surprised to discover his joy at having been liberated from Hera. He'd closed his two hundred eyes and had gone to sleep at his brother Cerberus's feet and was still sleeping there, even now.

There was still no sign of Hermes. Hip had come to agree with Than's theory: Thanatos had speculated that Hermes would be unwelcome on Mount Olympus after the role he'd played in helping the rebellion capture Ares, recover the helm, and save Hermie. But Thanatos had also said that the god of commerce and of thievery, of communication and of travel, could never act against his father; so, rather than join the rebellion, he likely fled somewhere to hide.

The other gods, including the three Titans from the Pit, were either sitting around the table or standing along the perimeter of the room. The younger gods had gone to rest. Iris was with Morpheus, Hestie was with Poros, and Therese was waiting for Hermie to wake up.

Hip stood not far from his parents, leaning with his back against the wall, arms and legs crossed. He wished he could sleep, like the one-hundred headed serpent, but there was no time for that now.

Jen had returned to Scylla in the cave at the Messina Strait. Hip was with them, lying on the bank, stroking Jen's hair.

"I'll wait outside the gates beneath the helm," Hades was saying. "It may take days, or it may take minutes, but sooner or later, someone will either go in or out, and that's when I'll make my move."

The gods around the table seemed content with the idea.

Poseidon, who stood beside Hip, said, "I appreciate your hospitality, Hades, but I think Amphitrite and I will go and round up as many of our people as we can, so they can help us when it's time."

Amphitrite added, "My sisters will want to be there, too, especially Metis."

Prometheus, who'd just entered the meeting late, said to Poseidon, "I'll go with you."

Athena stood from her chair. "I'll go, too."

Hip smiled. The goddess of wisdom had never seemed clingy before, but she seemed so now. Hip glanced across the room at Aphrodite, who was also smiling and who seemed to have drawn the same conclusion about her sister: Athena was in love.

"Thanatos will tell you when it's time," Persephone said to them.

"Once I'm inside, I'll wait until I'm alone with someone I can kill inconspicuously," Hades said, "'to signal Thanatos. Then he'll disintegrate and give everyone the word as I, still beneath the helm, open the gates to let you in."

"We'll wait for your word, Thanatos," Poseidon said before he and Amphitrite left, followed by Athena and Prometheus.

Alecto stroked her snake. "Zeus may have the help of Rhea and her Curetes and of the daughters of Ares, but there are few others at his side."

"Hera is there," Meg reminded her.

"And possibly Hermes," Demeter added.

"I doubt it," Hecate said. "Not after what he did last night."

"This will be a piece of cake," Crius said with a grin.

Apollo stood up. "Remember, our goal is to seize the palace, not to destroy it."

Artemis nodded. "We want minimal damage and as few casualties as possible."

"Because our goal is reform," Hades said. "Does everyone understand?"

At that moment, Pete entered the room with Lynn.

"Any news?" Tizzie asked them.

"She saw Poros again," Pete said. "Go ahead and tell them, Lynn. Don't be afraid. Close your eyes and take a deep breath."

Lynn was trembling. All eyes were on her. She did as Pete had said and closed her eyes. She took a deep breath. "It's like before," she began. "I see Poros approaching his father and asking Zeus to accept him."

"You're doing good," Pete said, holding her hand. "Keep going. What else do you see? Tell them what you told me."

"I see Zeus hurling a lightning bolt at Poros."

Gasps filled the room.

Apollo said, "Tell them the rest."

"Poros doesn't fall," she said. "He becomes illuminated with light."

Hip noticed Apollo nod his head, as if he'd seen it, too.

"Keep going, Lynn," Pete said. "Tell them what else you told me."

"I see Persephone jump into another goddess's mouth," Lynn said.

"What?" Persephone turned pale. "But why?"

"Which goddess?" Hades leaned forward. "What else do you see?"

"I don't know." Lynn opened her eyes. "That's it. There's nothing more."

"That's awful troubling," Iapetus said.

Pete squeezed Lynn's hand. "Now we're going to do that thing I told you about, okay?"

Tears streamed down Lynn's face, and her lips began to quiver. "Okay."

"Apollo?" Pete said. "Can you come stand with us?"

Apollo crossed the room and stood on the opposite side of Lynn from Pete.

"Apollo is the god of healing," Pete said to Lynn. "He'll heal you right up, as soon as we're done. It's going to hurt, I won't lie, but you can do this, okay? It's so important that we see all that we can."

Hip had a bad feeling. He began to understand what Pete was going to do. He knew Therese wouldn't like it, if she knew.

"Close your eyes, Lynn, okay?" Pete said.

Trembling like a leaf in the wind, Lynn nodded and closed her eyes, her face twisted with anxiety. "I'm ready," she said bravely.

Pete conjured his daggers and, as gently and quickly as he could, he pierced both of her eyes at once. Her blood spilled down his hands and his arms as she cried out in pain—a blood-curdling scream—and began to tremor. Then he took the daggers and gouged his own eyes, wincing and trembling as his blood joined Lynn's on his arms.

The two seers held hands, their heads bobbing. Apollo grabbed Lynn's hand and closed his eyes, too.

Together, as if they had one voice, Pete and Lynn muttered, "One, two, three, four. She's on the throne, she's at the door. She's in the sky, she's on the stair. The Queen of Dead is everywhere. As when Melinoe first breathed, everyone will be deceived. One, two, three, four. She's on the throne, she's at the door."

Pete and Lynn both collapsed, caught by Tizzie and Apollo. Apollo went to work, healing Lynn's eyes, as Hades said, "Wait. Is there more?"

Apollo shook his head and helped Lynn from the room.

Melinoe looked at her mother. "Why was my name mentioned?"

"I don't know," Persephone said, appearing as if she was in a daze. "I'm so confused."

"How can you be everywhere?" Meg wondered.

"Maybe she takes my place as Death, or Hip's as Sleep, and disintegrates."

"But what has that got to do with me?" Melinoe repeated.

"Hestie solved the last riddle," Persephone said. "Maybe she can help us with this one."

Hades took Persephone in his arms. "Than, bring Hestie here, will you? We can't proceed with our attack until we bring this vision to light. We need to protect your mother at all costs."

Demeter stood from the other end of the table and said, "For centuries, I've been wrong, my darling daughter, and I must apologize. Over these past few days, I've witnessed your devotion to Hades, to your children, and to the Underworld. I've watched as you've fiercely protected it despite my efforts to dissuade you. And I've seen Hades, whom I've despised until my heart has turned cold, fiercely protect you back. I apologize to you both for not seeing this before."

Persephone flew across the room to her mother and wrapped her arms around the goddess's neck. "Oh, Mother! Thank you for saying that!"

"This doesn't mean I'm giving up my six months with you, darling," Demeter added with a smile.

Persephone laughed. "But maybe we can come here and visit during the summer?"

"Let's get through this conflict first," Demeter said. "Then, we'll see."

CHAPTER TWENTY-FOUR

Storming Olympus

Hermie woke up and found Jinsoo sitting where his mother had been. Chidori was perched on his friend's shoulder, and Kitty was curled in his lap. Clifford had joined Noodle on the bed beside Hermie. Both dogs jerked awake when they felt Hermie move.

"Hermie?" Jinsoo said. "You okay?"

"Where's my mom?"

The boy shrugged.

"With the other gods," Clifford barked.

"How long have I been asleep?"

"I don't know," Jinsoo said.

Hermie sat up and pushed the covers off, causing Noodle and Clifford to rearrange themselves.

"Sorry," he said to the dogs.

"What are you doing?" Jinsoo asked.

"I'm getting up," Hermie said. "And I'm going to bring back your sister."

"Is that really possible?" Jinsoo asked as tears filled his eyes.

Hermie recalled what Hestie had said about giving Jinsoo false hope, but Hermie was determined to get Mina back.

"Yes," Hermie said as he slipped on his shoes.

"Can I come, too?" Jinsoo asked.

Hermie didn't see why not. "Sure." He went to the door. "Come on."

The animals followed Hermie and Jinsoo through the dark caverns along the Phlegethon, past the Fields of Elysium, past the fields of asphodel, and all the way to the home of the Fates.

Hermie knocked on the door and said to Jinsoo, "Let me do the talking."

The door swung open, and the wrinkled little face of Atropos popped out. "Goody!"

"Let them in!" Clotho called from behind her. "Hurry up, Atropos!"

Hermie should have remembered that they would expect him, but it was nonetheless jarring, even the second time around. "I came…"

"We know, we know," Lachesis said as he entered the room with Jinsoo and the animals behind him.

"Mina?" Jinsoo said.

Hermie turned to see why Jinsoo had said his sister's name and then saw her standing in the corner next to one of the archaic pinball machines.

"Mina?' Hermie said, echoing Jinsoo.

Mina smiled at them.

Hermie and Jinsoo ran across the room and hugged her. She felt solid, real, alive!

Hermie turned to the Fates. "I don't understand."

"This is when you give us your ultimatum," Atropos said.

"You will only give us our state-of-the-art entertainment facility if we give back Mina, right?" Clotho said in her throaty voice.

Hermie cocked his head to the side. "But if you were going to give her back all along, why make me speak to Arke about switching places?"

"Not everything is about *you*," Lachesis said.

"Arke needed to hear what you had to say," Clotho explained.

"And the other prisoners in the Pit needed a reprieve from their suffering," Atropos added.

"So, you see?" Lachesis asked. "It was all for a reason."

Hermie hugged Mina once more, feeling a little more awkward and shy than he had when he'd hugged her a few moments ago. He still couldn't believe his eyes. Jinsoo was crying so hard that he couldn't speak. Mina too, had begun to weep.

"This is where you give us what we want," Clotho prompted.

"Let's begin over there." Atropos pointed to the back of the room.

"And the big screen will go here." Lachesis waved her hand at the wall behind her.

Hermie laughed gleefully and got to work.

***

Hestie sat beside Poros on the sofa in her room, feeling the weight of the world on her shoulders.

"Atlas tweeted not to do that," Poros teased. "Remember?"

"This is serious," she said. "They were all looking at me like I was the key to everything. What if I can't figure this riddle out?"

"That's why we left the meeting room—to get away from all the pressure." He rubbed her shoulders. "Now relax. Take your time. You're the goddess of languages and of international relations. Gee, that's a mouthful."

"Poros."

"This riddle is like poetry. Poetry is language. Just take your time and think."

"Okay." She sat up on the edge of the sofa and stared at the piece of paper where Hecate had written the prophecy down. "Let's start with this part about Melinoe. 'As when Melinoe first breathed, everyone will be deceived.'"

Hestie knew the story of Melinoe. Her parents had told her about it when she and Hermie were seven or eight and had asked why they hadn't met her, like they had their father's other siblings. Melinoe was conceived when Zeus disguised himself as Hades and seduced Persephone. Zeus tried to kill Melinoe while she was in the womb, deforming her features.

"Zeus is going to disguise himself," Hestie said. "Like the night Melinoe first breathed."

Poros squeezed her shoulders. "That's it, Hestie. You're onto something."

Hestie read, "One, two, three, four. She's on the throne, she's at the door. She's in the sky, she's on the stair. The Queen of Dead is everywhere."

Then Hestie snapped her fingers and looked at Poros with wide eyes. "I know what it means."

***

When Hermie appeared to Thanatos with his previously dead girlfriend beside him, the god of death was angry. Why did he take it personally that he'd been wrong about bringing the girl back? But the look of happiness on his son's face and the expression of triumph in his son's eyes melted the anger away, and Thanatos was glad for him.

"Welcome back from the dead," Thanatos said to the girl. "Now, I better leave your presence before I undo whatever it is that Hermie has done."

Hours later, he sat with his family in the rooms that were officially his and Therese's again, since Tizzie and Pete had taken chambers closer to the Seers' Pit. It was only reasonable that *they* should move now that he and Therese were back. First, Thanatos had lived in these rooms for many, many centuries, so he had the better claim. And, second, now that Pete was the god of seers, it only made sense that he should be closer to them.

"Remember what we said," Therese was saying to Hermie and Hestie, who sat on a couch opposite her and Than. "Stay put. Protect Lynn,

Grammie, and Grampie and Mina and Jinsoo. Your father will be here, as long as he can be."

The mortals were hanging out together in another room, where Death wouldn't affect them.

"And Ladon will be helping Cerberus at the gate," Than added.

"Prometheus is on his way, too," Therese said. "He wants to help you protect the mortals, just in case the gates are breached."

"But they won't be," Than assured them.

There was really no way of knowing when his father would have the opportunity to enter Mount Olympus and take a life. He'd already been gone for hours, and, as Hades had said, it could even be days. But, for as long as he could, Thanatos wanted nothing more than to sit and visit with his family.

"Tell me more about your adventures aboard *The Marcella*," Than said to his kids.

The following day, Than was awakened from where he slept in his old bed beside Therese. Nike's soul called to him from Mount Olympus, which meant it was time. He woke Therese and disintegrated across the globe to alert the others.

The gods of the rebellion gathered outside the gates. The doors opened by an invisible source that they knew must be Hades beneath the helm. The rebels charged.

Thanatos and the other rebels were met by Curetes, Amazons, Rhea, Cupid, Psyche, Phobos, and Deimos. But the sheer numbers of the rebellion made it easy to overcome the smaller army, and it wasn't long before Than and his allies had fought through the courtyard and entered the palace doors.

With most of the loyalists either captured or fallen, only Hera, Zeus, Hebe, and a handful of Muses remained. Zeus and Hera stood side by side on their double throne with their swords drawn. As was the plan, Hades remained hidden beneath his helm.

Athena flew to stand before Zeus, her spear raised above her head. "Listen to me, Father. I have something to say to you before I unseat you!"

"Don't get ahead of yourself!" Zeus scoffed.

"Be careful, Athena," Metis said from Demeter and Persephone's double throne, where she stood with Clymene, Dione, and Amphitrite. "He's holding a lightning bolt. I can see it from here."

"And Hera has Poseidon's trident behind her back," Amphitrite said.

"We have you surrounded," Thanatos said to Zeus. "Put your weapons down."

"It's not over until it's over!" Hera screeched.

"Silence, you wench," Athena shouted. "I've long grown tired of your vicious, petty ways. I blame you for the shell of a god my father has become."

"How dare you!" Hera screeched again.

"While my mother resided in his belly, he had at least a modicum of wisdom," Athena continued. "But the god before me now is not fit to rule."

"You're breaking my heart, Athena," Zeus said solemnly.

"Father," Poros said, pushing through the crowd. "I beg you to let this be over. I beg you to accept me as your son and to allow us to live together in peace as a family."

Just as Lynn had seen it, and before Than or any of the other gods could intercept him, Zeus hurled his lightning bolt at Poros. Poros's luminosity filled the room and shot into the blue sky above them.

While everyone's eyes were on Poros, Zeus did exactly what Hestie had said he would: he turned himself and the other loyalists into the appearance of Persephone to confuse the members of the rebellion.

Had Hestie not been able to solve the riddle presented by the seers, Zeus would have had Hades and the members of the rebellion exactly where he wanted them—unable to identify their friend from their foes. However, because of Lynn's bravery, Pete's guidance, and Hestie's insight, Zeus's trick would fail. The queen of the dead knew to hide in Hephaestus's forge as soon as Zeus performed his trick, which meant that all of those with her likeness in the great hall were enemies to the rebellion.

"Please!" one of the Persephones said. "I'm over here."

"No!" another said. "I'm Persephone. Please, believe me!"

"Hades, don't you know your own wife!" another cried.

It would have been a nightmare without the prophecy.

Thanatos lifted his fist in the air, and the other gods of the rebellion vanquished them all with a swift throw of their spears or a stab of their swords. Even Poros, who wore the armor made by Hephaestus, drove his sword into one of them.

When the bodies dropped to the floor and took their natural form, Metis flew to where Zeus lay bleeding on the marble at Poros's feet. Metis stretched her mouth wide open and swallowed her old lover before he could escape.

"At last!" Metis shouted. "At last, I have my revenge!"

Upon seeing this, someone who'd been hiding behind Hera's throne and who was still wearing Persephone's image, screamed and climbed into the mouth of Metis after Zeus.

From the enemies still healing on the floor, Thanatos deduced that the person who'd gone after Zeus was Hera. Metis covered her mouth, to keep the unseated king and queen from escaping. The other members of the rebellion finished the job, and soon the other loyalists were cuffed.

Hades pulled off the helm of invisibility in the center of the room near Poros and shouted, "Mount Olympus has been taken! Hip, hip, hooray!"

Together, the members of the rebellion echoed, "Hip, hip, hooray!"

Laughing, Hip turned to Thanatos and said, "Well, it wasn't just me. I had a little help."

CHAPTER TWENTY-FIVE

The New Pantheon

Morpheus stood beside Athena in front of a grand altar where Zeus and Hera's double throne had once been. The Charities had decorated the great hall with morning glory and moonflower—Iris's favorites. Rows of chairs had been placed facing the altar inside the perimeter of thrones, and a red velvet carpet had been laid through the center, dividing the room in half.

Morpheus couldn't believe this day was finally here—the day Iris would become his wife.

Preceding her down the aisle were Aphrodite and her Charities, dressed in lovely gowns of gold meant to complement the golden hues of Iris's wings, hair, and lovely, bright eyes. The goddesses dropped white rose petals behind them to pave the way for the bride, while Apollo played his lyre.

As Morpheus anticipated the appearance of his betrothed, he met the smiles of all the beautiful faces in the crowd. His parents stood in the front row with Hades and Persephone, Than and Therese, Hestie, Poros, Hermie, Mina, and Jinsoo. Therese's sister, Lynn, and Carol and Richard sat in the next row with Scylla, restored to her godly form by Poros. Beside her were Hecate and, to everyone's surprise, Hermes, who'd shown up a few minutes before the wedding. The rest of the Underworld family, including Demeter, filled the rows behind them. Even Melinoe was there. Now that her hateful father, Zeus, was no longer a threat to her, she had decided to return to her home in the Underworld.

On the opposite side of the aisle were Poseidon and Amphitrite and Amphitrite's sisters: Metis, Dione, and Clymene. Beside Clymene stood Helios, her lover, and beside him, Rhode, his wife. Helios's children—Phaeton and the Heliades—had been rescued from Kerameikos and now stood in the row behind their parents with Prometheus. The rest of the rows on the bride's side were filled by Hephaestus and his family, Artemis and Callisto, various subjects of Poseidon and Amphitrite, and the Titans who'd been released from the Pit—Hyperion, Iapetus, and Crius. Asterion and Ariadne, who'd been found chained in the garage behind Zeus's chariot on the day the rebellion had overtaken Zeus, sat beside Dionysus in the back row, but the Maenads and Satyrs had not been invited. They'd planned their own party on Mount Kithairon.

Much to Morpheus's dismay, the Cyclopes had been invited under the condition that they refrained from eating the guests. But only Polyphemus had attended, because the others were too afraid to leave their island.

Had Hades not turned down the opportunity to run for the position of prime leader, he would have been standing near the altar beside Morpheus and would have officiated the ceremony; however, after being held prisoner in a bird cage on Mount Olympus for over a week, he'd said he wanted to spend as little time on Mount Olympus as possible. Athena and Poseidon had run against each other for the position, and Athena had been elected.

The first thing Athena did as prime leader was to pardon all oath breakers who swore on the River Styx because they were unfairly manipulated by her father. This not only spared Morpheus, who'd sworn to be loyal to Zeus under duress, but also Thanatos, who'd been unfairly treated by all the gods twenty years ago.

The second thing Athena did was lift Zeus's ban on procreation. Although Hera wasn't present to undo her infertility power on the gods, Artemis, who was also known to be a goddess of unborn children, became suddenly imbued with Hera's gifts the moment the old queen had been swallowed. At Athena's command, Artemis returned fertility to the gods and goddesses.

Unlike the last time Poseidon had lost to Athena, in a similar contest, centuries ago, when the people of Athens couldn't decide who should be their patron, Poseidon was a good sport. He had congratulated Athena and had said he would run against her again in a few hundred years, when her term was up.

Poseidon had agreed to sit on a tribunal with Hades and Hecate to determine the fate of both the Titans in the Pit and the loyalists to Zeus. Ares and his sons, who were being held in Tartarus with the other loyalists as they awaited punishment, had been sentenced to serve a year on the Holt Ranch in Colorado, helping Bobby Holt. Hestia had been sentenced to work as a cook in the orphanage in South Korea, where Mina and Jinsoo had once lived. Other various sentences were still being determined by the tribunal.

But Morpheus couldn't care less about all of that today. The only thing on his mind was his bride-to-be and the life they would have together this day forward as husband and wife.

***

To thank them for their part in the rebellion, Hephaestus had built Than and Therese a chariot of their own. He'd also built one for Hip and Jen. So, when it was time to return Lynn, Carol, and Richard to their home in Colorado and to transport Ares and his twin sons to the Holt Ranch, Therese and Jen were more than eager to drive.

Because of their effects on mortals, Than and Hip had to stay behind, which Therese thought was necessary, anyway, because there just wasn't enough room. She had Lynn, Carol, Richard, Hermie, and Hestie in her chariot, and Jen had Tizzie, Pete, Meg, Ares, Phobos, and Deimos in hers.

Jen and Hip had previously offered to let Morpheus borrow their chariot for his honeymoon with Iris, but both Morpheus and his wife preferred their wings. Therese was glad; otherwise, the entire crew going to Colorado would have had to squeeze into a single chariot, since Hades and Persephone had taken theirs for a much-deserved vacation. Hades had even received Demeter's blessing, so long as he promised to have Persephone back before summer's end.

Poseidon had given Therese and Jen each a pair of black geldings to pull their shiny new vehicles. Jen had named hers The General and Hershey, after two of her favorite horses from her childhood, and Therese had named hers Midnight and Thunder, just because. Therese had positioned Stormy between Midnight and Thunder and had appointed him as the leader.

Therese had told Jen to go on ahead of her to Colorado, because she wanted to give Carol, Richard, and Lynn the ride of their lives by taking them around the world to see some of her favorite places. Fortunately, the horses were spectacularly swift, and they were able to make the trip in less than four hours.

When they reached her childhood home in the San Juan mountains across from Lemon Reservoir, Therese parked the chariot, gave the horses each an apple, and walked with her family indoors.

"I've never been happier to be home," Lynn said as she collapsed on the couch.

"I can't thank you enough for your help," Therese said to her sister. "We might not have won without you."

Carol draped an arm around each of her grandchildren. "The god of technology and the goddess of languages and…what was it?"

"International relations," Hestie said.

"Are you sure that's what you want to call yourself?" Richard asked. "That's a…"

"Mouthful," Hestie said. "I've heard that before, Grampie."

"I think it sounds brilliant," Therese said. "It's no more complicated than the god of healing, prophecy, light, and music…or the god of commerce, theft, travel, and communication."

"Good point," Hermie said.

"Well, I'm proud of you whatever you call yourself," Carol said. "Both of you. And Lynn, too."

"Just don't become a god, Lynn," Richard said. "Promise me."

"You have nothing to worry about," Lynn said. "I like being a human just fine."

Therese glanced at her children, wondering if they would rather be mortal like their cousin, but the smiles on their faces told her they were happy with their fates.

"Is it true that the two of you plan to go back to sea?" Carol asked Hermie and Hestie.

Therese was filled with joy when her children's faces lit up with excitement.

"Yes," Hermie said. "I can't wait to set sail."

"Me, too," Hestie said.

"Hestie and I will be busy helping Prometheus, Mina, and Jinsoo serve third-world countries by delivering medicines and technology."

"And we'll also be diving for treasure," Hestie added.

"Not me," Hermie said. "I'll let the others do that part."

Therese and her aunt and uncle laughed.

"Promise you'll visit your ol' Grammie and Grampie from time to time," Richard said.

"Promise," Hestie said.

"We will," Hermie said.

Therese kissed Carol and then Richard. "We need to go." She leaned over and kissed Lynn, who was still collapsed on the couch. "We'll see you soon."

She watched her children say their goodbyes, and then they took the chariot to Jen's childhood home down the road. Therese parked and led her kids up the gravel drive to the pen, where Mr. and Mrs. Stern and Bobby were out meeting with Jen, Pete, Tizzy, and Meg, who had just released their prisoners, void of their powers, into Bobby's custody.

"You don't have to worry," Bobby was saying. "I'll keep an eye on them."

Meg surprised Therese by winking at Bobby and saying, "And I'll keep an eye on you, handsome."

***

When Hestie boarded *The Marcella II*, beneath the bright rays of Helios in the deep blue sky, she had the most peculiar feeling of *coming home*. The ship was docked in Patras. She and the others had just god traveled with Prometheus from the Underworld after a bittersweet goodbye with her family. Her feelings of sadness over leaving her parents vanished the moment she boarded the ship and followed Prometheus to the upper deck.

"This ship awesome!" Jinsoo said.

Chidori, perched on his shoulder, chirped her agreement. The other animals had stayed behind in the Underworld, but the bird had wanted to come, and she'd gotten her way.

"It bigger, Captain?" Mina asked of the ship.

"Yes, it is," Prometheus replied. "And you and Jinsoo get your own rooms."

"Yay!" Mina said with a huge smile.

"Where are we going first?" Hermie asked.

"To Athens to pick up some supplies," Prometheus said.

Poros combed his hand through his blond hair. "Please say we get to eat at Mr. Burger."

"Mr. Burger! Mr. Burger!" Mina and Jinsoo chanted.

Prometheus laughed. "That is, after all, where this little crew got started. It's only fitting we should return there to celebrate the maiden voyage of *The Marcella II*."

"Yes!" Poros said with his gray eyes shining.

"And from there we go where?" Hestie asked.

"From Athens, we sail to the Red Sea to help some small villages along the African coast."

"Then we dive for treasure?" Mina asked.

"Once we get to the Gulf of Oman, right, Captain?" Poros said.

"Right."

"Goody!" Mina shouted. Then she said, "That's what the Fates say, right, Hermie? Goody!"

Everyone laughed.

Then Mina asked, "Hey, Poros. When you make me and Jinsoo gods, too?"

Poros crossed his arms. "I'll tell you what. Next year, if you haven't changed your mind, I'll make you gods on your fifteenth birthday. Sound good?"

Mina clapped her hands, and Jinsoo blushed.

"What would you be the goddess of?" Hestie asked Mina.

Mina shrugged. "I know what Jinsoo be god of."

"What?" Jinsoo asked.

"Kimchi!" Mina said, laughing.

"No more kimchi!" Hermie said, laughing, too.

"Should we set sail for Athens?" the captain asked.

"Let's go!" Hermie cried.

Hermie followed Mina to the tack, and Hestie followed Jinsoo to the jib.

"Crank the winch!" the captain soon shouted.

As Hestie looked up at the sail billowing in the wind, she noticed an owl perched on top of the mast.

Hello, Athena, Hestie said telepathically. *And welcome aboard.*

THE END

Thank you for reading my story. I hope you enjoyed it! If so, please consider leaving a review. Reviews help my book to get discovered by new readers, which helps me.

Please enjoy the first chapter from a sequel to this saga called *The Marcella II: Vampires and Gods*.

<u>CHAPTER ONE</u>

A Rare Find

Hestie took a deep bite of the warm September air before she dove from the deck of the *Marcella II* into the Arabian Sea. She'd swum hundreds of feet on the heels of Poros when it dawned on her that she could breathe underwater.

"I'm a goddess," she reminded herself. "I'm the goddess of languages and international relations."

And, because she could, she said those words—though they were a mouthful—in seventy-five other languages as she descended.

Poros, son of Zeus and lord of the sky, led her down—nearly ten thousand feet toward the ocean floor.

Even though it had been four weeks since she and her brother, Hermie, had become the newest gods in the pantheon, she still hadn't grown used to the liberty of not having to wear a wet suit, diving gear, or mask. The weighted belt and flippers were the only accessories she and Poros needed, besides their swimming suits and the netted cross-body bags they wore to carry their finds.

They soon reached the uneven floor and picked through sand, rocks, and seashells. Unlike the last place they'd searched a few weeks ago, this place was desolate—not a living thing in sight.

After a while, Hestie approached a boulder the size of a Volkswagen Beetle. Poros swam up behind her just as she gave it a shove, revealing the mouth of a cave.

Did you know about this? she asked him telepathically.

Poros shook his head. His hair swished in the water like the short tentacles of a yellow sea anemone. *I've never searched this spot before.*

Together they peered into the darkness. Hestie was glad for the benefit of god-sight, which enabled her to see without a dot of light.

Within a few feet of the opening, the cave veered sharply to the left. It was impossible to know where it led or what it contained without entering it.

Should we go for it? Hestie asked.

We should stay on task. Jinsoo and Captain will be here any minute and will wonder where we've gone.

She rolled her eyes. Sometimes Poros could be too much like her brother.

You stay, she said. *I'm going in.*

Her job was to look for treasure, not to explore caves, and it was unlikely that any of the treasure from the *Camille*—a ship of Prometheus's which had sunk in the Arabian Sea in the 1970's—would have made it past the giant boulder and into this small cave. Nevertheless, she swam inside to have a look around.

She wasn't surprised when Poros followed.

The opening was only a few feet in diameter. Hestie propelled herself through the tunnel by pulling on the rocky floor beneath her. This helped her to avoid scraping her back along the top of the cave as it veered right.

Bracing herself for what might be waiting just around the bend, Hestie expected to find an eel, octopus, or other sea creature hiding in the crevices of the rock, but, as she veered left and right again, she found the cave to be as desolate as the rest of the area.

It came to a dead-end in a chamber not much bigger than her bathroom on the *Marcella II*.

This would make a great hiding place, she said to Poros.

For lovers? he asked with his brows lifted.

She smirked. *For treasure.*

She swam into his arms and gave him a kiss. It wasn't easy to do underwater, but, when he cupped her cheeks and kissed her again, she tightened the embrace and enjoyed the feel of his warm body against hers.

We better go look for Jinsoo and Captain, he said.

Mood killer.

Poros laughed.

As she was about to follow him from the cave, she noticed a small wooden box—no bigger than a shoe—tucked into a crevice.

What's this? she said.

She pulled it free.

Poros returned to her side as she opened it.

She gasped, nearly choking on the sudden intake of water.

The box was filled with gold coins.

Hermie sat beside Mina on the flybridge of the *Marcella II* and grinned at the look she was giving him.

"Let's just try it," he said. "If we ruin Jinsoo's kimchi, Captain will have no choice but to take us to shore for more food. And you know what that means."

She arched a brow. "Mr. Burger?"

"Or its equivalent," he said.

"I don't know. Captain might make us starve."

"He wouldn't."

"I thought you don't need as much food, now that you a god," she said in her broken English.

Hermie sighed. "I may not need it, but a burger sure sounds good. Doesn't it? Besides, I think that kimchi is expired."

"Kimchi don't expire for a long, long time."

Hermie cocked his head to the side. "I think that's more of an ideology than a fact."

Chidori chirped, "Hilarious! Hilarious!" from where she perched on the helm.

Mina giggled, even though, being mortal, she couldn't understand the language of animals. To her, the yellow canary's sounds were nothing more than tweets.

"In orphanage, one batch of kimchi last two month," Mina said.

"You're used to it," he said. "But I'm used to hamburgers and French fries and nachos and just about anything that isn't kimchi."

Mina climbed to her feet. "Okay. Let's do it."

"Really?" Hermie hadn't thought she would agree, and, now that she had, he was having second thoughts. He didn't want to make Prometheus angry. "I don't know. Maybe it's not such a good idea."

She sank back into her chair. "No. It bad idea. Captain will be mad. He don't like waste."

"You're right," Hermie said. "How long do you think they'll be gone?"

"Two hour. Three hour." She shrugged.

"That long?"

"Why? You want to watch *Naruto*?"

"We've seen every episode."

"So?"

"Not again!" Chidori chirped.

Hermie said to Mina, "You could have gone with the others."

"I want to stay with you!"

Becoming a god hadn't changed his dislike of swimming. He'd rather avoid encounters with slimy, creepy, and sharp-toothed creatures if there were other people willing to dive in his place. He was the god of technology, after all, and he preferred to be in front of a computer screen than almost anywhere else.

He gave Mina a once-over. She looked cute in her skimpy bathing suit with her black hair tied in pigtails. She had claimed to be working on her tan, but he sensed she enjoyed showing off.

"You want to play a game?" she asked. "I can get Jinsoo's *Yu-Gi-Oh* cards. Or, we could play *Urban Fighter.*"

He had a better idea but was too shy to say it.

"You want to kiss me?" she asked.

He laughed. "You read my mind. Want to sit on my lap?"

"Oooh. In Captain's chair? That funny. We make out in Captain's chair."

"Chidori, why don't you keep watch for Jinsoo and the others on the lower deck?"

"Fine," she chirped before flying away.

Hermie folded Mina onto his lap and pressed his lips to hers.

"You taste like kimchi," he said with a frown.

"Oh, stop saying kimchi and kiss me."

Unable to get past the sour taste in her mouth, he moved his lips to her neck.

"I like that," she said.

He chuckled. Every time they made out, Mina gave him a play-by-play of her feelings.

"That spot there," she said when he kissed her shoulder. "You make me crazy, Hermie!"

"But you're glad I brought you back from the dead?" he teased.

"Not again!" she said, chuckling. "How many time you want me to thank you?"

"I'm sorry. Never again."

"You said that yesterday!"

The sound of fluttering wings too large to be Chidori's made Hermie lift his head in time to see a gray owl land on the center mast.

He cleared his throat before saying, "Hello, Athena."

The owl flew from the mast to the bridge and morphed into the goddess of wisdom, her long black hair blowing away from her face as she turned her bright gray eyes on him.

"Sorry to interrupt," she said with a smile. "I have something for Poros."

She didn't look very sorry to Hermie as Mina jumped from his lap and returned to her own seat.

"He's not here," Hermie said of Athena's brother. "He's out diving."

"Is Prometheus diving, too?" Athena asked.

Hermie smiled. It wasn't the first time Athena had used her brother as an excuse to see Prometheus.

Mina nodded. "With Jinsoo. They be back in two hour or so."

"They're here! They're here!" Chidori chirped.

Just then, Prometheus emerged from the sea near the lower deck at the back of the boat, his dark curly hair and beard flattened by the water, until he shook it out like a dog, and the curls returned. Three other heads popped up with him.

Mina jumped to her feet. "They back already? That was fast!"

Athena flew to the lower deck to meet the divers. Hermie and Mina followed on foot.

"We found something!" Hestie cried as she climbed aboard.

"Oh, hi, Athena," Poros said, as he flew from the water to the lower deck.

"Hey, little brother."

Prometheus followed. "Hello, Athena. Welcome aboard."

As soon as Jinsoo climbed from the water and onto the deck, Chidori perched onto his shoulder.

Jinsoo grinned. "Hi, Chidori! Miss me?"

Chidori gave him a playful tweet.

"What did you find?" Athena asked.

Hestie took a small box from her bag and opened it.

Hermie and the others huddled close to get a view of its contents.

"Are we rich?" Mina asked.

"Those are ancient Persian darics," Athena said.

Prometheus took one from the box and turned it over in his hand. "That's exactly right. And each coin is worth over three thousand euros."

"How many coins are in there?" Jinsoo asked. "Fifty? A hundred?"

"Let's count and find out," Hestie suggested as Prometheus returned the coin to the box.

They followed Hestie up to the salon and into a u-shaped booth with windows overlooking the main deck on the bow. The teens sat around the table to help her count. Chidori remained on Jinsoo's shoulder, as usual.

While the others counted, Hermie listened to Prometheus and Athena, who were speaking together in the food prep space by the refrigerator—what to the other members of the crew was the *galley* but would always be a *kitchen* to Hermie.

"What brings you here?" Prometheus asked. "Not that you need an excuse for a visit."

"I found something else of my father's that I want Poros to have." Athena opened her palms to reveal a pair of what looked like silver cuffs. "I thought he might like these."

"Indeed." Prometheus took one of the cuffs and turned it over in his hand. "Fine white gold, is it?"

Athena shook her head. "It's adamantine. The strongest element there is—the only one that gods can't break."

"I've seen these cuffs before—on my own wrists, I believe."

"My father warded them, to prevent the wearer from conjuring weapons or from…"

"God travel. Yes, I know. Did you find his adamantine chains as well?" Prometheus asked with a frown. "The ones he used to chain me to a rock as his eagle ate my liver each day?"

"I kept those for myself, along with two other sets of cuffs just like these," she said.

"I don't think Poros will find them of any value—except sentimental, perhaps."

Athena furrowed her brows. "One never knows when one's enemies might need to be subdued."

"Your brother has no enemies."

"Don't be naïve," Athena said.

When Prometheus glanced his way, Hermie averted his eyes, back to the table and to the coin counting.

But Hermie listened as Athena added, "He's the lord of the sky and the most powerful of the Olympians. You don't think that warrants him a few enemies, especially now, while we're adjusting to the new order?"

Before Prometheus could reply, Hestie and the other teens cried out, "Sixty-seven!"

"How much is that worth, Captain?" Hestie asked.

Prometheus stepped out from behind a counter to give the coins a closer look. "I know a collector on the island of Malta who would give us a half a million euros for these coins."

"Wow!" Jinsoo cried. "That a lot, right?"

"Right," Poros said with a laugh.

"Wait a minute," Mina said. "If you are gods, why can't you *make* money? Why you dive for treasure and sell it?"

"I'm pretty sure Captain has already answered that question," Hermie said.

"Not for Mina and Jinsoo, I haven't," Prometheus said. "You see, Mina, if I create money out of nothing, the value of all money goes down."

"It's called inflation," Hermie added.

"So?" Mina said. "Who cares? More money is more money!"

"Would you rather have a hundred silver US dollars or a hundred pennies?" Hermie asked her.

"Dollars, of course!" Mina said.

"If gods make more money out of nothing, then the dollars will become pennies. They won't be worth dollars anymore. All money will go down in value."

"Oh!" she said. "I see! I see!"

"These coins will buy a lot of medical supplies and technology for communities in need," Prometheus said. "Good work, Hestie."

Hestie beamed.

"When you make me and Mina gods, Poros?" Jinsoo asked in his broken English. "It not fair, you know? My sister and I work so hard. Everything easy for you."

"Remember what I said?" Poros asked. "If you still want to become immortal on your fifteenth birthday, I'll do it then."

"That three more months," Jinsoo said.

"It's a big decision," Prometheus added.

"Are you sure that's a good idea?" Athena asked her brother. "You can't keep turning mortals into gods, Poros. There's a balance that must be maintained, and there are existing gods who will feel threatened when it's upset."

Poros's cheeks turned red. Hermie felt the blood rush to his own cheeks, too. Did Athena resent Poros for turning Hermie and Hestie into gods?

"Just these two," Poros said of Mina and Jinsoo. "No more after that. We couldn't have won against Zeus without them."

"They've got a point," Prometheus agreed.

"I suppose you can take it up with the council," Athena said. "You'll need the support of other gods to make it happen."

Poros shrugged.

"So, now what?" Athena asked. "Is the *Marcella II* heading for Malta?"

"Indeed, it is!" Prometheus smiled from ear to ear. Then he said, "Poros, pull up the anchor!"

"Yes, Captain!" Poros left for the lower deck.

"Mina and Jinsoo, prepare to hoist the mains!" Prometheus cried.

"On it, Captain!" Mina said as she followed her brother to the main deck.

"Hermie and Hestie, coil and stow the lines!"

"Yes, Captain!" Hestie said with a chuckle as she and Hermie followed the others.

As the teens prepared to sail, Prometheus and Athena flew to the flybridge.

Once they were travel-ready, Prometheus cried, "To Malta!"

249

Eva Pohler is a *USA Today* bestselling author of over thirty novels in multiple genres, including mysteries, thrillers, and young adult paranormal romance based on Greek mythology. Her books have been described as "addictive" and "sure to thrill"—*Kirkus Reviews*.

To learn more about Eva and her books, and to sign up to hear about new releases, and sales, please visit her website at www.evapohler.com.